THE DEVIL, THE DIVA & THE DEEP BLUE SEA

A Garnet Sullivan Live from Florida Novel

BY

MARGARET JEAN LANGSTAFF

THE DEVIL, THE DIVA & THE DEEP BLUE SEA

This is a work of fiction. Names, characters, places and incidents are the product of the author's imagination or are used fictitiously. Any resemblance to actual events, locales or persons, living or dead, is entirely coincidental.

THE DEVIL, THE DIVA & THE DEEP BLUE SEA
A Garnet Sullivan Live from Florida Novel
By Margaret Jean Langstaff

ISBN 978-0-9864492-0-8

Cedar Hill Press
Gainesville, FL & Nashville, TN
407 NW 122 St.
Gainesville, FL 32607

For my dear ole Daddy

Vampires, wizards, dragon-slayers—
pretty tame stuff when you live in a place like Florida.

CARL HIAASEN

TABLE OF CONTENTS

1

DRESSED TO KILL

✝ ✝ ✝

Dressed to kill and ready for action, Garnet leaned forward, eyes locked on the rough winding road, hands clenched white-knuckled around the jerking, bucking steering wheel. Underneath her new DKNY sundress every cell of her buffed, tanned and amply moisturized satin skin jiggled like shook jelly and was swathed in a cottony tingle. She was on a mission. Time was short. Her eyes narrowed as she raced through splotches of sunlight, widened in the shade of over-hanging trees. *Faster.*

A blur of green blew by on either side. Overnight, what was dead, brown and dusty had come back to life. Her old banged up VW convertible dodged a squirrel, put the pronto on a slow-mo armadillo, became airborne taking a lighter knot at full tilt. She banged back to earth into a deep wash-out, growled out of it spitting gravel and marl, and careened around a tight curve on two wheels. A possum fell out of a wind-tossed oak tree overhead and hit the windshield with a *thunk.* Muttering apologies, she yanked the steering wheel, swerved, ran off the road, then back on again and mama and her pouch of bug-eyed babies sailed off into deep grass and disappeared.

Misjudging a curve, she slid off the road into a ditch, bobbed, wobbled and rocked through cattails and sludge, greasy crud thwapping up from the muck onto her fenders and brackish water and weeds slapping the sides of the car up to the roof; then, as the swamp engulfed the car up to the floor-boards, she downshifted from fourth to first and the car coughed, strained and whined in pain. She smacked her forehead on the dashboard and roared out in second gear on two wheels.

Faster. Everybody was waiting for her. Chester was pissed. Incensed. His barrister orderliness and punctuality had a big problem with all of this. He'd been left holding the bag, an empty bag at that, with a crowd of hungry Gator fans swarming through the front door ready to party and watch some football.

Subsequent events could be nuclear. Garnet stomped the gas pedal harder, but it was already flattened and nearly snapped off from the force of impact from her unreasonable recently pedicured foot.

Faster. She stuck her nose out the window and inhaled. *Green.* Wonderful. After the record-breaking drought, a few thunderstorms and a weak tropical storm had dumped enough water on the landscape to paint it again with the colors of hope. Nine months of no rain had reduced it to a hard brown waste-land roamed by desperate wildlife. Anxious, jumpy homeowners watched their expensive sod turn to cinders and awoke to coyotes, deer, and opossums in their lawn sprinklers, dead birds, alligators and snakes in their swimming pools. Nighttime horizons glowed with inflammation. The days and nights became suffocating from the smoke of wildfires. Ashes from distant fires dusted cars, roads, mailboxes and everyone's clothes and hair. By mid-August all of Florida was on fire and covered with toxic smog. Everyone coughed. Voices rasped, Interstates were closed, public service announcements warned citizens to stay indoors. Neighborhoods went up in flames. The sound of sirens wailed around the clock.

But then one still hot smoky afternoon in late August everything changed. Dense black clouds flashing with lightning and bearing gales of wind and hail tore in from the Gulf. Every afternoon, the loud operatic squalls pounded and soaked the landscape with Wagnerian vehemence. Just like the good old days, golf games halted, shoppers got drenched dashing to their cars in parking lots, radio stations were knocked off the air by cloud to ground lightning, and some unlucky cows that had run for cover under the broad canopies of live oaks lit up like firecrackers and were fried, eyes wide open, when lightning hit the branches overhead. No one complained.

In two weeks Florida was doused with 28 inches of rain. Rather than saturate the topsoil and flood the creeks and rivers, the rain sank through the sandy topsoil and the sieve of the porous limestone underneath it into the aquifer that ran the length of the state. The ground was insatiable, the water table, dangerously low. Billions of gallons of H2O were needed to replenish it. The last few weeks were a drop in the bucket.

Even so, the Floridian Aquifer burped a profound "Thank you, ma'am."

She leaned her head out the window, tapped the brakes and slowed. *Pfisst.* It was a slow leak. *Faster.*

Forward. She glanced from side to side at the pine trees, checking the wind. Three hundred miles to the south a cat 4 hurricane was tearing up Cuba. Forecasters were laying bets it would plow through Havana and rip up the Florida Straits to clobber Miami in 48 hours.

But odds were that Punta Bella would get a pass. Fine with her. This was the first Saturday in September. Good times were coming back to Florida. The adrenaline rush was statewide. In her own little corner of Nutball Paradise, big party at her place in 45 minutes to watch the game on the new 50 yard-wide flat screen Chester had bought for the occasion. The piece d' resistance of her fete and the purpose of her present urgent errand? Her Uncle Tommy Covington's legendary barbeque.

She reached for her cell and made a sharp turn to the left. Tommy's lop-sided cracker house came into view when Chester picked up.

"I'm almost there."

"You damn well better hurry. People are already showing up."

"Eeeek."

She was out of her car trotting toward the house inhaling the inebriating fumes of Tommy's secret sauce.

"Thirty minutes max. I swear."

"I knew this was gonna happen, Garnet. You wear me out. Why do you always wait until the last minute? It's sick."

"Look, I'm sorry, okay? So what's the deal on the storm?"

"Still over Cuba, but picking up speed."

"It'll slow down before it hits the water again, might fizzle out, or hang a left, a right. We're still cool."

"We're a watch now. And Miami's ass is grass. They're evacuating the Keys."

"You never know till the lights go out."

Tommy stood in the doorway holding three huge mouth-watering platters of meat. But something was hinky in the picture. His toothless grin was missing. He looked half-way between mad and sad.

"Bad day, Tommy?"

"I seen this too many times. I watch the birds, they know."

She flipped her hair, tossed her head. "What the freak do the birds do?" All the trouble she'd gone to, the money she'd spent. Or *blown* as Chester had put it.

"They stop singin, they get real quiet and . . ." he jerked his head to the right, "See that? They start flyin back and forth frantic-like in flocks."

A flock of glassy-eyed brown wrens burst into view, settled for a few seconds in a pine tree, then shot off en masse in another direction. In five seconds they were back and settled on the roof of the house for an instant then took off like spastic remote-operated drones. In the distance she saw a flock of crows doing the same thing in the pine trees. The only sounds out here were the erratic whooshes and sudden exhalations of the zombie wind, the creaks of straining branches, the rattle and snap of palmetto fronds, the shocked flaps and flutters of terrified bird wings.

"We get any more rain like we been havin? That crater sinkhole yonder," he thumbed toward his backyard, "is gonna swallow my house."

"Gawd, didn't know you had one, Tom. Sorry." You could stick fork in her if she didn't get her butt back home fast. She hopped from foot to foot, nodded.

"Dadblasted ranchers pulling too much H2O outta the ground during the drought. Water table dropped sixteen damn feet."

The irony of the twenty pounds of meat in Tommy's hands from the same dadblasted ranchers' cows was not lost on her, but seemed to elude Tommy. She bit her tongue and joined in cursing them. Would it be too much for her to *lunge* for the platters and hightail it?

"I gave em a piece of my mind, you better believe it. And them having the nerve to come around askin to drill on *my* land. Jackasses."

"They had it comin, Tom." She started a jumpy little dance. "I'm going to be late, Tommy."

"What took you so blame long? You said eleven."

Garnet held out her hands and wiggled her orange and blue fingernails, shellacked by a pro an hour ago.

"I'll be derned."

"Took forever. Cost a fortune." She lifted a new Amalfi sandal.

"How 'bout that. Toesies too. *Women.*"

"Wish I didn't have to rush, Tommy, but Chester is going to fry me, I'm seriously late."

"Ya look real nice. Go on now. Have yourself a big time, honey."

She handed him a wad of bills and grabbed the platters.

"Whoa! This is too much!"

"It's worth twice that. Bye."

The Sauce was like a drug. No one knew what he put in it, crushed cricket legs or dried gator skin, who cared? She planted a peck on his cheek, made tracks.

"If you get into it driving, you'll get home a mess. It's sloppy."

"I'll be back soon, Uncle Tommy. We'll have a proper visit in a week or so. Love ya."

"Drive slow. *Slow*, heah?"

She shot out of the driveway both feet flat on the accelerator, leaving a tall rooster tail behind her. In her rear view mirror she saw a cloud of dust settle over Tommy Covington, hand raised in a silent, unsmiling good-bye.

When Garnet skidded sideways into her driveway, the hurricane was not on her radar. Ten cars were parked out front, run up helter-skelter on the right of way, braving citations, neighbor finger-shaking and side-swipes.

Chester was standing in the doorway, arms folded and glaring.

She licked her fingers, checked her face in the mirror.

"Garnet!"

"I'm coming!" She sailed toward him, nose in the air like Queen Elizabeth.

"You're not normal, you know."

"And *you* are?"

His knees buckled and a whirlwind of red hair blasted by him and slammed into her legs.

"No! Ringo! Chester! Grab him!"

"What's all that red stuff on your top?"

"Blood."

Ringo stood next to her, rigid and drooling. "Forget it, Ring." Chester waved her in. A sea of animated heads bobbed in the dim living room. Then the crowd saw her and her face flushed. Shouts and huzzas rang out for the eats and their hostess's fraternity sweetheart smiling face.

As the last strains of the National Anthem faded away, she held up the goods and announced "Go Gators!" She cocked her head. Was there an echo in the room? Her guests' roar shook the walls. *"Go Gators!"*

The heads jerked back to the TV and a hush fell over the room. A coin flashed end over end in the afternoon sunlight and fell to the ground. Everyone in the room turned to stone. Start the clock.

She sagged. That was a close one.

The Jonesing for a win was like a blue haze in the room. The Gators had a new coach, two feuding co-equal quarterbacks, a young shaky team, a tough schedule. Two back-to-back SEC championships had spoiled the fans, made them obnoxious. The press was bad.

She turned on her heel and fled to the kitchen. Whatever. There was a ball. Numbskulls in helmets ran back and forth. Everybody yelled, no matter what happened. She just wanted to throw a great party for her friends. *Go Gators!*

2

KICK-OFF

✛ ✛ ✛

Garnet arranged the snacks and tapas on her best Gator enhanced tablecloth (special order: hand-made damask linen, full color cameo portraits of starters, French Chantilly lace "pom-pom" fringe: $89.99 + tax & shipping). Then she covered everything with foil. Nobody would want to chow down until they'd knocked back some brew. But the platters of snacks and appetizers had already suffered serious depredations. The crab claws and shrimp were decimated; the guacamole bowl had been scraped clean. Only the waxy jacket of the brie was left. Ringo had plundered his own share unobserved. He was positioned for his next pilfer, standing next to the table with his nose on the table, the barbeque locked in his red cross-hairs. "NO!" He whined and slunk off in search of warm laps and absent-minded handouts.

As she was ransacking cabinets for replenishments, BFF Allison Highsmith slipped up behind her.

"I think I'm in L-O-V-E, honey."

Garnet jumped. "Allison! Don't *do* that."

Next was the ritual, the standard BFF drill. She looked her over, up and down, with exaggerated admiration. "Get outta town, girl! Since when does Dolce & Gabbana have an orange and blue line of sportswear? Just look at you!" Per the usual, Allison was in killer threads, designer "play clothes," and her tanned to perfection narrow neck was swathed with her signature single strand of pearls.

BFF leaned in closer wearing a peculiar smile. "Did you hear me, Garnet? I am in LOVE. Love!" She closed her eyes, held herself and swayed in ecstasy.

"You're WHAT?" A few of the babes in front of the tube glanced up, curious, and then looked away.

"Shhhh! Shut-up!" Allison hissed and stomped her tiny size five foot. A crease of irritation appeared between her perfect dark eyebrows. "Don't embarrass me, Garnet."

"You're doing a pretty good job of that yourself, sistah."

Allison expelled a staged sigh. "I'm serious."

"You? What, are you sick?"

Allison tossed back her head and took a long pull on her Corona. "No, I am not. I've never felt better in my life." She flung her arms out and twirled around like a top.

"Stop it! You're making me dizzy."

She slowed to snatch a shrimp tail from a serving platter and pop it between her pouty Plum Raisonette lips. "It's true!" She spun over to the fridge and flung open the door. "Do you have any curry sauce?"

"No curry today, try the cocktail sauce. New recipe."

Whirling across the floor like an ice skater, Allison plunged her shrimp into the dip on the counter. "Love! Love!"

"Slow down, will ya? Is there room in your heart for someone else besides Allison? You must have added on a wing or something."

Allison's face engorged with mock sensuality.

"Did you get collagen on your lips? Do you have an allergy?"

"Forget it, Garnet. You'll see."

"I give. Tell me. Who do you have the hots for?"

"Sheriff *Lance!*" She growled like a toy Poodle.

"You are too much. Your Mater and Pater will have him assassinated. How slumming of you." She looked around the room for Lance Dawtry, his handsome, earnest and squeaky-clean Defender of Everything face, all that is holy and sacred, like expensive cars, hulking ocean front mansions and well-born women, and the hoi polloi too, especially members of the Gator Nation. His nose was on the TV screen. His hands were on his knees. He was ready to suit up if need be. Lance had been the super stud in high school, the el primo football star, the quarterback arm to be on for the prom, the king of swoon. He had similar prowess years later, though his sweet blank simplicity, however hunky, made him at this later date far less interesting to the same babes, now more sophisticated and worldly.

"Whatever you say. You'll get over it."

Allison did a horsey bump and grind next to the kitchen sink. "Not soon, I hope, darlin'," she moaned. "I've never felt like this."

"Here. Help me with these plates. Let's go watch the game. Try to keep a lid on it, kid."

Allison stopped and picked up an open book that lay face down on the breakfast table. She frowned and flipped the pages. "God, I thought this sounded fun from the cover, but no way! You always read such serious hard stuff, Garnet! Why? And look at all those long words! I don't know half of 'em!"

"You would if you cut back on Twittering some and read something every now and then, honey bun."

"I don't have time to read."

Garnet stared at her.

"I don't." She put the book down. "All those boards I sit on, and now the Junior League . . ."

"I'm interested in the big leagues myself."

"Big leagues? That's a stitch! What *position* do you want to play?" She giggled. "Me, I always wanna be on top!"

"No surprise there. Just look at your *family's* position, bank balance. You've never been the missionary type, Allison. C'mon, let's go; they're hungry restless Gators out there."

"Like your hair that way."

"Thanks."

"Love your nails. Who did them?"

"Mo Ching at Spa Orchid. Allison, you're spilling the shrimp!"

"Sorry!"

No worries, Ringo to the rescue; the shrimp vanished from the carpet, tails and all.

The room was funeral home quiet, not a token roar from the fans in the stadium on the TV. Nobody doing the gator jaw chomp. Nobody doing—anything. MTSU had scored twice, UF zip. The tube showed a replay of the fourth Gator punt ten minutes into the game.

Garnet offered Fred Phillips, her editor and the sole proprietor of the undistinguished *Indian River Times* (the newly and most grandly thus re-named newspaper of local derision and disrepute, nee' *The Stuart Times*) some very nice, very expensive English Waterstone crackers and super-superior crab dip. Real, from fresh blue crab claws, eighteen freakin' dollars a pound. She smiled and awaited a compliment. Fred chewed thoughtfully, swallowed, eyes on the screen.

What? Was he a newspaper food critic now too?

"Not lookin' good, darlin'," he said at last under his breath, shaking his head. "This was supposed to be the year of the Gator?"

Fred, the sweet ole thing, he was developing a 'tude or something. She might as well have given him dip from her garbage disposal. "Aw, they'll come back, Fred, you know they will." Fred qua Fred had newsprint taste buds. She moved down the rows of the guests with the platter.

Terry Milligan took two fat crab claws and suffocated them in cocktail sauce. "So whadya think of that?" she whispered, cocking her head at Allison. Allison was licking Lance's ear.

Garnet moved on to the next guest. She noticed in passing that Ed and Germaine Connelly, sitting next to Terry Milligan and overhearing the exchange, were examining the crumbs on their plates, eyebrows frozen in the up position. She rearranged the platter and forged ahead.

"Oh, crap!" someone shouted, banging the coffee table with his fist. Garnet slumped. One more fumble or interception? Or did they run the wrong way again? Trip? Bump into each other? But no. The bad news was a bleeping red banner scrolling across the bottom of the screen from the National Weather Service. Hurricane Clancy had already walloped Cuba a good one, and was turbo-charging at 57 mph through open water aimed for a Miami bulls-eye. "No way!" she said. "Storms don't move that fast."

The banner was in a loopy loop and wouldn't quit. Sustained wind speed of 140 mph, gusts up to 155 mph. It was a news nugget that launched a spirited discussion about whether or not it was now a cat 5 storm. And was there a higher category? Climate change had intensified everything in these latitudes; all weather had become more extreme. Are your windows up? Do you have enough water? Enough batteries, candles? The various and competing merits of everyone's weather apps, the shortcomings of NOAA, blah biddy, blah-blah. The standard "yippy-kai-yay, a hurricane is on the way" that would evaporate fast if the storm got within a hundred miles of the merry-makers.

Already the evacuation arguments and posturing were heating up. *I will never leave my home on this island, I'd rather die than leave my dogs, I'm outta here tonight, I'm calling Orlando right now to get a room . . . Hurricane party at my place, everyone's invited. The cops could make you leave. No they can't. Do you remember the hurricane party at Jamie's last year? How Eddie took his pants off and ran outside during the eye and then that branch fell on him and . . . .*

Garnet popped out her laptop, hit the NOAA Hurricane Center. "Guys! SHADDUP a minute! It's still a four, according to the Saffir-Simpson wind index." She clammed up quick as she continued to read from the Hurricane Center online advisory. It was serious party pooper stuff, and she would put a damper on everything if the crew in front of the TV heard the details.

Catastrophic damage will occur.

There is a very high risk of injury or death to people, livestock, and pets due to flying and falling debris. Nearly all older (pre-1994) mobile homes will be destroyed. A high percentage of newer mobile homes also will be destroyed. Poorly constructed homes can sustain complete collapse of all walls as the loss of the roof structure. Well-built homes also can sustain severe damage with loss of most of the roof structure and/or some exterior walls . . . .

The hair on her neck stood up. The Atlantic Ocean was rather significantly just across the street. With a jolt she pictured Tommy Covington's old cracker house blown to bits in the wind. She closed the laptop and stood up.

"Still cat four?" Lance was roused from his football stupor by reference to the well-being of his county. "Thing'll peter out over south Florida. We're gonna be okay." Garnet sought his face in the crowded room and paused at the sight of Allison's arms and legs entwining his body like climbing vines.

"Hey, Allison! Get a room, why don't you?"

Allison semi-disengaged at the stream of titters and giggles that followed, but then buried her face in Lance's neck.

While helping Garnet serve the meal at half-time, Chester sidled up to her. "What the hell has gotten into Allison?"

"Lance doesn't seem to mind."

"She's making a fool out of herself"

"That's not illegal, honey. We all do from time to time. Even you! So get over it. The Gators made a great come back, eh?" They now had a comfortable lead on MTSU, everyone's pride and confidence was restored. High fives, back-slapping, beer bottles clinking into the trash, the rifling of ice chests had resumed. The Old South potato salad laden with eggs, onions, garlic, celery and Duke's mayonnaise was a hit, as was Chester's "super-secret recipe" green bean casserole (canned green beans + canned mushroom soup). Her fudge brownies were going fast. Happy campers everywhere she looked. Good party.

A flash of red shooting up the staircase interrupted her self-congratulations. She turned to the table. "Ringo!" She took the stairs two at a time and followed the trail of barbeque sauce all the way through the door to the master bedroom. "Bad boy!" She smacked him hard enough for a blink and a duck, though not for a yelp, and yanked the platter out of his mouth. But the damage had been done. The new coverlet was slimed. Ringo rolled over on his back in a good improv of a dead orangatang. A paroxysm of severe aggravation paralyzed her. Who was in charge here? But it soon passed. He had eyes that could marinate a brick.

With her head down and arms around the platter like a running back, she dashed to the kitchen. Lance caught her arm in the red zone. "Hey, what happened to the chicken?"

"All gone, Lance." She shook him loose. He could die from red dog virus. "Try the beef and pork—they're even better." She dumped the glop into a black plastic garbage bag before he could complain.

The final score was Gators 48-MTSU 14. They sucked, everybody agreed, and flubbed everything, fumbled, ran into each other going out for passes, tripped on loose shoelaces, tackled and blocked members of their own team, did everything dumb and stupid short of run the wrong way and score points for MTSU, but a "W" was a "W." The fans were sated. Maybe it would be the year of the Gator, after all. Take the NY Giants, for example; there was a precedent. And they still had the fan advantage: the Gator Nation.

Garnet and Chester were swamped in an orange and blue flood of compliments and thanks dispensed in the superflux of the moment by blissed out, stuffed-to-the-gills, staggering Gators waddling out the door headed for the primal sack. Some few paused to stammer that the wind seemed to have revved up and that the ocean across the street was roaring like a monster. A salty mist was in the air. But after such a cliffhanger game and party, no one was capable of processing, let alone formulating and uttering in speech, anything like a thought. Goodnight, Gator girls and boys. Only six more days, South Carolina sucks, you'll see, another mythic war of the worlds, bacchanalia rocks. Is there any beer left? Time for a beer run? Tear down the goal posts. We're Number One. Long live the Gator Nation, long live us.

Last out the door, Lance charged by them without a word, head down, and shoulders first, with Allison in his arms. The paramours tumbled into his cruiser and he flipped on the lights and siren, gunned the engine, and squealed out of the parking lot.

Garnet convulsed.

"What?" Chester snapped. "Totally inappropriate. People were embarrassed for them."

"Bizarro, for sure."

"Let's get this place cleaned up. I've got to prepare for court tomorrow."

She stiffened. "Check your calendar. Tomorrow's Sunday."

"Sorry, kid. It's a poor bastard who's been framed. Trial's at 8:00 a.m. sharp Monday." He threw his arms around her shoulders and ruffled her hair.

"Unless you're going for the last ditch appeal for a stay of execution, Chester, in my book, you working on a weekend amounts to a broken promise."

"There's this poor schmuck, a groundskeeper for a wealthy jerk in Vero. One of the other employees was cut to pieces on his property and the jerk claims my client had it in for him. He can't make bail. It's pathetic."

"I'd say you're pretty pathetic yourself trying to get me to buy into this."

"Have a heart, Garnet. Guy's got no record, not even a parking ticket. He's the sweetest, kindest poor SOB you'd ever meet. Speaks almost no English and is scared to death."

"What's the evidence?"

"The rich jerk's word and a bloody carving knife."

"C'mon."

"No prints on the knife and the lab says the blood was not human."

"Not human?"

"That's right."

"So where did the blood come from?"

"A buffalo."

"You sure it wasn't a beefalo? I hear they taste better."

"Do you want to hear about this or not?"

"No. But keep talking. Why haven't I heard about this?"

"Two reasons. Lance is way behind in his paperwork—and I know why after tonight—and the rich jerk paid everybody off to keep their mouths shut."

"That makes no sense. What's his motive? You're telling me a story, and not a very good one."

He looked away.

"But, hey. I need a story right now. The county is experiencing a shortage."

"That's all I can tell you. Go find your own copy for the paper."

"I am broke as a joke after this party!" She reached for his hand, but he yanked it away.

"You and your stories." He wandered off toward the bathroom.

Whoa, let it go. She swallowed her return salvo for that pissy warning shot across her bow. She didn't want to say something she'd regret and have to apologize for in the morning. She was over that.

He was half-way up the stairs. "Chester! Dammit! We need to get some batteries and other stuff!" The front door moaned and whistled in a gust of wind. "And plywood for the windows!"

Let it alone. Let it pass. She had her man back. That's all that really mattered. He was behaving, not drinking himself dead every night over the daily grind of his job defending feckless losers. He was now baring his soul to her, at least she thought it was his soul he was using as an exhibit for his monologues, something he had never done before. They laughed together more now than they yelled at each other. It had to work this time. If there was another guy out there with the stuff it took to put up with her, the stamina and wits, she hadn't run across him yet and she doubted she ever would.

Besides, she loved him with all her little bonkers heart.

Coverlet and sheets scrubbing in the washing machine, new linens on the bed, the house more or less spiffed, they headed for the beach with Ringo for his nightly dump.

The breakers were eight feet high and the roar of the ocean drowned all nuance. They held hands and walked. The sand was concrete, not a bird anywhere. The damp and fog pushed against every move they made. Ringo romped up and down the shoreline jazzed over the energy and noise in the air. Salt spray soaked their hair and clothing. They turned back.

"If this keeps up, every idiot teen surfer within 50 miles will be chasing those alpine waves tomorrow morning."

"Come to bed, my seething red head," Chester said from under the covers. Only his eyes were showing. "My storied sexy siren." He winked. He was cute even when he was trying to be cute.

She turned off the light, switched on the TV to the Weather Channel. Ringo slumped to the floor at the foot of the bed. She pumped up the volume.

"What *now*?" Chester croaked. "I'm beat, Garnet."

"It's turned east. It's veering off. It's going to miss us. It's going to miss Miami."

Chester sat up. The huge white whirling dervish on the screen was headed back out to empty water. It was about 100 miles due east of Fort Lauderdale and plowing away from Florida at 58 mph. The talking heads were smug and smiling as they delivered the news, taking credit for the salvation of Florida.

Chester flopped back onto the pillow. "Great. Now turn that thing off and let's get some sleep."

She thought of Tommy, the birds. Tomorrow the birds would be back to normal. Singing, flapping, pecking. She loved happy endings.

"Nitey-night, O Great One."

"'Nite."

"Great party even if it was a sucky game."

"Yeah."

"Can't get over Allison."

"Zip it, Garnet."

She tossed, pounded the pillow and kissed Chester on the cheek. It had been a good day and night. It was all one could ask, all one could expect. She awoke a few times and stared into the dark thinking she'd heard a muffled thump or bump, but couldn't place it. The wind still moaned, the windows still cracked and creaked in sync with it. But it would be gone in the morning. She rose early and went to the closest window. The wind had subsided, only a breeze whiffed through the trees now. It was going to be a great day. Beautiful. The sun was coming out.

With Chester still sleeping like a stone, she headed downstairs to make coffee, noting as she descended the heavy cleaning she was going to have to do to get the red sauce off the sandstone carpet. Alarm bells went off. "Ringo?" Her heart tanked. She found him in the kitchen asleep amid the shredded remains of the garbage bag and chewed up chicken bones.

He opened his eyes and wagged his tail.

"Oh, please, don't get up, you red-haired dimwit." She wanted to scream. So she did. Then she grabbed a spatula and smacked him on the butt and screamed again.

He looked at her. He didn't move. "I said, damn you!" He stretched and yawned, closed his eyes. He'd heard it many times before to no effect and besides it's hard to disturb a dog with a full stomach. In fact, *this* dog? It was hard to disturb him any time, in any way, under any circumstance whatsoever.

The slamming, banging, whamming, and clanking of dishes and pots and pans brought Chester downstairs. He rubbed his nose and scratched his head. "I stepped on a damn chicken bone barefoot coming down the stairs."

She didn't turn around. Whatever was in the sink, she was wasting it.

"So what's your problem?"

She pointed at it.

He yawned and stretched. "You aren't firm enough with him."

A pan flew out of her hand and grazed the top of his head. She slammed the dishwasher shut with her foot and slung another pan at his chest.

"I'm sorrrr . . ."

Garnet whirled around from the sink and gave him The Look. Chester froze. The subject was dropped.

3

LOSING

✞ ✞ ✞

It was raining again. The cloud to ground lightning was intense and the floor under her feet shuddered. She was standing in front of a display of plastic fly swatters in Publix lost in a reverie about how effective one of them would be in reforming Ringo's bad manners (not very). Maybe if she brandished it at him while screaming at the top of her lungs like a banshee? She had to do something. He was out of control. This morning Chester suggested obedience classes. She laughed in his face.

She picked up a yellow fly swatter. She wiggled it back and forth. The thin plastic flopped from side to side. Chester holed up in his dingy office on a sunny Sunday afternoon, a time they had reserved as sacred for the two of them? She felt slighted. Hurt. Betrayed would be next. She'd had tried to persuade him to work at home. Oh no, he had to focus like a laser, no distractions. She sneered at the innocent fly swatter, whacked herself on the thigh with it. Damn sneak. She fumbled for her Droid. To think he could out-smart her so easily.

She stared at her phone. She knew his working methods, papers would be strewn all over the desk, chairs, filing cabinets and all over the floor. She would park around the corner out of sight. Wear a floppy hat, a trench coat.

Big shades. Stroll down the sidewalk on cat's feet, muttering to herself like a homeless person, her Droid glued to her ear, gesticulating wildly. She started giggling. She'd punch the air vehemently a couple of times, and in front of his office, without slowing, hand on the key in her pocket, she'd swerve and charge the door. Slide the key home . . . turn the knob, and explode into his sanctum sanctorum. His head would jerk up from his papers, the color would drain from his face, and his lips would part. She cackled. *Yes.*

Busted.

She put the fly swatter back on the hook and was about to pitch her phone back into her purse when a call came in. Ole Fred. He was calling to thank them for the party. So old school in spite of being an ass. She dropped the phone in her purse, headed for the front of the store. As she was gliding by the cashiers, the thrill of the chase in her limbs, the phone rang again. Guilt got the better of her. She hadn't paid for the tablecloth and the rent was coming up.

"Hey, boss. Wassup?" Spit it out, Fred. She had a narrow window of opportunity to freak Chester. Fred hacked out some words.

"Sorry?"

"I said that something's happened to Tommy Covington. Cops are at his place."

"Bad?"

"I know it's Sunday and all. But I want you out there. Check it out."

"Why cops?"

"Where are you?"

She looked around. The rain had stopped. "At Publix on the beach. Is it really bad, Fred?" She found a wall and leaned on it.

"His fishing buddy Jasper Oates called it in. They were supposed to go bass fishing."

"Yeah, I know ole Jasper."

"Move it, get out there. It'll be wrapped up in yellow tape soon."

"Yellow?" Hadn't she just been examining a yellow fly swatter?

"They say he's dead, that somebody cut him up bad."

"Ridiculous!"

"Maybe." He hung up.

She did not remember getting into her car, nor did she remember exactly what else Fred had said. She did not feel the too bright sun in her eyes or remember the worried look on the gas station cashier's face when she stopped to gas up for the drive. She did not remember calling Chester and delivering the news to him in a monotone. If he had said anything in reply, it was lost in the frozen land of shock where nothing happens and everything is always the same.

She slid up sideways and slammed on the brakes. The first thing she saw was the dogs. They were straining against their leashes, some of them yelping. Tommy's old blue heeler sat alone on the front porch looking sad and confused. A deputy yelled, "Let 'em go!" and the dogs flew into the woods barking and wailing like mad. Their handlers took off after them, leaving only two or three badges at the house and a red-eyed anguished Jasper Oates on the front steps, his face buried in his hands.

"Where's Tommy?" She glared at the deputy.

"You kin to him or something?" His eyes turned cold at the tone of her voice.

"Yes. Damn right, I am." We all belong to the family of man, don't we? "So where the hell is he?"

The deputy reached out, touched her shoulder. "He's gone, honey."

"Where?"

The deputy looked ashamed. "I'm sorry for your loss. Tommy Covington is dead. His body is on its way to be pronounced."

"I don't understand."

"Neither do we yet, but we're working on it." He touched her shoulder again, this time gently, and walked off to the house and the ruin that was Jasper Oates.

Garnet had known and loved her Uncle Tommy Covington ever since she could remember. Her earliest memory of him was about puppies, an irresistible litter of baby black labs. Tommy had been a sometime patient of her late father, a local physician, one of a lost breed who still made house calls. She had ridden out to Tommy's place with her dad once when he looked in on his wife for some minor illness. Discovering the puppies and their mama on Tommy's front porch was heaven to her. She sat down in the middle of them and hugged, coddled and kissed them until her dad came out of the house with his black bag. Her was as charmed as she was by them, but nixed her pleas to take one home. She already had two dogs, three cats and a big white duck that hung out and pooped in their swimming pool. Before they left, Tommy had loaded them down with bags of fresh oranges, grapefruit and tangerines from his groves. Garnet stood before Tommy's mostly unchanged front porch and breathed the same crisp tart scent of citrus that had filled her father's car on their drive home so long ago, a fragrance now wafting from this year's fruit still hanging on the trees and ripening in Tommy's groves.

A deep depression and crazy swirl in the dirt and dust in front of the house caught her eye. Surrounded by a circle of crime scene tape, it was a record of Tommy's last acts. Tommy's struggle to live. A swath in the sand a frantic snow angel might have made. No red residue. No bloody hints or clues. She was no forensic anything, but she knew from her addiction to late night crime shows that cuts bleed out. Puncture wounds do not. They close up fast and the bleeding is internal. She marched up to the porch, passed by the two men and flopped down next to Tommy's old dog Diesel and put an arm around him.

"He didn't have no enemies," Jasper said, recovering from an embarrassing crying jag. He mopped his face with a rag, closed his eyes.

"This is total bullshit! Everyone loved Tommy!" Garnet heard herself shout. "He was so damn nice—and he was nice to everybody!" Whoever did this to him must be deranged. And he had nothing to steal, either. He lived a simple rural life, put no stock in fancy things, and couldn't care less about money as long as he had enough to get by on. She stroked white-muzzled Diesel's head and moved closer to him. He was shaking. Little bits of white foam had formed at the corners of his terrified mouth. She pulled him into her lap and held him in her arms.

The deputy was silent, looked over his notes. Then he looked up and addressed Garnet directly. "What about other next of kin? Who else should we notify? They may shed some light on what happened too."

"I'm not sure." Tommy's wife Sally had died over twenty years ago and they were childless. She had never heard him mention any other family.

"Uh, I think he has a sister in a nursing home somewheres in Polk County. Don't know where or what her name might be, though," Jasper said. "Come to think of it, she may have passed already. Tom may have said somethin' about that to me coupla years ago. Can't remember exactly."

Two deputies who had been scouring Tommy's house were at the front door.

"Find anything?"

"Nothin. No weapon, no blood. No nothin.'"

A rustling in the scrub next to the house changed the subject. Dogs and deputies began straggling out of the woods, looking beat and hot. They charged for the water coolers, and when re-hydrated, the men began loading the dogs and equipment back into the vans.

Garnet hurried over to a huddle they were having before leaving the scene. They looked defeated. Some were shaking their heads and kicking at the dirt. Tommy was a good old boy and everybody liked him. They were breaking up when the word "buffalo" stopped her in her tracks.

"Hey! Wait minute, guys! What is it about a buffalo? Did they see one in the woods or what?"

"Oh, that. It was nothing, Just a big old hairy bison who's got himself lost from some little hobby farm and a little cut up running around in the woods. The bad weather we had from down south probably spooked him and he broke through a fence. Anyway, he ain't hurt bad. Somebody'll be lookin' for him and find him."

She stared at the woods.

"Okay, now, don't you fret too much, hear? We'll be in touch, okay? Take care, little lady, try not to worry. We'll get him."

"The buffalo?"

"No, the man that murdered your uncle."

She pulled her cell out of her jeans pocket. She should have called Fred an hour ago.

"If I hadn't been crazy about your father and mother, I'd fire you right now. What the hell have you been doing out there all this time? I've left you five messages."

"They don't have anything, Fred. And I don't either. He's dead, that's all they know right now."

"Write something up, whatever you got, and file it tonight,"

She was hugging Jasper and telling him that Tommy was at peace now. She was telling him through hot tears that, yes, they would miss him something awful, but somehow they would figure out what happened and why. She was promising him, the poor old rough and stinky thing, that somehow, some way, something good was going to come out of this.

"I guess I'll make the arrangements. He ain't got nobody else to do it," Jasper said, pulling away.

His red haggard face was almost too much to bear. Garnet felt her heart try to rip out of her ribcage toward Jasper and she gasped for air. "I'll help, Jasper, just tell me what to do. Please? I'll at least chip in for the funeral."

"Naw, I'll handle it. I got it covered. Call me tomorrow. I'm in the book." He turned away from her and shuffled off toward his rusty dilapidated pickup. He cranked it and cranked it, and finally, after a backfire that would have skinned a bat out of hell, it started and he tore down the marl road in a cloud of dust and disquiet.

Then she was putting the catatonic Diesel in the passenger seat of her bug and heading home. Someone had to take care of him. The thoroughly discombobulated, disoriented country boy Diesel, probably never having been in a car before in his life, got motion sickness five minutes out and vomited all over the car—and her lap— the rest of the way back to her townhouse.

4

CAT FIGHT

✛ ✛ ✛

"Where are we supposed to sit?" Chester asked the question mildly, without a hint of sarcasm. He was on his best behavior. It helped some.

"Sit?" Sit?

"Yeah, you know, as in 'sit down?'"

"Oh, right." Ringo had taken over the couch and was stretched out full length in a deep sleep and whistling a tune through his nose. Diesel was in rebar-like semi-repose on the loveseat afraid to burp or do anything to call attention to himself. All of which meant that only one stiff, uncomfortable, though very good-looking, wingback chair in the room was available for human use. "I guess we can sit in the kitchen. Or we can lie down on the bed." Garnet ran her fingers through her hair and closed her eyes. A grinding headache had set in when she passed through the front door.

"Of course we can," Chester said. "Most of the time I'd rather lie down anyway."

"Sorry."

"Don't be. I understand. You did the right thing."

"I did?"

"You're a great kid, you know? I'm proud of you."

"Chester," she plowed ahead, not about to be disarmed. "I want to talk to you about all of this. I need to talk to you. Your case and Tommy's. Some similarities . . . ."

"Let's wait until tomorrow. Tomorrow everything will be clearer."

"No. There was this damn buffalo in the woods . . . ."

"Shhh. Later, honey."

"But you're in court tomorrow! Guess it'll have to wait till tomorrow night?"

"Maybe. We'll see." He headed up the stairs.

From the top of the stairs he shouted back down to her, "Answer your damn phone, Garnet! Life goes on. Or turn it off for godsake. It's making me crazy!"

She hadn't noticed it ringing. She pulled it out of her pocket. It was only the newly weird Allison calling repeatedly. No time or patience for that tonight. Lance, yeah, he had told her about what happened to Tommy. She'd become dutifully hysterical. She'd miss the barbeque. Go get laid again, Allison. You'll get over it. Phone silenced, she wrote up five hundred stupid stuttering words for Fred and shot them to him with a lame apologetic email. Chester was sound asleep. She didn't care if the dogs peed and crapped in the house tonight. She didn't have the energy to walk them on the beach by herself. And tonight she didn't want to be alone in the dark. The world had changed today.

In the midst of a fitful spasmodic sleep, she sat up with a cold start. She hadn't seen or heard a single bird at Tommy's place that afternoon. She stared into the dark. She thought she must be losing her mind. She wasn't looking for birds. She was looking for Tommy. But both were, as the deputy said, gone. So where did they go? Nothing just disappears, does it? It doesn't just vanish. Something had been damaged in her. She was reading too much into things. She was getting paranoid. This had to stop.

✢ ✢ ✢

Inspired by a brief encounter with the obvious and a few fleeting seconds of commonsense, Garnet found herself outside courtroom D at 8:10 the following morning. If Chester wouldn't cough up what he knew about the murder charges and evidence relative to his latest dumb schmuck case to her unmediated, Judge Theocritus Cudgel and DA Owen Duh Pecksniff (she had no idea what their real names were) would rip it out of him in public. She wasn't going to miss it.

She tried the door for a third time. Maybe she'd not pulled hard enough or missed a trick in the latch. An officious, pouty-lipped man with a white dangly county photo I.D. hurried by and she caught his shirtsleeve. "Oh, sorry." She had alarmed him. "But, please, is there something the matter with this door? I can't get in." She tugged on the unresponsive latch to demonstrate. The man shook her loose from his sleeve, stepped back to what he felt was a safe distance, and pointed to a tiny sign to the side of the door.

"'Closed Hearing?'" she read. "What does that mean?"

But the starched shirt was already briskly fleeing this illiterate and didn't offer to translate. You had to be so careful these days. Nuts were everywhere.

She sat down on a metal chair next to the door. To lay in wait or not to lay in wait? Chester had to come out sometime. He'd no doubt be irritated to see her stalking him. Too bad. His own fault. He sure wasn't going to divulge willingly the tiniest microscopic grain of anything about the case. But his client would be by his side. The Poor Schmuck would then have a face and a name. Not much, but worth something.

She checked her watch. Would it be worth an all-day stakeout? She looked up. Chester in his smart court duds and briefcase in hand stood right in front of her. Um. Must be one heck of a well-oiled door.

"Oh, hi."

"Hi."

"I was hoping we could catch a little breakfast together. Was waiting for you."

"That's funny." At least he was smiling. Sort of.

"Why is it funny?"

He kissed her cheek. "Have to beat it back to the office."

"Where's your client?"

"He didn't need to be here to file a motion to continue."

"Oh."

"Yeah. Oh."

"So do you have a few minutes?" She dropped her head and tried to look confused and needy. Didn't work anymore.

"You're too much. Later, my lovely." His broad back disappeared through the swinging glass doors into the bright sunlight.

That man could hustle with a hound on his heels. He'd had plenty of practice.

Lance looked as if he hadn't slept in a week. His normally chaotic desk had devolved further into a catastrophe-churned midden, a potential archeological dig for artifacts and relics of 21st century local law enforcement. His phone rang over and over again, but he never could find it, so the ringing always stopped and the calls went back to the switchboard. And the strangest part of the scene to Garnet was that he seemed oblivious to the wreckage and completely unashamed.

For half an hour she pestered him with questions, although it was clear he wasn't listening. If he had a mind left at all—something open to dispute—it was somewhere else.

At last she stood up. "Hey, you! Lance?" A pair of dull brown eyes rolled toward her. "Listen to me."

A woman in a green uniform just like Lance's strode into the office with a blank expression. She tossed a piece of paper on his desk. "You need to check this out, Chief." As if accustomed to receiving no acknowledgement, she was out the door in a flash.

His cell phone erupted in a noisy rendition of "Dixie." Lance picked up on the first ring. "Hi, darlin,'" he cooed—no other word for it. He scurried off to a muffled corner of his office.

Ever alert to the merest opportunity, like lightning Garnet hopped to the desk and snatched up its recent deposit, heretofore ignored by the Sheriff. Ha and aha. Now she was onto something. Yeah. Propinquity was the name of the game. You had to get in their faces. You had to be there. Lance's neglected, disorderly desk was the Holy Grail for a reporter. The only problem she'd ever had with it was one of access.

Lance still had his nose stuck in the corner, all hunched over in the act of phone sex, probably. "Lance?" No answer.

She stared at the page. Dadgummit, there were some terms she was going to have to Google. Propelled by an evil but irresistible idea, she ripped out of Lance's office and sped down the hall. When the copy machine insisted she enter a password, she stopped a green uniform and waved the paper back and forth in a blur, hoping he wouldn't notice the big blaring CONFIDENTIAL diagonal watermark on it. "Sheriff Dawtry wants me to make him a copy of this," she said. "But he didn't give me a code." Obliging nimble fingers unlocked the thing and Garnet soon held something she was dimly aware of being an illegal infraction of some sort, she didn't know what, but who would ever find out?

The sheet was back on the top of the debris on the desk in less than a minute and Lance never knew she had been gone. On the other hand, he probably never knew she was there, either. "You're busy, Lance. I'll catch up with you later." He didn't turn around. This was too easy. Getting some traction on what happened to Tommy made her feel much better, almost like her old self. "Bye-bye, Lance. Say hey to Allison for me, okay?"

Three hours on the beach with Ringo and Diesel further nourished her soul and helped restore her equilibrium. They walked, sat, lingered and sniffed until the sun slipped behind the dunes and a star-spangled crystal clear night was born. The ocean was at peace and softly withdrew from the shore as the tide went out, attracting in the final orange glow of the day a few hungry sandpipers in search of coquinas and sand fleas. Ringo faked a tired bark at them; Diesel hung back and stayed by her side. Venus took up her venerable position in the indigo blue overhead. Garnet and the boys walked slowly home.

Unannounced waves of disorienting grief still crippled her, but they were smaller now and further apart. The funeral would finally be the end of it, a kind of purging. Then it would be gone and the happy memories would come back like fresh flowers in what had been a wasteland in her gut.

She'd made great progress with her new darling Diesel baby. When she had first put a leash on him, he cratered and rolled over and stuck his legs up in the air paralyzed with fright. Poor little pooper, he'd never worn a leash in his life. Coaxing, sweet-talk and lots of smooches taught him in an hour that he didn't have anything to fear and he at last stood up and agreed to follow her. "You have more patience with dogs than anything else," the Great One had once observed. No argument there.

The homemade spaghetti was delicious paired with a musky fruity new episode of "Criminal Minds." Chester was detained at his office and she decided to be convincingly asleep when he got home. He wasn't going to tell her anything new, and with his sensitive nose and uncanny insight into her moods, he might easily sniff out a change in her; that is, her new intelligence. "You wear your heart on your sleeve, sweet-cakes. I can always tell when something's up." She knew she was a lousy liar and had always been poor at faking it, a professional and personal liability she had to work to overcome. Better to avoid him until she had this new stuff sorted out.

Hiding out, she sat quiet as a mouse in the gray flickering light from the tube in an otherwise dark room doing nothing but fork-to-mouth. She couldn't get enough of the pasta and continued to eat beyond the point of being over stuffed. This was a positive. Her appetite was back. She hadn't been able to eat for two days. Ringo and Diesel had been offered a dollop of the pasta. Diesel sniffed, eyed it suspiciously and then humbly begged off. He didn't do Italian. So Ringo made short work of polishing both plates which were now shining and spotless at her feet. His long pink tongue continued its relentless lick down.

"Stop it! Nothing's left! LIE DOWN!" He ignored her. She shot her fork at him. "DOWN!" And he was down. Wow! How 'bout that? Could be she was onto something. She'd have to practice that tone of voice, carry a fork around with her, maybe.

She had a few new vocab words as a result of the day's events. Biggies, Latinate. As they say on "Criminal Minds," the hunt was on. She was on the case. At last she knew what to do next. Equally satisfying to her was the fact that she and Fred had patched it up. Whatever had happened, she had recovered enough to understand she still had to live her life. Now that she had forward momentum, she had overcome her shock-mania and was willing to become methodical, take care of herself, her buddies and sweetheart—take care a bidness. Things would fall into place. She would go at it day after day like a bloodhound and track the monster all the way back to its lair. Fred would get his stories and they would be good. She felt sure of that.

Okay, it was underhanded, but in the present situation? More than justi-fied. They were supposed to have no secrets between them anymore, right? He was breaking the rules with his Dumb Schmuck case. The thought never would have occurred to her if Chester hadn't stayed out late, slept in that morning and had left his cell in the bathroom the night before. When it vibrated off the counter and hit the tile with a loud thump, what else was she supposed to do but drop her toothbrush and pick the thing up? Everything else that followed was so natural that she could hardly be blamed for it. Inquiring minds and all that. Natural curiosity fired by a sense of moral obli-gation, not to say journalistic bravado, trumped her scruples in a blink. She hit the All Calls button and nearly fell down the stairs in an urgent search of a pen and a piece of paper. Her heart was pounding in her ears and she felt faint with the serendipity and rush. She scrawled ten or twelve numbers on the back of an envelope then raced back up the stairs. When he woke up, the Great One would find his phone right where he'd left it—next to the potty.

She congratulated herself on her restraint, actually. She could have listened to his messages too, but didn't. Chester used the same password for every-thing: "garnet." But time was not on her side. He might have caught her. The aftermath of such an incident would be unthinkable.

She dragged Ringo and Diesel at breakneck speed around a twenty-foot swath of beach, then pulled on a wrinkled but clean pair of khaki shorts and the closest pair of sandals. She shot out the door in record time. It was getting hard for her to keep up with herself. An hour later Chester found a tall glass of orange juice and the sweetest ta-ta-have-a-great-day note from her on the kitchen table. She had to be off early. "Terrible deadlines today! Pizza and movie tonight, sugar? And don't forget the funeral!" He drained the glass scowling. There'd been a breach. He'd been hacked.

An investigative reporter with her nose to the ground locked on a scent exhibits a disquieting glee to other people. She comes across as unreasonably happy. No matter how grim the crime or subject, the thrill of the chase over-compensates for the effort involved and an irritating cheer accompanies her every syllable and act. Ordinary, normal folk intuitively resent this. Go figure.

Such a reporter goes on a characteristic yadda-yadda-whatever tare. Her senses are impaired by tunnel vision and myopia. Nothing registers but that which is relative to the case, the story. Over nice to everyone in order to better ignore them, she is insensible to irrelevant comments, no matter how pertinent the comments might be to other areas of life. Not even an IRS audit notice could have made her swerve off target.

Garnet was on professional autopilot, no hands on the wheel, when she slammed into a huge piece of stink that shut her boosters down. Allison's unexpected disheveled appearance in the line at the convenience store was the only immovable force that could have halted her forward thrust. Garnet squeezed the pack of sugar-free Trident in her hand into a two-dimensional pancake and stormed out behind her without paying for it. She had a responsibility here. The brat needed to be Baker-Acted before she committed social suicide. Resentment spilling out of her ears, Garnet followed her to Ordway's Meat n' Three. She wanted to get it over with now and fast.

She picked at her southwest chicken Caesar. She couldn't watch anymore. Allison was having an extended orgasm over the last lickspittle of her second super-sized triple fudge sundae.

"Refill?" the waitress asked, materializing at the right moment.

"Ummm . . ." Allison looked off into space and considered this with evident relish.

Garnet exploded, and the words blew out of her mouth like shrapnel, no stopping them or taking them back. "You are yesterday's puke, Allison! You're a cat in heat! Are you on drugs, bitch?" She fastened a glare on her that could strip paint off a wall. "What the hell has happened to you?"

Allison smiled and giggled. "Bite me, sugar. You're just jealous." She squirmed in her seat in delight.

"Ugh! I can't stand this, the very sight of you turns my stomach!" Garnet pushed away from the table and stood up, waving for the check.

"So too-too bad about Tommy, huh? What an old sweetie." She made a mock show of soap opera sorrow, scraping the bottom and sides of the glass flute like an addict. "So ya goin to the funeral? I was thinkin 'bout going myself."

Garnet slammed her butt back into the booth so hard Allison bounced up in the air off her cushion on the other side. This required a well-aimed, dead to rights riposte. A paralyzing moral impalement. And three days of strait-jacket time in a cork-lined room. She had a lawyer, The Great One, but she needed an M.D. to sign the papers too.

"Are your parents still in Europe?"

Allison licked her lips and thought a minute. "Ya know? I don't know." She tongued one side of her spoon and then the other. "Um, no way. Mama woulda been callin me. You know, her morning, noon and night drill. Could be they're in Nevis now. When they go there they just kick back. I don't hear from them."

"So when do you expect them back?"

Allison shrugged. "Ya know, I heard 'bout these lil blue pills? Have you heard of them? Vigor-Grow or Viber-Wow or somethin? For your honey? Wonder do they work or not . . ."

"You are absolutely disgusting, Allison. You need professional help."

She was on her feet again and strode to the cashier.

"Meow," her BFF called after her. "MEOW!"

Now she was truly alarmed. She had read about this behavior, this "syndrome." Her amateur, internet-based diagnosis and prognosis: horrible.

All ten of the little boxes on the online test for her BFF checked *yes*. She was in the promiscuous sex-crazed phase of the cycle. When she had more time, she needed to Google this some more. She needed to intervene. She would take it up with the Great One. With the adept application of the right amount of guilt, obligation and tearful pleading, Chester would realize he knew what to do and he would help her do what needed to be done. That safely shelved it for a while, back to business. She could only do much.

5

THEY WERE QUACKS

✛ ✛ ✛

Wellington Park was deserted. The lake glimmered and winked in the warm afternoon sun, its margins embroidered by a shifting latticework of white and Muscovy ducks. A single duck glided gracefully over the serene glassy surface like an out of context lyric to a song. Her old duck Herman's descendants must be here. This was the idyllic haven her father had found, close to his office and the hospital, where Herman would be able to poop to his heart's content without bacterial consequences to the Sullivan family swimming pool. She re-lived the ambiguous feelings she'd experienced as a response to his proposal. She'd caved quickly. She knew he was right.

The scribbling on the back of the envelope was barely recognizable as her own and was almost illegible even to her. That's what guilt will do to you. Forensic handwriting analysts no doubt knew this. She would take the list of phone numbers from the top and work her way down. No harm would be done. She would ask a few innocuous questions, that's all. Tell a little joke, insert a humanizing item like, "Damn, my feet are killing me today" or "My kids are driving me crazy" or "Here comes my boss! Tell me something, anything, so I can throw him a bone!"

She would play the role of an ignorant, over-worked factotum with a tyrant for a boss. She would ape (she had plenty of monkey in her for it) a simpleton subordinate of PD Chester Dare. Nothing more than an anonymous conduit of information. There was nothing wrong or ignoble with her plan. She slammed the lid on her over-active prickly conscience. What a whining inconvenience it could be. The damn jams it'd gotten her in.

"You have reached the Orlando INS call center. If you know your party's extension, please dial it now . . . ."

"Clovis Reddick at Peaceable Kingdom. Please leave a message."

Salsa music and a lady Latino accent: Alfredo y Lucy . . . su nombre y telephono."

"Bart Barnett, delivery and service entrance, Peaceable Kingdom. Leave a message."

"Uh, yeah, this is Jasper. Busy right now. State your business, leave a number."

Then a real live actual human voice! "Yeah, this is Lance . . . [He burped and yawned at length] Wassssupppp, buuuhhhd?" Garnet shot off her seat three inches and her hair stood on end. She threw the phone out the window as if it were a live grenade. It disappeared into the deep grass.

He never picks up. Must be an unlisted hotline he has for Chester. Did The Great One have one for Lance too? "Quack!" She glanced up. A large fat duck with a preposterously outsized orange bill, and white—just like her ole Herman—was furiously pecking away at her phone. "Quack!" He poked at it, flipped it, and turned it over and over. He thought it was a hand-out. Surely it wasn't trying to call anybody…. Or report a crime. "Quaaack!" The duck nailed it hard and the light dimmed on the phone. Thank God. Lance had hung up. Just another crank call from a quack.

"Quaaack!" Garnet yelled back, gripping the door-handle. "Scoot!" She hopped out to grab her phone and saw a horde of tail-wagging, waddling-at-top-speed duckaroos closing in on it. People fed these sons of a duck. Toss something out a window and bang. They ate it. Whatever it was.

She dove in. Freakin birdbrains. "Gimme that!" Five ducks were on it, then twenty, forty, sixty, flipping it over, shooting it around over the grass like a hockey puck. More were on the way. It was a stampede. Hundreds of ducks descended on her phone and it was lost in an epic melee, a churning sea of white. Panicked, she joined the fray, flinging soft fat heavy duck demons every which way, over her shoulder, to the side, to the front, back and over her head. "You SOBs!" Feathers and curses flew through the air. She chased the phone around, but never could quite grab it. Each time she lunged for it, the ducks jabbed her legs and crapped all over her feet. She tucked her head in and plowed through fat damp duck bodies. Something smelled awful and was awful familiar. Fifty more at a time piled on top of the rest, flapping, diving, madly paddling webbed flipper feet from their behinds, thrusting at the heaving, quivering, feathery mound of run amuck ducks, tossing the phone back and forth and up into the air, jumping for it, flinging it this way and that, skidding it everywhere in a wild frenzied search for the edible part. "Stop it! No! Stop!" Duckbills jabbed at her legs, flapped up and tried to bite her face. She flailed, fumbled, cussed her heart out and dove in again and again. "Dammit, you little bastards!" One hit her in the chest like a football and she fell down in surprise.

"I'm gonna kill all of you!" Duck poop was all over her feet and ankles. "Go ahead, quack your asses off! You are all dead ducks!" She wiped her feet back and forth over the grass, grimacing. "I mean it. Your asses are grass, man."

"Hey, you!" an elderly man shouted over the flapping, quacking din. He waded in and grabbed her by the arm, yanked her to her feet. "What do you think you are doing? Stop this immediately. Leave the poor ducks alone. I'm going to call PETA! I'm going to call the authorities!"

"They attacked me!" she screamed, scraping the crud off her feet.

He recoiled. "Hell they did."

"I'm tellin you, they ATTACKED ME IN A MOB."

"What did you do to provoke them?"

"Nothing! I was sitting in my car. I didn't do anything."

"You must have done something. That's not normal Carina Moschata behavior."

"What the hell is that?"

"This sub-type of Muscovy duck."

"Yeah, well, serial killing isn't exactly normal in homo sapiens either. Ever hear of mutants, eh? Genetic deviance, buster? Say what you will, but evolution happens, ya know, in life? In freakin 'nature?'" She looked down at her bird-fouled clothes, feet and sandals. "I mean, just look at me! Chromosomes!"

"Chromosomes?" He backed up several steps, pulled out his cell phone from his shorts.

"They stole my phone!"

The man retreated a more few steps. "You are not well, miss."

"Herman's great great great grandson was probably one of them too! Breaks my heart." She started to cry, which made her mad, which made her cry harder.

"Herman?"

"He was my little brother. Daddy brought him here and dumped him. Mother never said a word. It wasn't right. I mean, he was my little brother. I could have stopped him, but I didn't."

"It's going to be okay. Please try to relax and calm down." He tossed her his handkerchief which fluttered to the ground. A pair of ducks nailed it and raced off, yanking it back and forth between them, toward the lake.

"See?" she said. "*That's* what they do!"

The man had been fumbling with his phone and had missed it. "I beg your pardon?"

"Herman's not one of those pizza face punk creeps. He came from a good family!"

The man held up his phone and snapped her picture.

Garnet saw red and went for his phone. "You old geezer! Gimme that. That's illegal in Florida."

The silver haired dignified gentleman turned on his heel and tore back to his Mercedes, leaving an expensive pair of binoculars and a new bird guide-book behind him on the ground.

Garnet picked them up and trotted after him. He was rolling up his windows, had his cell phone against his ear.

"Wait! You could help me, you know!" Four pairs of eyes would be better than two. Damn grass was thick here.

"Get away!" He was on the phone talking to somebody, waving his arm.

She slammed the binoculars and book against his window. "You forgot these."

He screamed, and cried, "Get away now! Get away!"

She threw the goods to the ground and stomped off.

"My dear young lady! Please. Wait! The worst is over! Help is on the way!" he shouted after her. "Sit down. Rest. Try to remain calm."

She heard sirens in the distance and broke into a run.

She flew through the door shedding feathers with every step. Chester's eyes narrowed. "What happened to you?"

"Nothing."

"Oh. '*Nothing*' again? That's a relief." He picked one of 10,000 feathers out of her hair and held it up to the light. "Little old for pillow fights, aren't you?"

"I lost my phone."

"In a pillow fight?"

"We have to hurry. Gotta get dressed." She raced to the stairs.

"You better take a shower first, Garnet!" he shouted after her, holding his nose.

The funeral was sparsely attended. Most of the mourners were superannuated life-long friends and contemporaries of Tommy. They were dressed simply and were uncomfortable with the formality of the setting. Speechless with grief. Not an in-sympathy cliché or hollow he's-with-the-angels-now was uttered. Not one of his uptown fans and purchasers of his barbeque was in attendance. His secret recipe died with him. In that vein his former customers would mourn and thus would they remember Tommy—if they ever thought of him at all again.

Though Tommy had not been a Catholic, his old friend Father Ryan conducted the modest ecumenical service at St. Mary's. The Twenty-Third Psalm, St. Paul's bit "O death where is thy sting?" and "Ashes to ashes, dust to dust." A few simple old-timey Protestant hymns. Some of the mute old ladies dabbed at their eyes. Throughout, Garnet sat with her hands folded in her lap and thought of the puppies that day so long ago on his porch (she could still smell their milky "puppy breath"), the bright look on her father's face that day when he'd seen them, and with a quizzical half-smile on her own face, she mourned the loss of something larger than the passing of a single life. As people were filing out of the church, ancient Mr. Johnson stood up and tersely announced his wife had fixed a meal. He invited anyone interested to "come on over, have a bite and set a spell." Tommy had been cremated. Jasper drove away in his back-firing old pick-up with the no-frills urn. Garnet had the decency not to ask what he planned to do with it.

They drove home in silence, both lost in thought.

Once again she silently recited the state lab report, which she had memorized and now could quote verbatim, forensic gobbley-gook included. Tommy had suffered multiple puncture wounds to the face and neck, but none were more than 8 cm deep or had pierced an artery or vital organ. The autopsy revealed longstanding advanced heart disease of the congestive heart failure variety. Cause of death: sudden massive cardiac arrest. Did the attack scare him to death? Did the heart attack and his resulting vulnerability precipitate the attack? Was he already dead when the puncture wounds occurred? The weapon used in the attack was 10 cm at its pointed end and 4.3 cm at the top of the puncture wound. This was consistent with a wound made by a miner's pick, a hay hook or a tent tie-down.

Was the frantic flailing swirl Tommy had made in the sand in front of his house caused by the excruciating pain of a heart attack or by his attempts to fend off the attack?

"Could I borrow your phone for a minute, honey?"

"No, you may not."

"I have to check in with Fred. I know he's been calling me."

"Where's your own phone, brainiac?"

"At Wellington Park somewhere."

"I would ask what it's doing there, but I won't."

"Please? Fred is going to fire me for sure this time. I've got to call him."

He threw the phone into her lap. "Make it short."

Fred was annoyed with the lost phone update. But Fred was ballistic about her frequent use of the phrase "an anonymous source" in her recent squibs on the death of Mr. Covington. He demanded to know the sources.

"I'll send them tonight."

"No, now, Garnet. I want names now."

"I think the battery is going dead, Fred. Let me get to another phone." Where was the off button on this thing? She plopped the phone back into Chester's lap. "Thanks."

"'O what a tangled web we weave when first we practice to deceive.'"

"Love it."

"You would, drama queen." Chester suddenly swerved, turned around and headed west.

"Where are you going?"

"To find your stupid phone." Which they did by narrowing in on its location with repeated calls from Chester's jealously guarded phone. Numerous triangulations thereafter, her phone was found teed up on a lonely tuft of grass near the lake.

"Humph. Guess they lost interest in it."

"This could only happen to you."

"Is that supposed to be some kind of back-handed compliment?"

"No, it is not. Merely a statement of observable fact."

"Anyway . . . uh, um . . . I heard Day Glo got picked up for beating up some fans."

"It was self-defense."

"So it's true?"

Chester shrugged. "We suck."

"You mean the fans attacked him? Oh God. They were drunk or something."

"Ya think?" Chester turned on the radio.

"So what's up with the Schmuck? He still in the slammer?"

"Mind your own business."

That would be #1 one on the Room for Improvement List Chester handed her when they reconciled.

"Sorry."

6

A WALK IN THE WOODS

✛ ✛ ✛

If it was out here she was going to find it. Bison or human, nobody was going to buffalo Garnet Sullivan if she could help it. She pushed the stiff pine branch away from her face and stepped deeper into the woods. She released it after sliding by and it sprang back with a whispery muffled *thwiiiit*. A shocked cardinal peeped in the tree overhead and flapped away. Avoiding anything that might snap, crackle or pop underfoot was critical. Briefly she had considered bringing Ringo and Diesel with her. She often dragged Ringo along to scare off less domesticated life forms when she ventured into their space. But she'd dismissed this notion out of hand this morning and left the bums at home on the couch. If she found the buffalo, Ringo would harass it and screw up everything. And she didn't want to revive any painful memories in the still fragile Diesel. He was becoming her own little poopy pup. Why remind him of what he'd lost?

So she was out here on her own and she had the creeps. She was case-book phobic when it came to snakes and spiders—they freaked her at some basal level—no matter how small and non-poisonous—and they were everywhere lying in wait for her juicy essence, fangs poised to slake their evil appetites in her helpless and perfectly tanned flesh. The big brown hairy spiders with long legs and big black eyes on long stalks, the kind with dark hair that bristled every which way from their disgusting bodies—the subalterns of the species commonly denominated Housekeeper Spiders—were at their largest and most menacing in September. Yes, by September the monsters had sprung the yellow orange-red jewels of their hideous flaming maturity all over their bodies and were suspended everywhere dead center in their widely cast nets. As horrifying and grasping as a human hand, they draped their big dangly transparent webs from tree to tree and netted everything that tried to pass through.

Walking in the woods, an unsuspecting homo sapiens could easily find herself suddenly covered in sticky gossamer with an angry eight-ounce spider hopping and skittering all over her head and neck. They weren't poisonous, but so what? One could die of fright during such an encounter.

Her walk in the woods had been on her afternoon to-do list, but a few choice words from the Great One had shot it up to numero uno in the a.m. Nothing could make her cut and run, cringe and scurry out of his presence, faster than his prefacing a statement with "There comes a POINT, Garnet." The point—whatever it was—was something he'd been seething and fuming about until it became a live snake, a live or die issue in their relationship. It was a form of ultimatum and something she would be impaled upon if she stood there and listened to his indictment, something on which she would twist and squirm in pain and humiliation until she croaked her abject submissive agreement (which was usually a lie, an empty promise, wrung out of her under extreme duress) to whatever the point was. Maybe one other introductory remark had equal power to create in her an instinctive flight response when issued from his self-righteous, outraged mouth: "Are you *crazy?*" They had gotten to that point again and she was filled with dread at what might happen next. Anyway, here she was. Even snakes and spiders were preferable to The Point.

Tommy had one hundred and forty acres. Citrus groves covered about half of his homestead. The rest of the property was covered in dark dense formidable woods he'd just never gotten around to clearing and planting. Next to that? Hundreds of acres of abutting adjacent woods. She stopped in her tracks. A doe with a Bambi by her side silently slid across her path about fifty feet away. She hadn't smelled or heard her. She glanced up toward the treetops. A stout masked raccoon clung to a tree trunk and looked down at her, curious but motionless. He wasn't afraid—did he have rabies? As she was slowly putting one foot ahead of the other, a wrinkle and snap in the deep leaves ahead almost made her faint. *Snake.* She could have stepped on it.

She reached for a pine tree and paused, perspiration springing out all over her face and neck. Then she recoiled from the tree with a feral shriek. Birds burst out of the treetops without a sound and a noisy rustle in the branches on every side froze her in place. The thing hung from a branch less than a foot from her face in a big insouciant, look-at-me droop. Then it waved back and forth in front of her eyes. Her life passed in review (the best parts, the ones she'd miss), and it doubled up and flicked. Her blood-curdling wail rang through the woods, causing more loud rustling and shivering in the branches and leaves all around her. The thing snapped up once more and twisted in a kind of lazy confident threat, as if it enjoyed terrorizing her and was going to take its own sweet time before planting its fangs. She stared, unable to move a muscle, unable to muster one more scream. As she did, something about this serpentine death machine seemed incongruous. This was a snake with markings and coloration she'd never seen before—anywhere, not even in a book. Since when did snakes start having *hair?*

A deep growl from above yanked her eyes up to the thick branches overhead. And when did they start to *growl*—and have stripes like a *tiger?* Long-lashed Asiatic eyes looked down on her indifferently. A lush fuzz of white spikey whiskers twitched. The big cat ya-a-a-awned and closed its eyes. Nice teeth. Long, white, curved, pointed. What is it about ya-a-a-awns? They are contagious. Then they yawned in unison again the longest ya-a-a-a-awn. Yawning is comfy and disarming. Yawning creates an easy camaraderie betwixt yawners. Look at those amazing colors. Fascination slipped under her skin and suffused her senses. She sank to the ground onto the soft carpet of pine needles and dead leaves and indulged her hungry eyes for several minutes.

When her power of speech returned, she just had to ask. "So . . . . Have you seen a *buffalo* . . . around here . . . lately?"

The tiger stared down with golden slanted eyes and scratched its nose with its paw.

"Cat got your tongue? Hahaha! *Cat?* Get it? No?" Apparently not.

This cat, having missed the pun and bored, maybe, or disgusted, pulled itself up to a higher branch—moving like silk, like water—then to a higher branch and then to a higher—and without a sound vanished into a curtain of green.

Okay. It was a nice tiger. It didn't try to kill her. Maybe it wasn't hungry? Or maybe it was truly, genuinely nice? Had good manners? Reluctantly she left the woods. And more or less on tippy-toe. It wasn't wise to wander around in woods with a tiger in it, however nice.

A rotating circle of black up high against a blank blue sky was the last impression her expedition made upon her. Vultures casing a meal somewhere in the very woods she had left. Carrion birds. The last of the buffalo? Or a deer, maybe a coon? It could be anything; buzzards ate everything long as it was dead and smelly. These woods held enough surprises and secrets and fodder for stories to placate Fred for several frivolous lifetimes. Freddie was big on dead and smelly. What a goldmine. She would be back.

The tiger was exonerated, in Garnet's view, regardless of the teeth equals puncture wounds deduction. The tiger was after, she was sure of it, the buffalo, not Tommy. Nobody would believe it, though. Tipped off to the presence of tiger in Tommy's woods, even a lazy, non-aggressive one, Sheriff Lance would have the tiger dispatched in short order.

She was filling in the blanks too fast for comfort. Chester's client was Alfredo somebody lacking a green card, an illegal immigrant, charged with killing Eduardo Gutierrez, another lost soul lacking a green card, both of whom worked for some pretentious outfit called "The Peaceable Kingdom." The victim was a matter of public record. The accused was still under the protection of Chester's Mary Poppins' umbrella. The Lord and Master of the Peaceable Kingdom was a romantically out of touch with reality, nutz-for-animals wealthy man known as Clovis Reddick in Vero Beach. The case had drawn the attention of the INS. They wanted maybe to deport Alfredo.

Something bad had happened at the Peaceable Kingdom. Someone by the name of Eduardo Gutierrez was stabbed to death. But the tiger played no part in it, nor did Alfredo. She couldn't prove any of it, but she knew it in her bones. The recent high winds and torrential rain had frightened the animals out of their minds. All were exotic, imported, and un-acclimated to the Florida climate and its crazy weather. Barriers may have been broken. Natural enemies may have run through their contained areas and plowed through the fences. They may have intermingled. The tiger maybe ran away from the PK in pursuit of a frantic buffalo that tore through a fence during— she had to stop and think—what did they call that storm? So many come and go so fast, it's easy to lose track unless they're as destructive as an Andrew or a Katrina. But what about the buffalo blood on the carving knife, the putative murder weapon? Had they slaughtered a buffalo to feed to the tiger? That was as offensive to her as homicide. But it wasn't illegal if you owned the buffalo.

Anyway, she couldn't file stories about any of this. All of her information had been acquired beyond the pale. She had no credible "anonymous sources." She was the anonymous source. The "Are you crazy?" Garnet Sullivan. There comes a Point. Yes, and she was far more vulnerable at this point to *that* point, the point of which was for Chester's point to run her through to make *his* point, than she was to anything else. And that was the point, the pre-eminent point, she had to deal with first.

The three impatient ladies shifted from foot to foot and continued to ring the doorbell. Each wielded cleaning implements, a mop, vacuum, feather dusters, paper towels, buckets. Garnet peered through the peephole. They were in uniform. They were a military detail summoned to quell the chaos, to right an out of control situation and restore peace and harmony. And they wouldn't go away. She opened the door.

"Miz Sullivan?"

"Please come in." Something like this was bound to happen. There comes a point.

"Lord, have mercy. Where'd all the feathers come from?"

"Lotta dog hair on the furniture. This is going to take some time."

She'd heard enough and couldn't bear to watch them struggle with the mess. She put the dogs on their leashes. "Pretty day for the beach, guys. I'm outta here."

"He already paid us," one of them called after her.

"That's good. Have at it. Work your miracles." She slammed the door behind her.

The waves were sweet, small and frothy. Serene. The sun, less and less ferocious this time of year, was almost friendly, more warming than searing. The dogs put their noses to the ground, absorbed in a landscape of smells satisfying to them, consuming, curious. They were in a place she couldn't go. They wandered back and forth over the same ground, revisiting every grain of sand, full of infinite dog interest and delight. This was their life. How they enjoyed it. Her own head full of hornets, stinging shoulds, woulds, and coulds, and buzzing with ambiguities and enigmas, she watched and envied them their fully sensual approach to life. Warmed and made woozy by the sun, she finally stretched out on her towel, closed her eyes and wished that instead of the driven human bitch that she was, she had been born one of the canine variety.

Yeats said in his gem of a poem "The Choice" that one had to choose between perfection of the life or the work. She was nothing more than a small town reporter for a tiny to the point of insignificance newspaper. She had no notions of ever being rich or famous. She was dedicated, but not ambitious. She was ardent about issues and helpless people and animals in hopeless situations, but not in the pursuit of making a name for herself as a big time journalist. She knew that her work per se was not worth losing everything for, for it was ultimately silly and ephemeral. And there comes a point. Regret is a bitter pill to swallow. But she swallowed hard and finally got it down. As she was twisting painfully on the point, the afternoon slipped away from her.

✢ ✢ ✢

Chester stood in the living room and turned around beaming. "Oh, hey, *tiger!*" he said, seeing her for the first time.

En garde. This could not be a coincidence. His intuition about her plots, counter plots and thoughts was uncanny.

"Have a good day?" He put his arms around her.

She fell against him. "Yeah, I guess."

"Tired?"

"Chester, I'm sorry. I will do better."

"It's okay. Everything is good."

"I hardly recognize this place."

"Yeah, looks good. Smells good."

They hadn't made love in two weeks. The awkward questions burned in her throat. "You're not mad at me are you?"

He squeezed her. "No."

Ringo and Diesel stood at the door. In and out. In and out. They were compulsive about it. He had to be sick of this. "You don't have to go. I'll walk them by myself."

"No, I want to. I look forward to this every day."

She did not deserve the love of this fine and noble man. "I love you so much, Chester."

"Me too you."

"You do?" She couldn't imagine why.

With nothing submissible on Tommy's death for Fred, he put her on pavement beat. Sign ordinance hearings, next year's county budget hearings. Gradually she went numb with it. Her imagination got into a huff, had a hissy fit, and took off. She plodded and went through the motions and became very, very bored. She told herself she would pick up on the crime leads when it was safe, when she was less interested, when they didn't inflame her so much and drive her to do bad things, take stupid risks, when the pain of Tommy's death, the waste, the pointless loss, her regrets for not having taken the time to just be with him more, to stand in his light and his love while it was there and to return it as she should and wanted to, didn't cut her so badly every waking minute. Life or work? No brainer.

She pounded away on her laptop like a robot. Uninspired, flat verbiage, on time, every time, never missing a deadline. Five hundred words, *send*; 750 words, *send*. Fred was unusually quiet, remote, absorbed with administrative details about running the paper, and didn't offer any comment on her work one way or another. He sometimes had these spells of obsessive attention to the mechanics of newspaper publishing and they gave her breathers from his flogging and juicing over sending her on wild goose chases so he could get his thrills and chills from the safety and comfort of his own office.

Her most recent impalement on The Point had been such that Garnet held to her commitment and did not slip up or recant. She didn't feel herself, but she stuck it out. Like a sleepwalker, she put one foot in front of the other. She trudged to mile markers, tapped them and trudged back and hopped into bed with Chester at a decent hour every night. Days of simple tasks and minor satisfactions passed one after the other. She endured and survived without complaint or comment the nightmares about Tommy every night and surprised Chester with lunch delicacies and funny DVDs. She fought back her grief and remorse silently and bought the Great One three new shirts. They spooned in front of the TV after dinner. Diesel relaxed and revived, became part of the family. It was cramped in the townhouse, but Chester doted on him, and with all the TLC, he grew to be Ringo's good pal. Life was good, she supposed. Not a word passed between them about the Poor dumb Schmuck case. Not a word about the tiger. Not a word, after the funeral, about Tommy. Chester's phone records became sacrosanct. She was horrified at what she had done. She repented in sackcloth and ashes.

It was absolute hell on the inside and total dullsville superficially, but she was safe and so applied herself to playing the new role, one for which she knew she had no talent or aptitude and zero passion or interest. Like a cardboard cut-out, or a Stepford wife, she started cooking pies and cakes from scratch. She bought a bread machine and the aroma of fresh bread filled every room of the townhouse. She searched and found her mother's famous meatloaf recipe, her killer pot roast recipe. At the end of the day, Chester could barely load himself up the stairs to bed.

They stayed home on Saturdays and watched the Gator games alone. She cooked, he ate; they cheered, shouted, mumbled curses in a veritable swamp of touchy-feely agreeable togetherness, and on cue, without his asking, she dutifully got up and brought him another beer. They went shopping at Sam's together Saturday mornings and split hairs over coupons and sales. They drove home with bags and bags of groceries, satiated and silent. They made regular deposits in their joint savings account, astounded that they had money to save. They made slow sweet dreamy affectionate love nearly every night. Most mornings they woke up in each other's arms.

Then one sleepy quiet afternoon, less than thirty days after her reformation, Chester, lulled into a false sense of security about his domestic arrangements, made an observation that he would rue for many days thereafter. Sitting next to him on the couch watching a game and yelling "Go Gators!" at the top of her lungs, Garnet popped the button on the waistband of her shorts. "Oh, dammit," she said, getting up to look for a needle and thread.

"Pants getting a little tight on the old butt, huh, honey?" Chester said, laughing. "You're getting some kind of can on yourself these days, old girl!"

Garnet stopped in her tracks and stared. Chester rolled back and forth on the couch holding his stomach, tears streaming down his face. How hilarious! She, of all people, was "getting fat!"

Her eyes turned to ice. "Fat?"

He looked at her. "Oh, shit," he said. "You know I was just *teasing!*"

"No, you weren't."

"Honey, please, don't be like that . . . and don't look at me that way . . . You're . . . you're . . . just . . . about perfect."

"Meaning 'not *quite* perfect?'"

"You're perfect, okay? *Perfect.*"

She left the room. She disappeared into the difficult-to-disappear-in 1200 square foot townhouse for the rest of the day. After undressing, weighing herself, and scrutinizing her every inch, proportion and ratio in the bathroom mirror, then confirming and re-confirming everything with a tape measure, she admitted to the raw indisputable facts. Yes, to an embarrassing degree,

Chester was correct. But this came as no surprise once she owned up to it, for every woman knows if her pants are "tight"—and within a centimeter of how "tight." To inflict maximum pain and shame on herself for this unforgivable lapse and to inspire resolve for a speedy rectification of her degradation, she dragged out every pair of shorts, slacks and jeans she owned and tried them on, one by one, slowly with a severely critical eye in front of the merciless incriminating full-length mirror in the hallway. To make certain she got the full effect and didn't miss any damning evidence, she also dragged out two halogen floor lamps to shine on her sins and she turned and twisted for an hour in front of the mirror, wincing with tears in her eyes.

She flung a tasteless unadorned tuna sandwich on the table for Chester's dinner and left him to gag it down alone.

✢ ✢ ✢

Fifteen seconds after his fatal fat remark Garnet went on a draconian diet and developed an irresistible urge to seek out the tiger. Her mind hit reset and went into over-drive. Her imagination was restored with a florid vengeance. She had a plan. Adversity joined with righteous anger can be galvanizing.

It's all about leverage. She had to act fast. Shock and awe. Massive force. She went on a relentless hectoring crusade to save Allison. She had touched base with her to verify this was still a Major Moral Compunction and worth using her upper hand with Chester this way. It seemed a casual conversation and would have been innocent enough had Garnet not been one of the parties and if Allison hadn't been unable to talk about more than one subject.

"You know, Garnet, *I swear,* I've never had better sex!"

"Sorry? What does that have to do with sea salt, Allison?"

"I mean, sometimes, you know, I feel like a slut. But, hey, I'm a happy slut. Know what I mean? If screwin were *fattening,* I'd weigh 500 pounds!"

"That much? So you and Lance are still a 'thing?'"

"Long as his 'thing' is workin, heck yeah!"

"Clever girl."

50

"Now tell me the God's honest truth, Garnet, how many great orgasms have you had in an hour?"

"I lost count a long time ago."

"That many? I'm not there yet. Good gosh, I never even knew sex could be fun before now. I thought it was like football. The guys love it, we have to play along with them and fake it."

"When are Mums and Pops due back from Europe? Are they still in Provence?"

"Who cares? I have no clue. They leave messages, but I erase them as soon as I hear their voices."

"Back to the sea salt rub you got. Was it worth the money?"

"So how would you rate Chester in the sack on a scale of one to ten?"

Satisfied by her interrogation that her BFF had sunk even further into carnal depravity, Garnet pressed Chester's last hot button and he accelerated. It was a thread of an opportunity to redeem himself and at least she was talking to him about something now.

"I'll make a few calls. This is do-able."

"Then get it done, Chester."

"I'm on it, honey."

Chester had a healthy ego and a talent for coming to his senses in record time. She had a narrow window of opportunity. To keep him on task she continued to make herself scarce taking long drives with the dogs, spending hours at the beach with them, carrying her laptop to Starbucks to work. Everywhere she went the sad ghost of Tommy seemed to lurk in the shadows just out of sight—right next to the searing unforgettable image of her robust thighs in the hallway mirror.

7

CLASSIFIED

✝ ✝ ✝

Fred read the classified ad out loud for the second time. "$10,000 Reward. Missing since 9/5. 5 yr old female Bengal Tiger. Trained, non-aggressive. Answers to KALIMBA. Do not attempt to apprehend. 772-514-7131. Lv msg."

"Is it legit?"

"You sure you don't know anything about this?"

"How would I, why would I?"

"I pay you to know everything."

"I need a raise then. Knowing everything costs more, both you and me."

"I can't believe Martha took this over the phone and didn't give me a heads up."

"You know Martha, Freddie. She's obsessed with counting words and spaces, totally focused on using the calculator. Words and spaces, dollars and cents. She misses things. *Ka-ching*, that's her core skill set and her passion. It's the woman's *raison d'etre*."

"Call the damn number! What the hell are you waiting for? Get out there, see what's up! This is hot! Human interest! Animal lovers!"

"Headlines," she mumbled. Here we go again. She wanted to feed Fred to the tiger. She could muster some genuine enthusiasm for that.

"And you don't know anything about this? You're sure?"

"News to me, Fred."

She'd get Fred his scoop per his marching orders all right, but first she wanted to verify her own secret and "classified" scoop by taking a quick peek at the tiger again. Make sure it was still hanging around Tommy's woods and safe. Ten thousand dollars can be a real motivator to a lot of people. So she goosed it out there with no delay and ran straight into the woods, spiders and snakes be damned. She didn't have much time.

As she ducked under the branches and the shade of the trees covered her and hindered her vision, something cold and metallic jammed into her neck and a dirty calloused hand clamped over her mouth and yanked her backwards like a rag doll onto a sweaty and smelly heaving male chest.

"Don't talk, don't move."

She nodded.

"Hear me?"

She nodded. He was big. And he was old. She knew him. She'd known him a long time, since she was a little girl. But not like this.

"Purty blue eyes, purty. Just like your mama." He twisted her head around on her neck tight. "Do we understand each other, Miss Garnet?" He loosened his grip some.

"Yessir, Mr. Johnson."

"Don't do anything silly and ya won't get hurt."

"Okay."

The poor old guy looked fierce and hyper, like he was going to fall apart any second. She better not push it. She tried a little levity to defuse the situation. "*Me*? Silly? Mr. Johnson, really! How silly!"

"What are you doing out here, missy? Huh?" His eyes were nutty. Something was off. He was angry and alarmed. Weird. Jumpy.

She rubbed her numb lips and tried to read him better. "I was just out here for old time's sake, I guess. You know, paying my respects to Uncle Tommy. Kinda came out here to sort of see him, talk to him."

He waved the gun and snarled. "Pshaw! Go along now! Crazy little thing! Git 'for I shoot your purty little head off!"

"Are you okay, Mr. Johnson? Has something upset you?"

"Get your skinny little ass outta here! Now!" He pointed the gun at her and cocked it.

She was in no position to argue. "Okay. It's all right. Calm down, don't worry. I'm going. Bye now." She turned and walked away slowly looking at the ground and her leaden reluctant feet. Halfway to her car, she stopped and looked back. "What are *you* doing out here, Mr. Johnson? What's going on?"

He snarled at her. "*Git!*" he snapped and fired an earth-shaking shot that caromed around the old house, rang through the clearing and echoed throughout the woods. Her eyes opened wide as the ground jumped at her feet.

"Hey, it's *me*, Garnet, Mr. Johnson! Me! What's the gun for? Huh? What have *I* done? What's the matter?" she said backing up fast.

He closed his eyes, squeezed the trigger and fired again, pinging her front bumper.

She jumped in the bug, floored it and got Lance on the phone 30 seconds later. That old jackass must be after the tiger.

"No way! That old fart? He can barely walk. Nah, must be someone else, Garnet."

A few nuclear powered obscenities flew out of her mouth.

"Listen to you. Take a powder. We'll pick him up. But you need to file a report."

"Do it now or you'll be sorry."

✝ ✝ ✝

The Peaceable Kingdom, ten miles due west of Vero Beach, was surrounded by a twelve-foot high hurricane fence topped with three loops of razor wire.

The wrought iron gate ended in spear-like thrusts toward the sky. It was a pleasant sunny happy afternoon, the birds were singing, the air smelled good, there was the nicest little breeze. You'd have to work at it to be unhappy on a day like this. But Garnet sensed this was not a happy place. Stopped before the gate, she got a bad vibe she couldn't shake.

Clovis Reddick was a nervous little man, a mumbler and a stutterer. His eyes darted and blinked with nervous tics and twitches. She sat through ten minutes of his mewing, fussing, fidgeting, rearranging things on his desk, shrieking at staff on his intercom in the voice of a six year-old girl about tea service, petit fours, scones, and photos from the "vault." Then she snapped and whipped out a clipping of his classified ad.

"What's this all about, Mr. Reddick?" She had gotten over petit fours at 14 after her first cotillion.

He must have been expecting this, because he kicked into a stammering rapid recital of a press release. He said he was an exotic wildlife fancier. He had many fine specimens from every part of the globe. All kinds of animals, large and small, carnivorous and vegetarian. His eyes rolled around the room and he sighed in billows fulsomely.

"A Wildlife 'fancier?' Fancy that! That's an odd expression for an operation the size of yours, Mr. Reddick." He winced and she bit her lip. "Sorry, didn't mean it the way it sounded."

"Miss Sullivan, are you an animal lover?"

"You might say that."

"These animals are my children. They are my life."

Moreover, however, and furthermore, there was "Mother." He lived with and cared for his 98-year-old invalid Mater. Mater herself was a wildlife enthusiast and he owed his passion to her. Her mother, his "Grand Dame, dead for centuries now, good Lord, don't you know, how time flies, tempus fugit, time's winged chariot, all that rot," had been an original investor in Standard Oil.

"Old Nelson Rockefeller, the first one I mean, the one who gave dimes to guttersnipe in New York? Don't you know, they had been engaged once, but Grandmother insisted on going on safari to bag some elephant and he got tired of waiting and married another society belle. He'd given her stock options as an engagement gift. She exercised them for 10 dollars a pop and here we are today. Shrewd one she was, Grandmother."

At this he shut his mouth, spun away from his mahogany desk and looked at his feet. Suddenly he pulled a monogramed handkerchief from his safari vest and honked.

"Bloody sinuses. Forgive me. But maybe you can understand? I have to find Kalimba. She is everything to me."

Several awkward silent minutes passed. He was embarrassed and she was embarrassed for him. This man had to be the most "exotic" life form on the place. She'd never encountered anyone with so many palsies, tremors and twitches. This little creature was angst itself. His spiel was spin by someone who couldn't so much as spin a top as a kid. Riddled with anxiety, hyper-sensitive about the oddball image he knew he projected, and on the hot seat for the fact that a Bengal tiger he owned was loose in the community, he was pathologically craven and groveling. She expected him to disintegrate on the spot any second. She didn't want to be the one who flipped the switch and blew his last fuses, so she held her tongue, sat still and just waited to see what would happen next.

Reddick's starched safari togs were two sizes too large for him. He moved around in them as if he were in a small cage. His neck had shortened like a tortoise's at her "fancier" remark, then it seeped out ever so slowly again, as his eyes filled with hope at her uncritical calm and patience. She couldn't help feeling sorry for him and wanting to comfort him. As he relaxed a bit, she leaned toward him. "Mr. Reddick, listen. I know where you're coming from. I get it. I am often misunderstood myself. I know how it hurts. You can trust me. Whatever you say here will be off the record. I promise."

She placed her notebook, pen and camera on the table and folded her hands. "Sorry to have interrupted you. Go ahead. You'll feel better if you get it off your chest. You couldn't find a more compassionate pair of ears." She pulled the back of her ears forward until they stuck out from her head like big wing nuts. "Seriously?" She winked. "If I can help, I will."

He sniffed and giggled. "You will?"

She nodded and winked again. "So tell me about Kalimba. Will you show me where she was kept?"

Wrong thing to say! Reddick shrank. His head dropped, his chin hit his chest and he receded into his clothes.

"Are you okay?"

He raised his eyes. He was weeping. He swung his flabby little arm into the air. "Something bad will happen to her. People are afraid of tigers!"

Garnet's heart banged against her ribs. This was painful to watch. "Please, Mr. Reddick, don't worry. I just know she's all right. I have a very strong feeling about it." She reached out for him but he fell back.

"Thank you for your kindness. Oh me, where was I? Well, we re-located here from Santa Fe, New Mexico two years ago, my awful chronic sinus problem, such a bore. Doctors advised it, heavens, no idea, it hasn't helped one iota."

"Gads." She fumbled with her camera. "I had no idea bison were this massive." Suckers kept shuffling off every time she almost had them in focus. Bite of grass, two to three steps, bite of grass.

"They are very docile," Reddick said. "You could approach them more closely, if that would help."

"So how many do you have?" All she saw through the lens was a huge coffee colored hairy hump. Where was the zoom thingy? As she was pushing buttons, a wet sneeze-snort sprayed her face. A glossy black nose the size of a bowling ball was in the viewfinder.

They walked in a slow silent lockstep toward the big cat runs.

"You certainly don't manage all of this yourself, Mr. Reddick."

"I have help. Right now I'm a little short-handed."

"Is it hard to find qualified personnel?"

He blinked hard but refused to bite on her bait and quickly changed the subject. "Now then let me show you the lions. All are from Africa and were bred and reared in the wild."

"Is that a good thing?"

He crimped at the waist and giggled into his hand. "Oh, I don't want any pussy-foots! I like my kitties with some spirit!"

"Good one!" She forced a polite titter. "You are quite the punster, very clever!"

✛ ✛ ✛

They met at Johnny's Crab Shack. The tide was out and the air smelled awful. Rotting fish, algae.

Garnet was ravenous. "I wish they'd hurry up. I haven't eaten all day."

"That stupid diet. Now you're getting too thin. Moderation, Garnet, has always been a challenge for you. You need to work on it." Chester swabbed up the last of the smoked mullet dip with a wad of bread.

"Stop looking at me that way. I haven't turned into a damn toothpick. I'm not anorexic, you know, just disciplined and goal oriented." If she had to have her jaw wired shut, she was never going to give him another opportunity to say she was getting fat.

He shook his head. "Right. So rough day?"

"No, not really."

"Wish I could say the same."

"Oh?"

"Yeah."

"We need to get out, Chester, have a little fun. I think we should go to Terry's game party Saturday."

"I would actually like to see that game live."

She frowned. "Then go."

"It's not that long a drive."

"No."

The waitress was serving their crab cakes and shrimp. "Tennessee's gonna be tough, Chester. Why go all that way to see them lose?"

"We can leave Friday after work. I'll drive. You can sleep."

"No. I have to work. Too hot anyway." She wanted to talk to him about Allison. But he was beat. It could wait.

"May I have one of your shrimp?"

He stabbed her hand with his fork. "One."

"Gees."

"If we knock off Tennessee we're back on the AP list."

"Maybe."

"Sick of this rain."

"Me too."

"I need to talk to you about some things."

"I'm on the case, honey. Lighten up on Allison's problem for 15 minutes every now and then. Dig in. I want to go to bed."

8

THE FRITZ

✝ ✝ ✝

The rain had been coming down in steel sheets all morning. Three tropical depressions were skulking around the Caribbean and making runs at the east coast Florida shorelines, but only bouncing off again so far. Undeterred by the potentially disastrous weather, Chester and his buds took off for Gainesville—the Gator Swamp—in high spirits on Thursday afternoon, having whipped and roused one another into a manic fandango at the prospect of a Big Game in Ben Hill Griffin Stadium minus the ladies (and thus the ordinary rules and regs of comportment). Garnet just hoped they wouldn't get arrested or fall out of the stands.

She sat at her laptop and went over her notes one more time. During the last several days she had scrounged, sifted and embellished the facts sufficiently to write a compelling story for Fred on the alleged murder at Peaceable Kingdom, and it was nigh Pulitzer-worthy prose in her humble opinion. He'd been dogging her about it for two weeks and she had to dish up something soon or he'd pop his cork again. Problem was, of course, Chester and his mysterious defense strategy for Alfredo Gomez (she'd gotten his full name finally off a "misplaced," now found, police blotter entry at the sheriff's office). Alfredo, unable to post bail, was still behind bars at the county jail. She put in a request to see him three days ago, but had received no word yet. The justifiable opportunities for procrastination on filing the story were plentiful and made sense. She should wait until she knew more, until she heard the accused's side of the story, until she pulled something like a statement—anything—out of the jittery evasive Mr. Reddick. But these concerns counted as nothing in the big scheme of things because no one waited to get the *whole* story if that someone was a professional journalist. You had to run with what you had.

Garnet was tormented by a sneaky underhanded way out of the conundrum, but she was supposed to have stopped that sort of behavior—wasn't she? She could file the story Friday night while Chester was swilling suds in the Swamp and yelling his head off with 89,999 other fans, and he might not find out until it was "old news." To wit, not worth having a hissy fit about. But she knew that he would know instantly that she had cadged the run date and the upshot of that would be not good in their domestic bliss department. How could she expect him to toe the line if she didn't? So, bottom line, pros and cons shifted and sorted and flogged, she was damned if she did and damned if she didn't. Funny, she paused to reflect, how much of life is like this. Her life, anyway.

Ten days ago she'd stuck her neck out with a squib about Tommy's cause of death—an apparent heart attack preceded by advanced congestive heart failure—and Fred printed it. He'd demanded the source and she 'fessed up: Lance's messy desk. She'd pilfered it and copied it. She produced the proof for him, the copy she'd made. He frowned, but ran with it. That kind of source, while a little on the shady side, was unassailable, and he had no problem using the phrase "According to an anonymous but well-placed and credible source" as the lead. As further evidence of Lance's professionally damaging cupidity, not a peep had issued from the sheriff's department after it appeared in the paper. They must have gotten some calls about it, she thought, yes, she was sure of it. But if Lance was still engrossed with, not to say enwrapped by, the sexually woozy Allison, he wasn't looking at his messages at the office. The day he did, if he ever recovered, would be a tough day for the Sheriff, and she almost felt sorry for him thinking about it. But he was a Teflon kind of a guy. Everyone in the county loved him so much they could forgive him for almost anything, particularly a hot, distracting romance.

She glanced across her desk at her scribbled list of doctors she'd been trying to contact to get a diagnosis on Allison that would hold up in court. She crumpled it up and tossed it into the trash. Most names had been scratched through; it was essentially worthless. Her crusade to save Allison and thus maybe salvage Lance's reputation too, had come to a dead halt. She'd phoned ten docs and ten docs had said, hell no. None wanted to stick their noses into the high falutin' Highsmith family private matters. The doctors were, one and all, members of the Pelican Yacht Club. Many golfed with Morris, Allison's old man. It was a matter of caste and propriety. A couple of medics told her pointedly it was none of her damn business either and that if she knew was good for her, she'd drop it and look the other way, just let it play itself out. If Allison needed a time out in a cork lined room, her parents or some blood relatives should initiate the process and file the papers not some equally nutty "BFF," a term she'd had to explain to more than one M.D. Since there were only twelve doctors in all of Punta Bella, odds were the X-rated soap opera entitled "Allison Screws Sir Lance a Lot" was going to be a ribald public phenom until its natural torrid and embarrassing end.

She checked her voice mail again for the third time in five minutes and the hair on the back of her neck came to attention. An alarming unfamiliar voice, a voice as obnoxious and strident as fingernails on a blackboard shrieked, "Dr. Hiram Beignet Fritzwold returning your call. BLAM."

Garnet jumped out of her chair and dumped the over-stuffed trash basket out onto the floor, kicked the crumpled papers and wrappers around with her bare foot in a frantic search, and with her other set of toes fended off the newly roused and curious Ringo and Diesel. With trembling hands she retrieved the wadded up list and smoothed it out on her desk. Yes. There it was. Must be him, albeit number twelve on the list. Dr. Fritzwold, her very last choice. A retired dermatologist.

So what? He was still a doctor, right?

"FRITZ! Put your GD glass down and get up off your lazy ass! Someone wants to talk to you."

"ME? Talk to *me?*"

"Put the glass down, Fritz."

"Shut the hell up, Ruth. I'm coming."

Receiver hits the floor, shuffling, groaning, it's dropped again. Then "Hello. Hiram Beignet Fritzwold, M.D. at your service."

"Dr. Fri . . ."

"Wait. First I must tell you that I am retired from the practice of dermatology."

"Uh, okay. That's skin, right?"

"Warts and all, my dear."

Garnet held the phone away from her ear, tapped her head with it, and decided she wasn't dreaming. "Yessir, this may be another exercise in futility . . . ."

"Ah, my favorite kind of exercise. Toning. Keeps the mind sharp."

Seriously, seriously. "My name is Garnet Sullivan and . . . ."

"Yes. I knew your father. Fine doctor. Our last consult was on a 76-year-old case of undescended testicles. Male, of course."

"Wow. Of course."

Her father had been an Internist. Provided the testicles were, as it were, *un*-descended, that may have fallen into his purview, but she wasn't 100 percent on it.

"I think he wrote a paper for *JAMA* on it. Very strange case."

"Yeah. I bet. Anyway, reason I'm calling . . . ."

"Is because you're at the end of the list, isn't it? Everyone else said nyet, nada, no way, f*ck off, ersatz, NO."

Head banging time again. What the hay was going on here? Word must travel fast through the Me Doctor grapevine.

"So, Miss Sullivan, wassup?"

"Well . . . not sure where to start with this . . ."

"By the way, you can call me Fritz."

"Okay, Fritz, Dr. Fritz, anyway, I have a friend I am very concerned about. Her name is Allison . . . ."

"Highsmith."

Boink. She slipped from her chair to the floor. Ringo and Diesel plodded over and plopped down on top of her. "Oooooumph."

"And she's gone . . ."

"*Crazy.* Hahahahahaha!"

"I was going to say sort of 'off the deep end.'"

"Hahahahaha! Aha. I am *quite* familiar with the syndrome."

"How did you know?"

"*Know,* my dear? The Fritz knows everything. I've lost my license several times for '*knowing* too much.'"

"I can imagine." She remembered now. This guy was a living legend in the Punta Bella medical community. It was so long ago, though, she assumed he'd be dead. As a kid she'd heard a rumor about a large black cauldron he kept simmering into which he'd throw whatever caught his whim, snakes and spiders, Drain-O, then use the broth to "experiment" with on unsuspecting patients. "Double, double, toil and trouble," a witch's brew kinda deal. It was enough to terrify any kid who heard about it enough to be willing to die before "going to the dermatologist." She had overheard her parents laughing about "Fritz's brew" more than once. And this was one and the same: Hiram the Fritz? Good grief. Now what?

"Of course you can imagine, dearest, because you have the right and oh so tight genes."

She looked down. Safe. She wasn't even wearing jeans.

And dadgummit, a man, even a madman, with these legendary talents could prove very useful in helping her negotiate her way out of the several imbroglios she had recently created for herself.

"Forgive me, but I need to ask . . . ."

"Yes. I am still licensed to practice medicine in Florida. Believe it or not. *Haha!* Those old stiff necks in Tallahassee never could *prove* a damn thing. Couldn't make a ONE of their charges stick. Get me?"

How he ever got a license in the first place was still an unsolved mystery in town. But no matter. All righty, then. Things were lookin up.

"Perhaps we could meet somewhere, Dr. Fritz, you know, over a cup of coffee or something? This is rather difficult for me to explain on the phone."

"No. I don't drink anything but Beefeater's."

"Only gin? Not even water?"

"Sometimes my wife slips it into the gin behind my back, curse the demented old bag. And of course the ice cubes melt."

"Right. So, hey, how 'bout we . . ."

No, no, no. Turned out there was only one place in the county the Fritz would go to for a "consult." That settled, they made a date.

She sent Fred a decent pile of rubbish he could print about the death at the Peaceable Kingdom, along with a teaser email alluding to the hot juicy stories to follow. "This guy Clovis Reddick at PK is a total hoot. More soon. Promise. Yes, there is a tiger on the loose. A real T-I-G-E-R with stripes and everything. And BTW, *please* send my check early if you can. I'm broke as a joke. Thanks. XOXO, Garnet."

Earlier Chester had texted her that he and the guys had made it to Gainesville and were staying with his rummy old frat bro Harry. Not to worry. Things wouldn't get outta hand. Harry had "mellowed" a lot. Like hell he had.

9

WARTS & ALL

✛ ✛ ✛

She wasn't a member, but the Moose Lodge on US1 made a special exception because her last name was Sullivan ("the old doc's kid"). The 76 year-old man whose hidden testicles her father had routed out like a buried archeological treasure, and brought to light as if they were astounding artifacts of the Pleistocene period, had been a huge Moose, a highly revered lodge donor, patron, hero. A massive testicle-shaped bronze plaque dedicated to his memory and celebrating his bravado (e.g., "balls") hung in a prominent location right over the bar with a spotlight trained on it for all to see and to facilitate lifting a reverent toast, hoist a frosted mug, to for as long as Moose were Moose and Men were Men.

Nevertheless, the three octogenarian bouncer Moose at the door officiously and tediously examined Garnet's I.D.'s, frisked her rather too personally, tried to confiscate her cell phone and iPod, and called over a contingent of glowering, suspicious Moose consiglieri to further consult, verify and approve her credentials. After fifteen minutes of leering lewd fun transacted in a secret obtuse Moose language, a looming, hirsute Moose major domo conducted her into the dark cavern in which she expected to find The Fritz hanging upside down from some rafter.

She stumbled around in the murk bumping into tables and feeling the soles of her shoes make contact with various smelly adhesive substances on the bare concrete floor. The scene was be-fogged floor to ceiling with thick gray strata of tobacco smoke of the cheap cigar variety, and laced with ancient body odors and the reek of countless spilled drinks from days gone by. From huge loud speakers at the four corners of the massive non-descript echoey room Sinatra was crooning his old mafia era stuff at deafening decibels. The sole waitress on duty was a hump-backed senior citizen with a giant old style hearing aid stuck in her ear and, though a fellow red head, was no help whatsoever. She could not comprehend a single word Garnet said. "What? What's that? Come again?" Garnet finally mouthed a giant "Thank You" and wandered away.

An ear-splitting howl proved to be the only clue to the location of her new mentor. She wended her way in its direction as if homing in on a siren call to hell.

She was unprepared for the specter awaiting her in the innermost recesses of Moosedom. As she followed the voice through the slurry dark, a white shrunken prune of a face topped with a wild cascade of blue-black hair and punctuated with a matching blue-black razor thin mustache emerged gradually out of the mist. It was a sight that would stop a raging Moose dead in its tracks. Doc's erratic Prince Valiant hair-do was in dire need of a color "touch up," for an inch and a half of stiff snowy white roots sprang away from his scalp in an unearthly ominous corona suggestive of Lucifer himself.

He didn't get up. He pointed to a spot next to him in the booth. He thundered, "SIT."

When she recoiled, he responded, "Sit down, dammit. Are ye deef?"

When she at last, against her every instinct, reluctantly slid onto the bench next to him, he added, "Look at *you*. The spittin image of your daddy."

"Don't say that. I'm a girl."

"Yes, you are. And a pretty one. Now relax. I ordered you a sloe gin fizz."

"What's that?"

"It's a girly drink. You'll like it."

"I'd rather have a glass of Francis Ford Coppola pinot noir—2008, if they have it."

He laughed. And laughed.

She took a deep breath. "So I don't know where to start with this. But bottom line, Dr. Fritzwold, my friend Allison is off her nut. She's turned into a nympho and she's taken down the sheriff and . . ."

"And you need a physician to sign the papers that she's psycho. You want to Baker Act her butt. A nice long three-day time out. With complimentary meds and arts and crafts classes—if she behaves."

"Uh, yeah, I guess that's pretty much it."

"Ah, yes, been there myself a few times. Humorless place. And no G.D. gin, either."

"You don't mean . . .?"

"Oh, yeah, I've been locked up in the bin. And more than once. Not recently, though." He winked and squeezed her knee.

"That's good, I guess."

"It's not all bad. The food is crap, but I always found the nurses, shall we say, 'indulgent?'" Another knee squeeze. "Nursies love doctors, ya know. Especially *crazy* ones!"

"Yeah, I guess." Eeeew. Yuk.

"So out with it, tell me more."

"So anyway, Dr. Fritzwold, I'm not sure you can help me. I mean, you're a dermatologist. I don't know if a judge . . ."

"Done it before, don't know why I can't do it again."

"But maybe that was a long time ago?"

"I have to see the patient first. Let's get down to business here. I have to do this by the book. Check her vitals. All that rigmarole. Tonsils, ears, find her spleen, do a rectal, a vaginal . . ."

"Oh no, all *that*?"

"Damn right. Follow all the P's and Q's. No short-cuts. Can't afford anymore 'infractions.' Know what I mean? One more and I'm SOL. Peer review, all that shit."

A red bubbly thing appeared on the table in front of her. It didn't look safe. A static white froth sat like an inert toxic substance on top of a rosy red gelid solution. It was in a tall glass and had a parasol and straw in it like the

Shirley Temple cocktails her parents ordered for her while they were enjoying their martinis at a restaurant.

The Fritz raised his glass. "Down the hatch!"

She took a sip. Just to be polite.

"Your daddy would be proud of you."

"Dad didn't drink much, if that's what you mean."

"It's not."

The warm glow of a sloe gin came over her. "Say, do you know anything about, uh, *tigers?* Or maybe *buffalo?*" It didn't taste too bad. Kind of like cherry kool-aide spiked with two shots of gasoline and a spritz of kerosene.

The Fritz leaned stiffly, rigid as a fence post, into her side in the booth. He swung his arm around her shoulders and placed a damp hand on her thigh, nodding maniacally as she spoke, seemingly getting her point way ahead of her delivery, maybe getting her point before she knew what it was herself. He expostulated in Latin and Greek at certain junctures and finished her sentences for her. He had a plan and an answer for everything.

"Waitress! Waitress!" he yelled, holding up his empty glass and waving it as a remonstrance at her snail's pace service. When the poor old shuffling thing at last wobbled up tableside, he said, "Take your *hormones*, woman! If you had, you wouldn't have turned into a stooped over old toad!"

Cringing and grinning, Garnet mumbled apologetically, "He's kidding. Don't mind him."

"No, I am not. This woman needs an estrogen IV, damn her wrinkled old hide."

"Shut up, Dr. Fritz."

"Get a move on, granny, we need some drinks here! Or are you blind too?"

"My God, Dr. Fritzwold! That's mean! Stop it!"

He smacked the back of her head. "You're a softie, just like your daddy. Wise up, kiddo."

Hours of hooting Latinate delirium ensued peppered with stories of his time in North Africa in dubya dubya two "seeding" the "Krauts" with big cats wired for reconnaissance, "Jaguars, they're the best, natural born spies and killers," stories of warts the size of bowling balls "excised masterfully with my secret chemical serum leaving absolutely no scar," plots by the board of medical examiners to "curtail" his leading edge practice and research practices. He had her attention. She sat in the foul dark, watching his sputum-flecked jabbering, twitching lips, her mind ricocheting like a pinball, as one improbable scheme, heinous act, shocking scurrilous statement, and scatological jibe issued from them after another, a flood of blab and arcane reference carrying all before it, a Sargasso Sea of erudite garbage, a swamp of vomited verbiage. She was impressed, yes, but by *what?*

He paused and drained his tumbler of Beefeater's.

"*Huh,*" she said. "Wow."

He slammed the empty glass down on the table and turned to her. "Take off your clothes!"

"What?"

"I want to check you for suspicious growths."

"I don't have any!"

"I'm the best mole man in Florida, the skin cancer capital of the US of A!" he crowed. "Melanoma made me a rich man! I'll remove your crud right here *gratis,* dearie! Won't hurt a bit. Waitress! Bring me a steak knife!"

Five minutes later, with Fritz already off on another tare, a steak knife was unceremoniously flung onto the table. He held it up. "What the hell is this? Where's the beef?"

"No idea." While he was haranguing the waitress for yet another round, Garnet slipped it into her purse.

Well into hour number three, by dint of continually forcing him back to the issues of burning interest to her, and fortified by the Pink Parasol Pulverizers, they began to make some progress. Yes, he wanted to see the tiger, the sooner the better.

"Why the hell not tonight, right now, eh?"

"Tomorrow would actually work better for me, Dr. Fritzwold."

"Female, you say? Interesting. Unpredictable, very dangerous." And "Yes. Absolutely," Allison was obviously manic, needed to be locked up for her own good. They needed to be quick about it, and stealthy. No telling what she might do at this end of the cycle. Garnet needed to take her credit cards away post haste before Allison found herself in front of a bankruptcy judge and landed in the poorhouse. "Spend, spend, spend! Maniacs are EXCESSIVE, I tell you. Remember that, excessive in everything they do! Buffalo, eh? Figures. Tigers love bison meat. Love it!"

And the murder at the Peaceable Kingdom? "Darlin, do you have a BRAIN inside that pretty red head of yours?"

"Well, ex-*cuse* me? [hic hic] I *did* graduate [hic] cum laude, Phi [hic] Beta Kappa . . . You you [hic] you—whatever you *are* . . ."

"They WANT you to think the tiger did it! She's the back-up if they can't pin it on the spic!"

"Huh. No *kidding?*" Hiccups gone.

"Bastards were probably abusing her anyway. Bestiality perverts and such."

Garnet swooned and her head fell forward onto the table with a thump. "*Oh no!*"

"Either way, justifiable homicide, hot stuff. Mark my words."

"So you think Clovis Reddick is covering for Kalimba? Or what the hell *do* you mean?"

"Ya know the law will whack that tiger, one way or another."

"No!"

Fritz cupped her chin in his hands. "Why, my lovely, do they have to nab the tiger, though, eh? I'm not gonna talk. You gonna talk?"

She pulled away. "Hell no."

"No sweat. Stick with me, kid. I ain't been caught yet."

She had no idea what he was talking about, but the rosy glow of dawning solutions was blooming, unaccountably, on her cheeks. The Fritz! She wanted to dance. He was psychic! Intuitive! Brilliant! Uncanny. Dangerous. Inebriating. Funny too. What a stroke of luck. Problems solved. She had found a Merlin, and he was her very *own* Merlin. Look out. There's a new sheriff in town.

Leaking sloe gin from her gills and pores and unable to gag down another drop, at midnight Garnet rolled out the door of the Moose Lodge on rubber legs, leaving the Fritz behind to continue his avid pursuit of brain pickling and eureka moments. Under a street light she saw the light. She held onto the lamppost. The sidewalk was moving, the stars overhead were swirling in joy and jubilation. Her lips felt fat and her feet felt . . . nothing.

"Cabbie!"

In the next 24 hours she and the Fritz were going to track down Allison for a cursory look-see so he could pull off their plan "by the book," check on the tiger, the sweet mistreated Kalimba, and do a bunch of other super important things she couldn't remember just then. It would be the adventure of a lifetime.

Seven hours later she woke up with a head the size of a basketball on top of the covers, fully dressed, one shoe on, one shoe off, and sandbagged on either side by sacked out Ringo and Diesel. The sunshine streaming in the window was brutally offensive. Yeah, it'd stopped raining, but this was much worse. She could stand a few clouds this morning. She staggered to the bathroom with her eyes closed, bumping against furniture and bouncing off the walls. Through a blue haze of pain she realized she had to call yet another cab to get back to Moose Land to pick up her car. In a rush she swallowed eight Tylenol with six glasses of water, fully aware she might be over-dosing. It hardly mattered. If the pain kept up, she would be in the ER anyway.

From the dim backseat of the cab on the ride back she realized with a jolt that she'd missed the game on TV yesterday. She didn't know who had won. This was not good vis-a-vis Chester etcetera. So quick. After the Tennessee game, was Florida #1 in the SEC—or not? And who got MVP? Help! What were the critical plays?

Lacking this info in Florida on a Sunday during football season made her a suspicious character. If she hadn't been watching the game on Saturday night, what exactly had she been doing? And with whom?

The only thing she had going for her was the absolute assurance that Chester and his buds were in a similar mental state of disarray about the particulars of their activities of the previous 12 hours, albeit in possession of the game score and the stats.

The cabbie wore a white turban and was listening to staticky sitar music on a small transistor radio. Gusts of sandalwood incense blew into her pale face from the front seat A/C vents. Yeah, he was an unlikely informant, but what the heck.

"So, hey, just wondering, did you happen to watch the game yesterday?" she mildly inquired of the turban.

Rapid nodding. "Go Gators!"

"Yeah, great game."

"We number one!" Even though he was shooting through heavy traffic at 65 mph, he turned around and grinned at her. "Tenn-lee-see sucks!"

"Yeah, man. Whoops!" Horns were blaring, cars swerving sharply to avoid them. "Oh, no! Watch out!" She covered her eyes and sank into the seat.

A few minutes later, she had to ask. "I didn't get to see the last ten minutes of the game. So what was the final score, anyway?" She braced herself for another swerve.

A sparkling expanse of huge, perfectly white teeth faced her. Out of them came the incredible words, "One towsund to nutting! Go Gators!"

Talk about running up the score. She covered her head and ducked. They sideswiped a mailbox then careened on two wheels to the other side of the road.

"We are champs! We number one! Go Gators!"

Man, she had to admit, the shoe was on the other foot, if she wasn't behind the wheel. "Oh my God! Watch out! You're on the wrong side of the road!" She put her head in her lap, grabbed her knees and prepared for impact.

The turban bobbed and jerked in hysterical mirth. "I forget! I tink I in India! Dis side, dat side, what deefrance is dat? Haha!" Then Swami-Gator flashed another dazzling smile, nearly blinding her, "It great to be a Gator, no?"

"Yes! Watch where you're going, for godsake!" Even if she did survive this cab ride, she was doomed. Cursed. All the Sunday papers would be sold out by now. Then two gin-soaked brain cells woke up and whispered snidely in her over-wrought, sensitive, ring-dinging ears: "It's online, stupid. Check it out." Right. She would. Preferably before the Great One got home.

The cabbie pulled up to the curb in front of the Moose Lodge, hopped out and dashed around to open her door. "Dank you berry much, lady. You are very fine young missy. Yes?" His hand shot out towards her. "Please. My card. You need a ride again? Call me? Please?"

Her eyes swam, the words ran together, sloe gin seemed to be oozing out of her every orifice. She opened and closed her eyes and held the card away from her at arm's length, squinting and blinking. Buried in the dense colorful foliage of red roses and green curlicues on the cabbie's business card were the words, "Chutney Patel, Esq., Chauffeur, Man Friday, Speedy Go-For."

"At your service, very nice lady!" he said, with a heartfelt gusto that nearly blew her over and clicking his heels several times like castanets.

"You bet," she said listing right, then left, then tilting dangerously backwards while attempting to place one foot in front of the other. She took a deep breath. Then another.

"You okay, missy? Feel good?"

She thought and chose her words carefully. "Yes. Fine. Absolutely." She handed him the money with a giant tip, because arithmetic eluded her in her present condition. "Thanks very much." She turned to go, but her feet were uncooperative.

"Lady? Please?"

She turned around very slowly and carefully. He was huddled over, hands prayerfully folded, eyes closed, humming and swaying from side to side as if caught up in a strange, extreme emotion, some kind of trance.

"We meet again. I see. I know dees tings. You see some day."

"Wonderful. Bye now."

"Go Gators!" He clicked his heels together again and saluted her smartly in the best traditional British Raj manner. "God save the Queen!"

"You can say that again." She told herself the first step is always the hardest. One hundred blinding accusatory sun-shiny asphalt yards separated her from the bug. At three steps per yard, she'd be there before the sun went down, if she were lucky. She hoped she'd be lucky. "Bye now. Thank you," she guessed.

"We number one!" He cried after her.

Go Garnet! You can do it, you can do it, you can! One baby step at a time.

10

THE BLAME GAME

She had a hangover for three days. Chester didn't notice because he had one too. They dodged and ducked each other for 72 hours, writhing in silent pain, wracked with shame and soaked in guilt.

His text had said, "Great game. Almost home. Naptime."

She fell into bed next to him oblivious to his wall-shaking snore and the brown piles dotting the living room floor. At 9 p.m. Ringo and Diesel ripped open and consumed the contents of a 20-pound Beneful bag and, for desert, ate the orchid on the coffee table that Chester had given her for Valentine's Day. And the potting soil. And the sphagnum moss. Then they peed on the porcelain pot it had come in. They were thoughtful enough, however, to leave the little white card that had been stuck in it on the carpet in the center of the room, the dear sweet card that said, "Try to keep it on the blacktop, Honey? Love, C.D."

Chester stood at the foot of the bed and tugged at her big toe through the covers. "Hey, I bought us a new NOAA weather radio today."

She didn't open her eyes. "Good for you. Brilliant. You're a genius."

"When do you want to go to Home Depot, get the plywood, duct tape, other stuff?"

"I'll have to get back to you on that."

"It was your damn idea."

He glanced at the TV which was semi-permanently fixed on the Weather Channel this time of year, then at her. "Is that whopper mess of suds in our neighborhood?"

She groaned and rolled over, pulled the sheets up around her ears. "Is it cold in here to you?" Maybe he hadn't seen the story yet. Her story that named names, spilled all the meager beans there were to spill at this stage. But maybe he had. He could detonate without warning any moment. It was a favorite tactic of his.

His penitential fully completed legal forms and motions for Allison's impoundment were smoldering on the corner of her desk. All she needed was the signature and affidavit of a licensed M.D., an M.D. licensed to practice medicine in Florida.

"Yeah, I guess it is sorta chilly in here. So anyway, catfish, there's this geriatric weirdo at the door who says he's a doctor and has come to pick you up for your appointment."

"There is?"

"Yes. He has a car and driver. He said to tell you to hurry, that 'time was of the essence.'"

"He did?"

"So are you sick or something? What's this all about, nitwit?" Then he snapped his fingers. "Ahh. Gotcha. Allison."

She hopped out of bed, circled him, nose down, then circled the room nose down, found her shoes under the bed, hit the head, stubbed her toe on the tub, yelped, raked a hairbrush through woody woodpecker hair, cussed it, and stumbled down the stairs, Chester, Ringo and Diesel in tow.

"Honey?"

Two cold noses nudged the back of her knees when she turned the doorknob. "Jeese, Chester. I can't believe you made him wait outside. How rude!" Gave him a pissy look.

"Are you kidding? The guy has all the markers. Are you sure he's a real medical doctor?"

She flung the door open wide. It was a dark and starless night. There was a brief interregnum in the downpour that had resumed with a vengeance that afternoon. The ocean roared across the street. Salt spray filled the air. A1A was a wasteland of tarry black leading to nowhere, a route that no one saw fit to take at this particular time on this particular night. A lone seagull screamed. A dead palm frond floated down from an inked-out invisible tree and dropped with a muffled clatter near her feet. Then a sudden isolated gust of wind scuttled it out of sight. All she saw was black vapor with two long high beam headlights aimed at her as if they were brilliant probing searching eyes.

"Dr. Fritz?" Ringo pawed at the back of her calf and whined and Diesel licked her hand. "Hello?"

From behind the headlights a disembodied voice, shrill and obnoxious, screeched, "Let's roll, bitch! Hump it!"

Chester shoved her back into the townhouse and threw himself in front of her in the doorway. "Hey, you S.O.B.! Watch your mouth!"

Garnet shushed him like a silly little boy, "Chester! Be nice!" She threaded her way around him and slipped into the murk. "I'll call you if I'm going to be late, sugar. Don't worry. He's cool. It's all right."

The front door slammed like thunder behind her and the porch light snapped off, speeding her steps into the night. Confident she was on familiar ground, heck, she didn't need a light. She knew what she was doing, where she was going. She tripped on a speed bump and stumbled on a coconut before she banged her shins into the side of the limo.

"Where's the damn door on this . . . hearse?"

Six feet above her a turbaned head said, "Halloooo, missy! So very nice lady! We meet again!" He bowed deeply at the waist. "You need a ride, yes?" He held the back door open for her. "Please? Yes?"

She tumbled into the black hole like Alice after the bunny rabbit and smacked headlong into The Fritz.

"Miss me, honey pie?" He put a moist palm on her thigh. "Huh?"

The Fritz was wearing a voluminous black Zorro cape with a stiff turned up collar that almost covered his ears and was caparisoned with a snazzy red wool beret pulled down low over his forehead. He held a huge empty Sherlock Holmesian pipe between his teeth through which he chattered unstintingly, rather like tapping out Morse code, vocables with no inflection, tonal modulation or emphasis. His subject? The advantages of ambush and surprise in medically evaluating a "major nutcase." Their mission was a night raid, a surprise attack on Allison whilst engaged *in flagrante delicto* in nymphomaniacal deportment. He had it all figured out. Not to worry. No problemo. Just do what he said. Pay attention to his signals and cues. He'd done this many times before and rescued hundreds of lost souls from sexual incineration and financial ruin. He bolstered his exposition of his strategy with a graffiti blizzard of historical records and stats, famous battlefield logistics from the dawn of civilization up to and including the war in Afghanistan. He quoted Alexander the Great, Charlemagne, Ethelred the Redless, Napoleon, Bismarck, Winston Churchill and Chairman Mao, then added flying buttresses to his bolsterment with passages and citations from Lao Tzu, Caesar Augustus, the Emperor Constantine, Dame Julia of Norwich, Machiavelli, Meister Eckhart, Robert E. Lee and Teddy Roosevelt, Field Marshall Rommel, Generals Patton-MacArthur-Eisenhower (somewhat conflating them), Thomas Edison and Eleanor Roosevelt.

For some reason, like a mental hiccup, he kept coming back to the Battle of Salamis, a much studied and admired fifth century BC naval battle, a very cunning Greek outmaneuver of a vastly superior Persian fleet that saved the Greeks' asses—and Greece—big time, but the metaphor, not to say the implication, was lost on Garnet. She had no intention of carrying their mission out into the Atlantic Ocean, nor the Indian River, nor into a plastic wading pool, for that matter. And damned if she was gonna ask for further explication. Yeah, that was September 480 BC, but this is September nearly three thousand years later. Whatever his persuasive powers and charisma, The Fritz would never convince her that he was Themistocles reincarnate and the only oar he'd ever see her paddle was the one paddling her own little canoe.

Wait a minute. What was going on here?

They were moving forward down a dark two-lane road at a very high speed. "Okay, Fritz, listen to me." Oddly, he stopped chattering about the Maginot Line and mustard gas and closed his mouth.

"She probably isn't home. She's probably off with Lance banging away in some bower of bliss. And if she is actually home with Lance, this could make her mad. I mean, like, really *mad*. Not to mention pissing off Lance too. Not a good idea. Not. He's the SHERIFF. He's the law."

Then she noticed that Chutney Patel, Esq., Chauffeur, Man Friday and Speedy Go-For was driving 75 mph down the narrow blacktop with no headlights. They were hurtling south into a black void; they were, essentially, human shots in the dark.

"Quibbles! Pissant details and distractions!" The Fritz stabbed the air with the end of his pipe and popped her on the head with it. "I am a man of *action*! I shall not be deterred. And the time for action is *now*. Ripeness is *all*, cupcake. Hear me?"

How could she not? "Wait a minute, Fritz; let's slow down and . . ." A curdling sensation gripped her stomach, her temples started to throb, and the chill of an instinctual prescience flooded her. "But . . ."

"Shaddup. Now *you* listen to *me*, hot stuff!" Pipe locked between his teeth, he grabbed her by the shoulders and shook her until her teeth rattled. "Going bonkers creates a special *cunning* in some people, you know! They can become extremely *clever* at out-smarting and eluding mental health professionals. They are often extremely *effective* at making the very people who are trying to help them appear to be the lunatics!"

She pushed him away. "I'm a little uncomfortable with all this *drama*, Dr. Fritz. With all due respect, something about this strikes me as . . ."

He clamped his hand over her mouth. "Silence! I am the expert here, Pollyanna. Do you want my help or not?"

She nodded.

"Then, it's now or never."

He yanked the pipe from his mouth and pounded on the plastic partition to the driver. "Chutney, my man, more A/C! It's hotter than hell back here! Ramp that friggin' thing all the way up!"

The car lurched left then right. "Okee-dokee, kind sir!"

"And hit the gas, you New Delhi towel-head! Floor it! Pedal to the metal, Patel! Do the funky Buddha! Let's haul *ass!*"

Garnet's head snapped back with the sudden forward thrust, but the Fritz leaned forward, hunched and rigid with dark purpose, into the night. They were flying south down a deserted undeveloped stretch of A1A at 95 mph with, yes—she couldn't believe it—no headlights, taking, as Fritz termed it, "evasive action," dense clouds of Love Bugs smacking into the windshield by the millions and smearing their tarry liquefaction across the glass. A gnarled hand fumbled with her shaking right knee.

"What? Cat got your tongue, sugar pants?"

She swallowed hard, but her heart remained stuck to her tonsils.

"Relax, kid. This'll be over quick, like lickety-split, you'll see. We'll have her butt in the bin in no time flat." The Fritz took another long pull on one of the many silver flasks Chutney had passed him from the front seat. "Aaah," he burped, "nothing like the thrill of the chase, eh? So loosen up, sister, relax, I say. As they tell every whining sucker wimp in the ER, 'The worst is over.' *Hahaha!*"

Out maneuvered, Garnet caved and leaned into her latest tangent. Miles and miles of dark desolate banks of palmetto scrub whizzed by in a dizzying panorama. At last lights from towering condominiums began streaming past the windows and she started hopping up and down in silent panic, making time out signs with frantic hands in front of the good doctor's smiling catatonic face. Finally he noticed.

He banged his sleuthing pipe once like a rifle shot on the partition and shrieked, "*Whoa!*" Hyper alert and ever eager to please, Chutney Patel, Esq., Chauffeur, Man Friday, Speedy Go-For, instantly hit the brakes and his passengers sailed off their seats, flew through the air, and fell—thump—onto the floor.

"Turn left at the light, Dumbo!" Fritz bellowed from the floorboards, slumped over and buried in the folds of his cape. "LEFT! NOW!"

"No problemo, kind sir."

The car teetered, veered, fishtailed and leaned 150 degrees into a left turn at 70 MPH. On their hands and knees, the passengers, propelled by nuclear reactor level centrifugal force, skidded across the sandalwood-scented floor mats in the opposite direction, and slammed into the vinyl door panel, making a lasting impression on it with their respective skulls. The limo's front bumper thunked into three concrete barrier pilings at the entrance of the swank Ocean Avenue One silo and came to a shuddering steamy halt, exuding the odors of burned rubber, ruined brake pads, and a dangerously over-heated radiator.

"Is this thing on fire, Fritz?"

"Nah. It's cool." Fritz crawled over to the door and kicked it open, flinging his cape over one shoulder. "Okay. Showtime," he said, tumbling out of the limo onto the red carpet and into the glare of the extravagant entrance floodlights. He took a deep draught of his 90 proof nectar, boinked Garnet on the head with his empty flask, and pushed himself up to his feet.

"You brought your camera, right?"

She sat on the sidewalk, legs folded Indian style like a kid, hands in her lap. She had to be dreaming. But maybe the thump on the head had knocked some sense into her? From a wondering hazy daze she mumbled, "Sooooo . . . ummmm . . . are you, like, crazy or something?"

"On your feet, woman! To the ramparts! Battle of Salamis! 'One if by land, two if by sea.'" He charged the haughty ornate doors, head down, cape flaring and flapping out behind him, sleuth pipe sticking out from his jutting chin like a poisonous insect proboscis.

As if sucked in by a powerful swirling vortex, or shot through a pneumatic tube, she flew through the revolving doors in his wake. "Wait."

"Remember the Alamo!"

11

DIFFERENTIAL DIAGNOSIS

The doorman recognized her and winked, smiled and waved her in, but he did a double-take on The Fritz. He was a little too outré cloak-and-dagger, disheveled homeless looking, an alphabet soup of alarming odds and ends. "Sir? If you don't mind . . . ?" He caught up with them at the elevator and made them come back to his station and sign in: name, address, phone number, who they were visiting, time of arrival.

"How about that! All the way from Rochester, Minnesota. Mayo Clinic. Wow. Welcome to Florida, Dr. Schrump," he said looking at his clipboard. "I hope Miss Highsmith isn't ill . . .?"

"Nothing Dr. Feel-good can't handle, my good man," Fritz said, dashing for the elevator, alert to the fact that further inquiry would only confirm the doorman's worst suspicions. Holding the folding doors open, he bellowed like a rutting bull, "Nurse! Step on it! Up, up and away!"

Allison met them at the door wrapped in towels and covered with sweet-smelling froth. She had been taking a bubble bath.

"Oh my God. Hi, Garnet." Her sudsy eyebrows pinched together and met in the center of her forehead. "I didn't know you were coming. Is something, like, the matter? Or, uh, something?"

Fritz leaned into her, poked her ribs with his bony elbow and muttered, "Salamis" under his gin-soaked breath.

"The matter?" She looked at The Fritz. She looked at her BFF. "Heavens, no. We . . . ."

"What fun! So come on in, come on in . . . don't stand out there in the hallway . . . ." She swung the 17th century imported Italian mahogany door wide and smiled a warm welcome, motioning them inside. "What a surprise. I was unwinding, getting ready to put on my nightie . . . ."

Garnet, experiencing an intense depersonalization sensation, feeling as if she were floating above the scene and bobbing off the ceiling like a helium-filled balloon, drifted over the marble foyer. Her dread had been transformed into a pathological detachment, a hypostatic dreamlike state of denial. For some reason she laughed.

"What's so funny?"

"Oh, nothing. Nothing, just that . . . *Allison!* I want you to meet," her head whipped around to The Fritz standing next to her like a shady demented character out of one of Poe's stories. His recently applied black eye-patch (hastily, on the way up in the elevator to the penthouse) had slid down to the bridge of his nose, and lay there like a mysterious disengaged prosthesis in need of repositioning. Her head jerked in shock at the sight, and she instantly shoved it back in place, poking him hard in the eye, "I'd like to introduce you to a wonderful new *friend* of mine."

"Oh, yeah?" Allison smiled pleasantly and politely. Waiting. Expectant. Innocent. Vulnerable. Trusting. Willing to believe almost anything Garnet uttered. A friend of Garnet's was a friend of hers, for sure. She looked like a little lamb with the glistening white bubble bath bubbles all over her. Her pretty brown eyes open wide, habitually willing to believe the best in people. That people were essentially *good.* "Soooo?"

"Allison, this is Dr. Fri . . . uh . . . Dr. Schrump." She glanced at Fritz. He was studying his nails and chewing on the end of his pipe. "He is a famous sex research expert and has a clinical practice at . . ."

"Salamis" Fritz whispered.

Her eyebrows shot up in wonder. "At *Mayo* in Rochester! Minnesota, I mean. You know, THE Mayo Clinic. Up *North!*"

Allison looked rather blank as she processed this info. Then she said sweetly, "No. Really? That's pretty famous, huh?"

"Yes, really. And, yes, quite renowned."

"Wow. How cool."

"Anyway, I thought you'd enjoy talking to him. He's only here overnight. He's on his way to . . . " She turned to Fritz. His eyes were closed and he was humming the William Tell Overture. Rather loudly, as it happened. "He's on his way to . . . New Delhi to consult with a . . . doctor there about . . . " Fritz pushed past both of them and strode into the living room. . . . "A Buddhist Princess who has a problem with her . . ." Fritz waved his pipe at her angrily (e.g., No! No! No!). "Her *pipe*, I mean, *pipes* . . . and, uh, you know, it's very complicated, a very rare condition, BUT a condition on which he is the world expert. So anyway . . ."

"Amazing! I have problems with *my pipes* too!"

"Get outta town! Really?"

"Yessiree, they been actin up lately. Givin me fits."

The Fritz cackled hideously like a spectral old crow from the couch facing the giant plate glass windows, windows which offered a spectacular breathtaking panoramic view of the storm-tossed waves of the Atlantic Ocean 100 feet below.

"What wonderful *synchronicity!*" Garnet sang at the top of her lungs.

"What the freak is that?"

"Listen, Allison, cut to the chase. I've got this neat idea. See, I'm doing a feature for the paper on him and it . . . uh . . . will be syndicated. You, know Fred, he'll milk it for all it's worth, celeb M.D., world famous sexologist. Fred!" She rolled her eyes. "He is so mercenary."

Allison nodded rapidly, trying to keep up. "'Syndicated,' Garnet? Oh, no! I didn't know Fred was in the mafia!"

"No, no, no, that means, oh hell, that he'll sell it to other papers."

"Oh."

"So here's my concept, Allison. I want to do a video of you and Dr. . . . . Mayo Schrump having a little Q & A together. I mean, you're a healthy, normal, beautiful young woman, sexually . . . active and I know it would be a hit, definitely go viral and probably help people who need help, people who have pipe problems too, but can't afford the treatment, certainly not the services of," she spun around to check on The Fritz. He was checking out the bar, pouring three tall drinks for himself. "Shoot, few could afford the expertise if someone of the stature of Dr. Schrump."

"Cool! I'm in!" She ran off to the hallway. "Let me get some clothes on, put on some make-up? Eeeek! This'll be fun!"

"And you'll be doing a real service to *humanity,* Allison!" Garnet shouted after her. "Your life will make a *difference!*"

"Yeah, man!" Allison yodeled down the dark hallway. "Get Dr. Schrump a drink? Chips and dip! Give me ten?"

"Okay! But hurry!"

Fritz stretched out on the couch, beret over his eyes, and chortled like an evil troll as Garnet paced the living room. Suddenly, there was a horrible crash and rattle in the back of the penthouse. Allison shrieked and tore back into the room holding in one hand her ripped from the plug curling iron and in the other her make-up mirror, both trailing their wires.

"Wait! Oh, my God! Wait. Wait a minute. Guys! Guys!" Her face was ashen, her eyes frozen wide in shock.

Face it, this was so ludicrous even Allison wouldn't swallow it. "Yeah?"

"Garnet, you mean this is Dr. *Schrump?*"

Garnet nodded. The Fritz was staring out the plate glass windows peering into the maelstrom, the chaotic watery abyss, far, far below. "Those windows don't open, Dr. Frump, uh, Schrump," she said.

Allison started dancing from foot to foot. "Garnet! No way! Did you really say *Schrump?* From *Rochester,* Minnesota? A *doctor* named Schrump?"

"Why do you ask, Allison?"

"No way!" she squealed, nearly dropping her towels. "How very weird!" She jumped up and down. "This is like, amazing, man. *Mother's* maiden name is Schrump! She grew up in Rochester! She has a cousin who is a physician at Mayo!"

Garnet's verbal acuity decamped her cranium. Her tongue stuck to the roof of her mouth. Her eyes swiveled left and clamped on The Fritz like tongs. His longish raven hair with the snowy root system sprang away from his skull as if he'd been struck by lightning.

It's a small, small world, after all.

"So what's your point, Allison?"

Before Allison could say a word, The Fritz suddenly whirled around from the windows, and in a gale of fluttering, twisting black folds, his cape flying out from around his splintery physique in a dark fustian flourish, declaimed explosively, flinging his hands high in the air over his head like Mephistopheles:

"*Homo Ecce!* Behold the Man!"

"What?" Allison gasped, stepping back. "You *are?*"

Garnet stared. "What? Who? Frederick *Nietzsche?*"

"No." The Fritz whipped off his eye patch in a revelatory flourish, threw it behind him and bowed deeply from the waist.

"Smedley S. Schrump, M.D., himself, the one, *the only.*"

He snapped back up like a jack-in-the box and his black eyes bulged forward and swam in their sockets like catfish. "SURPRISE!"

He smiled a snaky smile that seemed to have a life of its own; it wrapped around his head and throbbed and pulsed, slithered and kinked, wriggled and snapped. It was an alarming non-human alien thing that the average person would instantly hit with a shovel or an axe, then shoot with a hand gun or shotgun, then spray with insecticide, stomp to pieces, hack to cellular bits, pour Holy Water over, then soak in gasoline and burn outside, then bury in some public garbage dump, then maybe call a priest about to get further advice about the defenestration and purification of one's home, mind and soul.

Goodness, Garnet thought. Were those fangs?

"Oh my God, I can't believe it!" Allison cried.

The Fritz then swept the red beret off his pate and cried, *"Dulcet ET VERITAS!"*

"Uncle Smeddy? Is it really you?"

Fritz licked his nasty old lips. "Yes, my dear. *Himself.*"

"It's been years and *years.*"

"Too, too long," The Fritz oozed.

"Oh my gosh, knock me friggin' out!" Allison gathered her towels around her and ran up to him, closed her eyes and planted a big fat darling kiss on his loathsome cheek. "Missed you, Uncle Smeddy," she blinked through tears.

"Me too you, little gum drop. Me too *you*."

"Where have you *been* all this time?" She took his hand and looked up at him with adoring little girl eyes.

The Fritz swayed slowly back and forth above her like a cobra. Through a sinister, soul-shriveling Vincent Price smile he hissed something unintelligible.

"Where?" Allison piped with her upper pipes.

"I said, dear, *Salamissss*."

"Oh." Allison's wide eyes stayed on The Fritz, mesmerized, her juicy young bod bowing out toward The Fritz as if he were a large evil magnet.

Crap, crap, crap. Garnet had TMJ from grinding her teeth.

"It's where they make *salami*, Allison!" she blared through the megaphone of panic.

"No way."

"Way! Bologna, too! And pepperoni also, if I'm not mistaken!"

"Huh. I didn't know that."

"Yep. It's quite the hot bed for sausage, you know." Sausage? Hot bed? Those damn Greeks.

"I guess . . . if you say so."

"Correction!" She ran up and put her hand in front of Allison's motionless dreamy eyes. "Sorreee. Bologna is from ITALY. I misspoke. Now get dressed, kid. We gotta hustle here."

"Put on something red and real cute, gum drop, for old uncle Smeddy, wouldja?"

Allison toddled off.

"You disgust me, you turd."

They sat on the couch.

Allison tore back into the living room. "Mother is gonna freakin go crazy when she hears you're here, Uncle Smeddy! I'm calling her right now." She ran out of the room giggling and squealing.

"Let me handle this." The Fritz had donned his beret once more, but at a different, more cocky-cavalier angle.

"My God, Smedley S. Schrump, M.D. is a real person. You have mooned the gods with this one, Fritz. You are dead meat."

"He's not any more real than I am. And far less imaginative. I've been around a lot longer than he has too, have a much bigger rep. I'm a legend in my own time. You might say, with no exaggeration whatsoever, that I'm a Legend in Time qua Time, if you follow me."

"Bullshit. It's illegal to pretend you're a real person when you're not. Hell, I mean someone else who is real and you're not. It's about identity theft. Being an imposter."

"I'm thirsty."

"You are a fraud, a fake and a corrupter of innocence."

"Thank you, Ruth Bader Ginsberg."

"You are the vilest person I've ever met."

"Get up off your sweet puss and get me a drink or three."

Allison shot back into the room with a news blast. "It's 4 a.m. in Barcelona, but I left her a long message! She gets up early! We'll hear from her soon!"

"Hurry, Allison. We're running out of time. Dr. Schrump has a flight to catch."

When her scrumptious bronzed flesh had disappeared, The Fritz put a hot palm on her thigh. "You're a pretty good little liar yourself, cupcake."

She smacked him so hard his beret flew off. "You make me sick."

"Ditto, miss goody two-shoes." She hopped to the wet bar, filled a glass with the first bottle she found. "Swipe her cell, flush it down the john."

"Impossible."

"Nothing is impossible if you stick with *me*, you luscious creamy thing. You'll see."

"Oh my *God.*"

"He's not here. He's in a meeting. Wanna leave a message?"

12

YESTERDAY'S TWEET

✦ ✦ ✦

"I've got it. I turned it off. It's in my purse."

"Now we're cookin, sweet cakes."

"Get me outta here. You're not funny anymore. Or cute. Or interesting. You are repulsive and vulgar."

"Too much, huh? I over-did it?"

"Are you for real?"

"Are you? You have your own documented firecracker moments and flame-outs. You ain't no saint yourself. . . "

"Turn it down? Lighten up?"

"You mean well, sugar pie. That much is clear. You don't want to piss anybody off, you hate fights and confrontations, will do almost anything to avoid hurting anybody's feelings—lie, cheat, duck, disappear, hide—you . . . you . . . you wanna *help*, do what you *can*, make a . . . small, what's the word today? Oh, yeah, hahaha, make a '*contribution*.' Listen, sweetheart, you're okay, ok?"

Garnet stormed to the window. Five sea gulls shot by at 85 mph followed by a wide-eyed pelican, an old floppy straw sun hat, a worn out flip flop and . . . her father's sad exhausted face, the face he wore after he lost a patient . . . her heart fluttered and turned over.

"Admirable sentiments, poor strategy. Life makes mincemeat outta people like you."

"Go to hell."

"Hell? Home, sweet home. I have a *pad* there, sugar, with my name on the door. Oh yeah, I'm a hellion, but so are you. I'm here on a day pass. Work release program, you know."

She spun around. "Who *are* you? You sure as hell aren't who I thought you were."

"That's what they all say, hot lips. Are *you* who you think you are?"

"Something smells in here." She checked the bottom of her shoes.

"So tell me. How old was your old man when he croaked?"

Her eyes narrowed. "Sixty-seven. Why?"

He grimaced. Yeah, I remember now. What a waste. "I ain't givin you no stats, sister, but I am one *hell* of a lot older'n than that."

"So?"

"Make of it what you will."

"You are evil."

"Nope. I'm a realist. But harken and attend. You are in the fast lane, the good intentions lane, the passing, as it were, lane, right behind your daddy. We all end up dead sooner or later and in the same place. Me? I'm suckin the lees long as I can, hangin by a thread, maybe, but hangin around, getting things done, helping out, having fun. It's worked so far. I go on and on."

Her eyes flared. She marched up to him, got in his face. "No. I think you died a long time ago, Fritz. You're a rotten fake and a total flake." She held her nose and sneered. "You *stink*."

Allison sashayed back into the room, looking down, and one hand on her hip, her pelvis swinging from side to side in a perfect runway model routine.

"So? How do I look? Huh?"

" FABuloussssssss. You remind me of the gorgeoussss galssss . . . in . . . Salmaaamissss."

"I do?"

"Yeah, little lady, the red-hot hottiessss . . . at . . . the temple."

Allison smiled and blinked. "Okay, then, I guess I'm ready now. What do you want me to do?"

"For starters, pull up the front of your dress, Allison! Your boobs are hanging out."

"So? At least they're *real.*"

"What's *that* supposed to mean?"

Allison smirked. "Garnet, you know I *know* . . ."

Garnet fell on her and yanked her plunging neckline up to her moist, glistening, over-glossed rubyesque lips. "There. Much better. This is for a *family* audience, Allison!"

"Hey!"

"Ladies, ladies, now, now. Allison, you darlin little poopy pot. Sit down right here next to old Uncle Smeddy." The Fritz patted the cushion next to him. She plopped her succulent pissed off buns down next to him and in a flash he dragged her butt onto his lap and dandled her on his knee. "Wanna ride the horsie, gum drop?"

"Doctor Schrump, please!"

"What? No harm here. She's my favorite little . . ." Allison looked up at him, awed and infantile. "Ummmm," he closed his eyes and inhaled ecstatically, "Ya smell sooo *good*, honey. She's my favorite lil . . . poopy poontang NIECE." He bared his teeth and sank them into her neck.

"Owchie, Uncle Smeddy!"

"*Quiet!* Listen up. This is the drill." Garnet fumbled with the camera, flung it into a chair, fussed with everything in the room, ran back and forth, fluffed a throw pillow, smoothed Allison's hair, shook out Fritz's beret for bugs and lint—and hair ("Uh, oh. You must be going *bald*, Dr. Schrump. Look at all that hair. Too bad, too bad."), stomped on his toes, twice, powdered Allison's nose, powdered her own nose, powdered a vase, knocked a cobweb or two down.

"All righty. Look sharp."

"Is there a script or somethin, Garnet? Can I see it?"

"No. Absolutely not. This is all about honesty and candor. Truth. This is a REALITY show, Allison, for heaven sakes. Shit. Just be your*self.*"

Garnet twisted and turned the icons around on top of the camera. Gees. She should have practiced with this damn thing before she rolled in here. "So, hot stuff, anyway, how's the dude, you know, Lance? Ya'll having any fun? Set any new records? How many notches in your headboard as of today?"

"Lance?"

"Yeah, your studly stud, your rack stallion." Garnet looked up, puzzled at Allison's puzzled face.

"Oh. Him. I have no clue. We broke up. Didn't I tell you?"

Garnet dropped the camera. "No. When? Why?"

"He got boring. Boring is boring. Who wants to be bored?"

Garnet was rarely bored. She could count the times she'd been bored on the fingers of one hand. "Not me."

"We had nothing in common. You were right. We had zero to talk about."

"*Talk* about?" Fact was, Allison usually had nothing to say. "Poor Lance."

Allison shrugged. "No big deal. It was just sex. I'm over it. Yesterday's tweet."

"Tweet? You said you were in love with him."

"Garnet, how many times have you been in love? Love can last a week or a lifetime. I saw you fall in and out of love lotsa times in less than five minutes before Chester." She laughed. "Remember that dork Thane? You wanted to marry him till he opened his mouth. I mean, you know, to actually *say* something." She winked.

Garnet's eyes fell to the camera where it had landed on the carpet. It was whirring like an insect. The black soulless lens was aimed at her dispassionately, objectively. She raised her eyes to get Fritz's take on the deal. Did Allison's boredom constitute a recovery? But the couch was empty. Only an ornery red beret slouched in the spot where he'd sat.

He probably had to take a leak. Or check his notes. Or . . .

"I'm ready when you are." Allison yawned. "Getting kinda late. So what do you want me to say? Will this be on TV? You Tube?"

"Hold that thought. Be right back."

Garnet knocked on the powder room door. Knocked-knocked on every other door of the multitude of doors in the sumptuous penthouse, looked under every bed, peered in every closet. "Fritz? Fritz!"

"What in the ding-dong are you doin, Garnet?"

"Did you happen to see where Dr. Fritz went?"

"Who's that?"

"Fritz? The Fritz is Dr. Schrump's professional nickname! It's what his colleagues call him . . . it refers to a *procedure* he, uh, developed . . . very revolutionary . . . a huge medical breakthrough . . . He's up for the Nobel in Medicine. A PROCEDURE. . . to . . . *repair* . . . female pipes that have been . . . on, you know, in layman's terms, in popular parlance, that is, pipes that have gone on the 'fritz,' for one reason or another." She glared at poopy poontang.

"Huh?"

"Yeah, it's a condition that occurs in some susceptible women and most often from *abuse and overuse of their pipes.*"

"Wow. I'll be darned. So *that* must be what happened to *me.*"

"Yes. That would appear to be the case. But what do I know? I'm not a doctor."

"I'll have to ask Uncle Smeddy about this! Lucky for me he showed up at the right time!"

"Yes, highly . . . fortuitous."

"It's like someone was watching out for me." She folded her hands, bowed her head and closed her eyes. "Thank you, Lord. 'Now I lay me down to sleep, I pray the Lord my soul to keep. . . '"

"Allison, pay attention! So did you see where your Uncle Smutty went?"

"Oh, he ran out the door a few minutes ago. He saw something out the window on the beach, got all excited, banged his pipe on the window, then hauled ass. I don't remember him being, whatdaya call it? Like so 'Ick-centric?'"

"Eccentric?"

"It is a *word,* isn't it? I think I heard it in a movie once. Yeah, I did. In the 'Nutty Professor,' maybe or 'Planet of the Apes.'"

"Geniuses are like that, dummy. They live at a higher altitude than we normals, way, way up there where the air is very thin. He probably had an emergency." Garnet skipped to the picture window and looked down. A dark chiaroscuro chaos of gloom and doom, wind-tormented waves, airborne sea foam, white caps, froth. A lunatic indigo watercolor.

Allison tittered. "*Emergency?* I didn't know sex doctors could have emergencies."

"Ha. Are you kidding? Sure. All the time. His beeper went off. That's what happened." His beeper was always going off. In fact, he was the most off his beeper bat brain she'd ever encountered.

"Are you pulling my leg, Garnet?"

"No. Absolutely not. It could be a ten-hour erection, lots of those today with Viagra overdoses, or maybe a prolapsed uterus, there's an epidemic of those going around, and they are highly contagious, according to eHarmony. They have to be precisely re-folded, carefully tucked and gathered, packed and stuffed back in like parachutes in their sacks by specialists like Dr. Schrump. My God. Serious stuff. Life-threatening. He consults for hospitals and celebs all over the world."

Where *was* that dirt bag? Was he coming back?

Garnet rattled on buying time. "Shoot, some sheik in Saudi Arabia may have gotten his wiener outta whack or . . . or Prince Charles—Holy God. All the jams and fixes he gets himself into with his . . . uh . . . *tampon* fetish."

"I didn't know he had one. For real?"

"Allison. It's in the papers all the time, if you'd read them. Hell, he got one stuck in his *ear* last year."

"No way."

"Way. It had to be surgically removed. Finally they had to pull it out through his nose with forceps."

"Ow. I bet that hurt. What size was it?"

"Size? No idea, but next time you see a pic of the Prince? Check out his nostrils. One of them now has the diameter of . . . uh . . . oh . . . a tail-pipe on a muffler, if you get my drift."

"No shit?"

"No shit."

An hour later, Allison drove her home. She had recovered from the joyful surprise of the sudden reappearance in her life of her dear Uncle Smeddy and had turned her energies and attention to now bemoaning his equally sudden "ick-centric" disappearance.

"I sure wish I could find my phone, Garnet. This is a real pain in the butt. I can't wait to tell Mama about all of this."

"It'll turn up, kid," Garnet said from a morass of guilt as she felt the phone in her purse vibrating with an incoming call. "Don't worry."

Chester came in from walking the dogs on the beach. They bounded up the stairs ahead of him, flopped on top her, all sandy and sticky, soaked with salt spray and sea water, and stood over her, compulsively covering her with slurpy, stinky kisses. It was tough pretending she was asleep under the circumstances, so she tried instead to pretend she was dead, hoping to hit the mark by raising—or lowering, as the case may be—the bar. She wished she were dead anyway. Maybe she could bring on the escape from her mortal coils and embroils by assuming the position.

Silent and motionless as a stone she listened as his feet hit the stairs slowly one at a time with the chilling thuds of inevitability, rising higher and higher, coming closer and closer, growing louder and louder, announcing her moment of execution. It was the goose-bump inducing Frankenstein goose-estep of a Disastrous Destiny Deserved. She really had really done it now. Really.

He shut off the lights, undressed in the dark and rolled into bed next to her with a groan. Her heart stopped. He pounded the pillow, stretched, cracked his knuckles, groped around under the sheets and pinched her butt.

"So how'd it go?"

"Good news or bad news first?"

"Good."

"Allison isn't crazy anymore."

"And the bad stuff?"

"It would take HOURS to tell you about that."

"Okay, summarize."

"I made an ass out of myself again. I'm in a tight spot. A very tight spot. I have put a noose, you might say, around my neck."

"Is that all?" He fumbled around under the covers, found her hand and squeezed it.

"Once Allison figures out what I pulled on her tonight, she won't ever speak to me again."

"I think you give her too much credit. She can't figure out which end of a screw driver to use without a private tutor."

"God knows, I meant well."

"You always do, honey. Anyway, peas and carrots, you guys, Mutt and Jeff, Shirley and Laverne. You'll go on together forever into the sunset, of that I'm certain."

"And that freaky doctor? That son of a bitch is totally psychotic. He thinks he's the devil. And he's vicious, sneaky and malevolent; sometimes I think he *might* be. Man, if they're in town, I find 'em, don't I? Or is it that they find me?"

"There is a pattern there of sorts. You might take some time to slow down and reflect on that someday."

"I love you so much, Chester. I'm such an idiot."

"*Ah, contraire, Mon Cher.* And if those are your catastrophes for the day, I would say you have behaved exceptionally well. Given, that is, your track record."

"You saw my schmuck piece for the paper?"

"Yep."

"You're not mad?"

"Nope. Expected it."

"I heard we're under a hurricane watch."

"So we are. And a sinkhole watch, I should say, perhaps not official, but it's pretty damn evident the state of Florida is sinking. Craters and canyons are opening everywhere."

"Oh, God, it's too much."

"And we can't—most of all, *you* can't—do a damn thing about it. So let's go to sleep, get a good rest and see what happens tomorrow."

"And wake up bright eyed and bushy-tailed."

"How about refreshed, restored, calm, clear-headed and rational instead? Let's shoot for that for a change, okay?"

"Chester! You make it sound like a high school homework assignment. Now I can't sleep worrying about getting all that done before morning."

"Nighty-night, darling."

"Love you."

Chester clamped his hand over her mouth and held it there. "Love you. Good night."

13

RUBY BEGONIA

+ + +

"What are you cackling about?" Chester leaned over her shoulder and peered into the screen of her laptop.

She slammed it shut. "Nothing. Go away. I'm trying to work."

"Right."

"Beat it. I'm serious."

"Coulda fooled me."

"Close the door behind you."

"Consider it closed." BLAM.

She flipped her laptop back open along with her grin.

Garnet was full of beans and getting more buzzed every minute. Some recent developments had been quite positive. Some good news for a change. Yes, granted, she'd had a complete moral, ethical and spiritual meltdown the other night at Allison's. She'd gone over the line, over the top and overboard. Yes, she was burning with shame over her behavior, her duplicity, the alarming ease with which she spun falsehoods and fairy tales to bamboozle her best friend, and far worse, the ease with which that pile of feces Fritz had conned and persuaded her to enlist his so-called expertise to save Allison from herself. Clearly, she, "Garnet the Good" *herself* had been a more needy urgent case requiring such a rescue, and the leaden irony of that fact and her remorse over that realization hung around her now jailed and repentant heart like a ball and chain.

But she had applied herself to the matters at hand, matters to which she might "matter," e.g., be "of help." She had made a reconnoitering mission out to Tommy's old place the night before to check on the tiger, and there, hidden in the bushes in the dark, had observed some curious things worth reporting to Fred. He could damn well put these onions in his pipe and smoke 'em. But he couldn't, if he had a shred of journalistic integrity, actually print them. She leaned into her laptop screen and re-read her write up of what her skulking around had discovered. He probably wouldn't think her lampoon was funny, but why not tease him, screw with his head a little? He was sending her all over on all kinds of wild goose chases trying to cover the two murder cases. She knew what to do, where to go and when, far better than he did, but he was the boss and the boss called the shots. She was sick of it. Maybe it was time to respond in kind, maybe it was time to hit old Fred between his eyes with some of her own Mother Goose.

"Tyger, Tyger Burnin' Bright by Thet Air Sinkhole on Thet Air Night"
A Poem
By
Ruby Begonia

Lo, my goodness, who'da thunk.
Lord, I swear, I wasn't drunk.
Sneakin' round last night I saw
Somethin thet made me drop my jaw.
Whilst I wuz thru a winder peerin,
A peepin Thomasina, but God-fearin,
Mister Johnson, he appears
In Tommy's house pacin floors,
Dumpin files and tossin drawers . . . .

In a stunning feat of truly bad writing, she had managed to drag this poet-aster tripe out ad nauseum for over 100 turgid lines. She smirked at this perverse accomplishment and weirdly congratulated herself for her efforts, for gutting it out to such length. It had taken hours. She had revised the quality *downward* several times, a first for her. Didn't she have anything better to do? The thought had occurred to her more than once as she struggled hard to sound dumb and illiterate for the prank. Was this a reasonable use of her time? For other than sticking it to Fred, it really wasn't even all that much fun. Writing this shit was *hard*, man. It was work.

As she dealt with the guilt of the guilty pleasure, wholly absorbed and amazed by the awfulness she had wrought, the pure dreck she'd produced, her phone, she noticed suddenly, was skidding across her desk and she jumped. For a nanosecond she'd recoiled, expecting it to levitate and spew obscenities and vomitus. God. What that creep Fritz had done to her head. Scenes and dreams worthy of *The Exorcist* now lurked everywhere in the shadows of her brain, multiplying daily, just waiting for the slightest opportunity, the merest suggestion, to rush out and scare the crap out of her.

"Oh, hi, Fred. What's new?"

"My, you're certainly full of the *devil* these days, aren't you?"

She jumped to her feet. "What on earth are you talking about?"

"Don't get me wrong, I think it's cute. Maybe we can use this rhyming flair of yours, that wit, for something on the Leisure and Lifestyle page. Didn't know you had it in you."

"Oh, that. Yeah, that was just a joke, you know. I was just tweaking your old nosey nose to deliver some recent observations, some new intelligence, as it were."

"So I've never really been good at reading poetry, Garnet, but it seems to me from reading this, uh, poem of yours that you are trying to tell me that Johnson is not only ransacking and tossing Tommy's old place but also grilling goddam sirloin steaks outside and feeding them to that tiger."

"You got it. 'A' plus, Fred."

"Are you shitting me, kid? He's really calling her 'Kitty' and feeding her prime cuts? Don't waste my time, smart-ass. The truth. Now."

"Weird, huh? Yes, it's true. I swear. Saw it with my own two eyes. Hell of a surprise, eh? Knocked me out." She sat down and breathed. "And know what else, Freddie? I think the old guy is actually shaking the place down for Tommy's secret barbeque sauce recipe. That was the only valuable thing he had that I can think of anyway."

"No, kidding."

"Yeah." The bad dreams of Tommy had slowly subsided like a dark tide withdrawing from the shore. It was what it was; her job was to find out how it had happened, if she could.

"That's sweet. That's sad."

"Yeah. I kinda hope he finds it too. I hope it didn't die, you know, with him."

"That'd be a shame."

"Yes, it would. But he also may be up to something else too. I have a funny feeling about it. He has a very hyper protective, sheltering, caring spirit about him out there, as if he's hovering over it kind of like a mother hen. Might be cool if he found the secret recipe, could be a money-maker for him. Tommy sold a lot of barbeque in his day."

"Very true. But why the gun? Why shoot at you? And Lance? You know he let him go, never brought him in to book him. Believed the cock and bull, whatever it was, Johnson handed him, not you."

"That's Lance for you, his typical M.O. You never know what he's gonna believe or swallow. For a cop he's as gullible as they come. Mr. Unsophisticated himself. And he's pissed at me about something or the other too. Who knows? I can't worry about it. I have bigger things on my mind."

"Oh clearly! Things like poetry, practical jokes? Shit, I sure as hell wouldn't want you to fritter away your time on the practical mundane business of journalism or doing your job, earning your keep around here."

She was used to it. She let it pass. Arguing with Fred would be an even more unforgivable, egregious waste of time and effort than trying to find words that rhymed with 'tiger,' 'kitty' or 'yummy.' "Fred, just shut up for a minute. Listen to me. Don't you *dare* tell anyone that the tiger is at Tommy's, okay? You wouldn't actually try to collect that 10 K reward Clovis Reddick is advertising for her recovery yourself, would you?"

"I hadn't even thought of it."

"Well, don't, Fred. You'll get the tiger killed, if you do. And if that happens, I quit, hear me?"

"Promise? Then maybe I should reconsider."

"Go to hell, Fred."

"So why would it get her killed? I thought the dingbat wanted her back, that she was some kind of living trophy to him."

"I think there's more to it, but I can't say right now. I'll have to fill you in later when I know more."

"As in 'when,' kid? When?"

"Tomorrow maybe. No later than in a few days. Back atcha. Later, boss. Cheers."

14

THE BASTARDS

✣ ✣ ✣

The Fritz's Moose Lodge ravings about "pinning" the murder of the "spic"—
and the death of Tommy, by implication, on the tiger, the beautiful lady
Kalimba—had stuck in her head the moment he'd uttered them, and his rant
and accusations had continued ringing in her ears ever since. It was both an
absurd and a tantalizing idea.

But who would have such a motive? Tommy and Gutierrez, the
groundskeeper who was killed at Peaceable Kingdom, a crime for which
Chester's newest "poor schmuck" client was charged . . . those two men could
not have been more different or physically farther apart and still be in the
same county.

One was a good ole boy redneck, a rural, unsophisticated elderly white
man with a heart of gold, whom everyone loved, who had lots of friends, both
new and old, of all ages, and who was considered universally by everyone who
knew him or knew of him as a stalwart, upstanding sweet old guy, not a mean
bone in his body, a good man who had a well-earned longstanding sterling
reputation in the area. He was an old time southerner through and through,
everybody respected him, smiled when they heard his name mentioned, and
spoke highly of him. The other was a Latino nobody, an illegal immigrant

without a green card or a dime to his name, Spanish speaking, illiterate, completely ignorant of the customs and ways of this country, a poor man with no means or connections to the community whatsoever. Gutierrez had been around here only a few months at most and no one was real sure how he got here, or exactly when, either, whereas Tommy Covington had lived here all his life and the old timers knew all his "people," including his ma and pa.

Neither one deserved to die and it pissed her off that the law had fallen flat in finding out what happened and catching the slime that took their lives. For all the pompous official verbiage in the coroner's cause of death report about "congestive heart failure" and "sudden massive coronary," Garnet didn't buy it. Tommy was a tough old bird. Nimble, limber, fit and strong, steady on his legs. His complexion was good, his handshake firm. His gaze clear and his concentration and memory impeccable as far as she could tell. His mind was good and his judgment sound. He still had his driver's license. Heck, he didn't even have to wear glasses. He was no frail, whisper of a man about to give up the ghost.

Why and how a young Latino who couldn't have been older than 23 or 24, and who was in good physical shape, a man who worked outdoors with his hands, who had a strong back, and presumably was coordinated, and had good reflexes, had natural wits and moves good enough to work around wild animals as a care taker, how he could have been surprised and over-powered to the point that someone could murder him in a location that he knew well and at which he was well known and employed . . . Something there didn't add up. The murder weapon had buffalo blood on it? C'mon. Should they check the dead man's blood type and DNA? Was he a buffalo disguised as a human being? Was his mother or father a buffalo? Get real.

Her cogitations and ruminations were interrupted by a painful memory. She had more skin in this game than she had known until now. This was more than a story. Without gadflies, harridans and avenging furies, and yeah, NAGS, bastards always got away with stuff. Nothing got done, papers piled up, got filed and people soon forgot.

She hated bastards on principle. In fact, it was a well-known fact that she highly intolerant of bastards as a class of people, and if she could get away with it, she would set em straight herself. She'd tried to do that once when she was five years old. That little bastard had gotten away from her and had run home bawling his eyes out, and she instead had gotten in a whole lot of trouble herself for her noble efforts when, crying, screaming and bleeding from a tiny scratch above his eye, he returned with his pissed off mother who demanded her daddy fix him up right then and there or she'd sue. That nascent bastard had killed a small green tree frog for fun and laughed about it, and then went after another one. She wasn't going to stand for it and so she'd popped him a good one with the first stick she could find. Today he was serving two life sentences for his habit in Raiford Penitentiary. As many bastards do, he'd started with small animals, moved on to small people, and upped his appetites for size of kill as he improved his killing skills. She shoulda hit him harder. She still wishes she had banged a crater into his hateful head. What a difference it would have made.

Anyway, she'd learned she had to be devious, indirect. There were laws, police, and they were supposed to take care of those things. But she also learned you had to ride them and make their lives a living hell until they caught the bastards—or they wouldn't. She had a repertoire of trademark "Garnet" methods she'd developed over the years to do just that.

"Me again."

"Yeah, Fred. What now?"

"Got something for ya. Want to you to check this out. Peter Panzer. Ever heard of him? In Immokalee?"

"Ugh. *Tank*, he was called Tank at UF when I was there. An offensive lineman. Suited him, he was as big as tank, pushed through everyone, scorched earth you know, ruinous, impossible stop. And disgusting, downright offensive."

"Guess he hasn't changed much."

"No he's still offensive, even more so, I hear, and ruinous. A cattleman. Big bucks, inherited from family dumb clucks thousands of acres west of I 95, married another dumb cluck of similar heritage, expanded it by twice, bribes everyone in Tallahassee, is a member in good standing of the Bull Gators, etcetera."

"I take it you never dated him, went to bed with him then?"

"Oh, my God, Fred. That's a nauseating thought."

"He's making a big stink to faculty, royally pissing em off, at UF of late. They're up in arms, as it were, over his recent shenanigans."

"That's hysterical. He hasn't the faculties to do much of anything, even to speak plain English to a faculty member. Sucker can't do anything I know of but, you know, but eat, sleep, screw and raise cows."

"He's donated 10 mil to build and fund a big new Florida water institute at UF. They're naming it after him, 'The Peter Panzer Floridian Aquifer Institute.' Now, of course, The Audubon Society has jumped into the fray, the Sierra Club, the EPA is investigating the wells on his property, all the greenies are piling on, but this is Florida. *Plus,* dearie! *Get this*: He's got an application with the St. Johns Water Management District to pump an *additional twenty million gallons per day* outta the aquifer to water his friggin cows! How's that for balls? And you and I both know he has a better than even chance of making everyone look like fools and getting everything he wants and more."

"Well, this *is* Florida. Don't act so surprised, boss. But what an obscene joke. That means the bastard is guilty as hell of something and I think I have an idea or two on the matter."

"So get going! Sic him! Get him! Bring him down, girl! I want to break the story, scoop the big guys on this." He held his breath. He knew she wouldn't disappoint him.

Garnet stifled a groan. It was off to the races again.

Fred lived vicariously through her reckless random behavior, indulged his repressed urges, fueled his fantasies and his dreams denied of valorous assaults on all that was wrong with the world, a life that he'd long foregone at this point, the career he hoped for but never got around to, a life lived at full tilt, a zestful fist-swinging, brawling balls out approach to life that put truth at the top of the list, no matter what, come what may.

In his orderly corner office on the quiet uneventful Banyan Way, Fred the Editor sat behind his neat clean desk and pulled her strings, yanked her chain, poked her with pins and hot pokers, to see what would happen, what she'd do. He knew it'd be a cliff-hanger and over the top. He plotted and planned how and when to stick it to her, experimented, looked for issues and morsels suitable and suggestive. His own journalism career had deteriorated to a daily effort to inflame Garnet's fervors and fevers, wind her up and send her off into deep grass like a bird dog, places he'd never dare go himself, Lord, no, places he was too sensible and conventional to go himself. She had job iron-clad job security because of Fred's insecurities and his remorse and shame at having let life pass him by. He went to the movie "Garnet" every day, and sat on the edge of his seat, in suspense, thrilling to her exploits and hyperbolic hyperventilating reports. He juiced on her rousing rhetoric, jeremiads and expletives, her exercised moral indignations. He loved to hear her "talk dirty" and cuss, provided these bombshells were fired at subjects or individuals he deemed deserving of them. He got off on all of it. It kept him alive. She'd discovered this way before he had. She played him like a violin and for a while they had made beautiful music together.

"His ass is grass, boss. I'm on it. Consider it done, Freddie. I'll make your mullet wrapper famous. 'Florida Newsman of the Year: Fred Phillips of the Indian River Mullet Wrapper, Bass Fishin, Frog Giggin, Swamp Crawlin, Hog Killin, Skunk Skinin, Gator Wrastlin, Turkey Holler Chronicle.'

"Your paper will line more bird and rabbit cages and train more puppies to pee outside than any other newspaper in the great state of Florida next year, Fred, I swear, or my name's not Ruby Begonia. You have my solemn word.'"

"Cute. Funny. I'll count on it, then. So what about Johnson?"

"Fred, that was just 20 minutes ago! I'm fast, but not that fast. Hang loose for an hour or two at least. I have to put on make-up, do my hair, decide what to wear first, requisites for crime solvin and bad guy bustin. Chill, big guy! Later, Gator."

"Hey, Ruby? Hear me loud and clear now, honey bun. Make it sooner rather than later, *Ruby Begonia*, or I'll print that rhyming tripe of yours and put your real name on it."

"You wouldn't."

"You got three days. Understand?"

"That's blackmail, you know."

"Bye, Ruby Begonia. Get to work."

So what was the plan? She needed a plan.

She had shitload of work to do and, under the influence of The Fritz's battlefield obsessions, had become almost *Fritzoid* and obsessed herself with military strategy and tactics, particularly with Napoleon's logistical mistakes, his attacking on too many fronts, underestimating the deadly Russian winter, and also what an old Brit windbag with one arm could do with his big mouth, big ideas, a few ships and good men. Code name *Waterloo*.

Discretion, not digression, was the better part of valor. It increased exponentially one's chances of success. Discretion results from one's being discreete (not the other discrete; that means separate, individual, isolated, a kind of particle in space—although, sure, she often felt like a particle in space, that is, discrete, an erstwhile desert island, a mote in God's eye, a fly on the butt of the universe; but the drill down here, the goal, was circumspection, prudence, caution, qualities that played to decisions and actions that often were sly, sneaky, along the lines of machinations that in their most potent form were Machiavellian. That was definitely more Garnet and more useful in the present situation. Where was the OED? Discretion, indiscretion—and so forth and so on. It was an extended reverie and daydream that culminated in indigestion and which was yet another digression.

She had to pick her fights, know her enemy, slow down and be rational. She hated that. So she filed her nails, ate some celery sticks, weighed herself, was pleased with her diminution coinciding with Chester's contrition, ("You're getting too skinny. Your hipbones stick out. I'm afraid I'm gonna cut myself on 'em."), went to the beach with the dogs, drank some wine, cleaned the kitchen and fell asleep on the couch trying to establish, as were, her real priorities. Not that they were *the real* priorities. Oh forgeddabouddit. She woke up at 5:30 p.m. and wondered where she was and what had happened. She'd had a dream equivalent of *The Rime of the Ancient Mariner*. What had she done?

Had she shot an albatross? More to the point, was she wearing it as a stinky accessory around her neck? That was a tiny secret anxiety she always had on waking. What have I *done*? Will I regret it? Yet this waking caution was not her style, no. She picked up the OED from the carpet and put it back on the shelf. Discretion, strategy, poof! Out the window.

Far better to be natural, herself, create noise, confusion, turmoil, dust-ups, just be Garnet and see what happens. She liked suspense. Didn't everyone? Wondering what would happen next? So forward, march! To the ramparts. What did she *feel* like doing? What did she feel was important, right now, this very minute? Trust your instincts, girl, your most persuasive, if not most precise or reliable, navigators. They'll get you *somewhere*, so let's get going.

15

DON'T FORGET TO FLOSS

✝ ✝ ✝

One ringy-dingy, two ringy-dingies. Finally The Ruth picked up.

"He is traveling."

"May I ask, Mrs. Fritzwold, when you expect him back?"

"You may. Go ahead. Ask."

"When do you expect him back?"

"Back here? Back where? Back there?"

"Uh, back home? Here?"

"What do you mean by that, young lady? Is he living with you?"

"Oh, no! Oh my God, no! No, no, no! He's not living here, no. Not with me. Oh no. What a thought! I did not mean to offend you, Mrs. Fritzwold. Please. Don't misunderstand me. I would like to talk to Dr. Fritzwold for a few minutes about a subject of mutual interest."

"That's disgusting."

"I'm sorry. I think you misunderstand me. He and I are doing some research together relative to a medical syndrome. He is consulting with me about an illness."

"Like hell he is."

"I have or had a dear friend who was seriously ill and I . . . ."

"He killed her?"

"Killed her? Oh my God, no, or not that I know . . . "

The good doctor's wife lowered her voice to a ghastly whisper. "So what did he do to her?"

"Nothing! I mean, as far as I know . . ."

"Where was this, when did this happen?"

"A few days ago, but he left unexpectedly and I . . . ."

"That's Fritz for you; he clears out when they're closing in on him. He can fly, you know, like the wind. He can walk on water. I saw him turn into a dragon fly once, then a bird ate him and he came out the other end, the birdie's behind, slick as a whistle, and flew away. It was one of his better stunts!"

"Who?"

"Fritz. Who the hell are we talking about here? Santa Claus?"

"I'm a little confused, Mrs. Fritzwold. I meant to say who was, or is, closing in on him?"

"Who? Santa Claus? This is October. Check your calendar, miss. The Huns have invaded Cleveland and I'm out of celery!"

"I'm very sorry to hear that, Mrs. Fritzwold, but please, how can I reach Dr. Fritzwold? Do you have a phone number I could call, maybe?"

"He gave me my pill, brushed my hair, packed up a case of gin and told me he was going for a walk on the beach. If you know what I mean? The beach? Believe me, *I* know what that means, after all these years."

"What does it mean?"

"What?"

"That he went for a walk on the beach?"

"Oh that. They couldn't prove it."

"Prove *what*?"

"Please get to the point. I'm busy with the little people."

"Of course you are. May I leave my number?"

"I am sure, honey, he has got your number and a whole lot more than you'll ever know. Look out! The British are coming!"

"I'm sorry?"

"You should be."

Obviously Fritz was a bigger expert on insanity than she had known.

The beach! Allison! Garnet ran out the front door, slammed it in the faces of Ringo and Diesel so hard they yelped in pain, pumped her legs like an Olympic sprinter across A1A and skidded on her butt down the dunes through the sea oats, sea grapes, sand spurs, backwash of driftwood, Styrofoam cups and trash washed up from the last high tide, staggered to the water line and, gasping, looked north and south.

"Allison!"

A flock of sand pipers took flight and wheeled over her head, landing a few yards away. It was almost dark. The beach was deserted. The tide was out. There was an irritable four-foot chop on the water beyond the six-foot breakers banging the shore. The wind was blowing flicks of foam off the white caps. Nary a veteran pelican or sea gull found the ocean suitable for paddling, be-straddling or diving for dinner. And it was starting to rain again.

She ran back home. She dialed Allison's number with shaky spastic fingers. Allison didn't answer. But there was a persistent ringing noise emanating from her purse on the coffee table. How could that be when she had her phone in her hand? She approached the purse stealthily. It could be a trick of the senses, a stressed-induced auditory hallucination—or a purse bomb.

(Hadn't she read about purse bombs somewhere? No great shakes to rig up a purse bomb relative to shoe bombs, underwear bombs, one would think. Wait. Why anyone want to bomb her purse? It was a cool Coach purse. She'd had a lot of compliments about it. Chester had given it to her. Jealousy, perhaps. Or a planned obsolescence scheme by Coach? She'd only had it three months. You don't throw down $300 every three months for a purse, I don't care how flush you are. That's pushing the marketing envelope, marketing suicide.).

But! It could be a weather thing; atmospheric conditions distort sounds, throw sound waves off their ordinary path. Light curved, Einstein proved that ages ago, but no. It stopped. Her purse stopped ringing when Allison's outgoing voice mail message came on, when Allison's voice was in her ear saying, "Hey! Wassup? Sorry I can't pick up. I must be out shoppin or rockin. Leave your number, I'll call ya right back."

Crap.

She sat down. "Ow!" She got up. She picked the sand spurs out of her butt for ten minutes while trying to figure out what to do next.

Chester came home with a heavy briefcase and a heavy mind as Garnet was standing under the bright fluorescent lights in the kitchen, the best light in the townhouse, with her shorts and panties down around her ankles and a hand mirror in her hand, head wrenched around at a very unnatural angle, the other hand holding a pair of tweezers. Frowning and squinting, muscles trembling from the effort and concentration, she slowly pinched the tweezers together over the left cheek of her derriere.

"Oh dammit to hell!" She shrew the tweezers on the floor. "Holy freakin crap!"

"What are you doing?"

She spun around.

"Chester! Thank God! Quick! Now! Hurry!"

Still hobbled by her underwear, she hopped over to him, yanked his briefcase from his hand, threw it into the hallway and flung herself onto his chest.

"Someone is trying to kill Allison!"

"Nice time to be flossing your butt then, kiddo."

"Hurry!"

She hopped to the door, pulling up her pants. Come on, I'll tell you everything on the way. I was too scared to go alone. What are you waiting for? Dammit, Chester! She'll be *dead* by the time we get there! Oh, God this is all my fault! If this doesn't get me sent to hell forever nothing will! *Hurry!*"

"Hold it. You? *You* were too scared to go alone? Where? Why?"

"Allison's! Okay, you, freakin *anal* lawyer. Questions! Always! Questions! All your stupid questions! If she dies, it's your fault. Don't say I didn't warn you."

Garnet slammed into his old BMW, fumbled with the door and rolled onto the seat. Chester walked over and closed her door, a detail she had overlooked.

The vast endless black interminable length of the A1A asphalt that lay ahead of them, the terrifying terra incognito to the crime scene right out of Law and Order SVU, was too much. Garnet started banging her head on the dashboard. "No. No no no no."

"Start talking."

She did.

"So why didn't you call the cops?"

"Cops?"

"The police, ya know? The sheriff's department? You've heard of them?"

"I don't know. It all happened so fast. Maybe it was the sandspurs."

"The sandspurs?"

"You are hopeless. In my butt! The freaking damn sandspurs in my *butt*."

"Understandable, I suppose, to other residents of Bedlam."

"What? Hurry! Why are you going so slow?"

"I'm going 45 mph, the posted speed limit."

"It's people like you, cold-hearted creeps like you, that get people killed. It's that attitude that has ruined this country. The cancer of callous indifference. Oh my God. I can't stand it."

"What happened?"

"Where?"

"I have no idea. You tell me."

"What are you talking about? I can't believe you. You, of all people."

"What happened to Allison?"

"I don't know! Oh my God. Allison! Hold on, were coming!"

"Slow down, Garnet."

"Slow *down*? At a time like this?"

Chester called Lance. In a New York minute, several green and white cruisers with wailing sirens and blue lights passed them en route to Ocean One.

"Hurry! They're going to beat us there!"

"Hope so."

"Are you out of you mind, Chester?"

"No. Are you?"

"This is Allison we're talking about! Our Allison!"

"Oh, *our* Allison. Well, then." He slowed way down and turned on the radio.

"They won't let us see the body if we don't beat them there." She'd dropped her voice several octaves. The other higher scale having proved ineffective, she might as well try the "I-am-going-to-commit-suicide-over-this" range, and why not? She might.

"Body?"

She folded her arms, whipped her head to the right window, and refused to look at him. He'd see soon enough. He would suffer from guilt and remorse for the rest of his life. She hoped one day to be able to forgive him, but she doubted he'd ever be able to forgive himself.

Allison had been taking a bubble bath and listening to music when the deputies showed up. She didn't hear the doorbell. So they axed, splintered and broke down the hand carved ornate 17th century imported Italian mahogany front door, and in fine swat team fashion, guns drawn, fingers on the triggers, crouched, with tasers, smoke bombs and mace canisters at the ready, kicked in the bathroom door and yelled, "Throw down your weapons and get on the floor! Now!"

Up to her neck in fragrant bubbles and warm water in her own home and her own private bathroom on quiet week night, with soothing music playing, scented candles flickering around the tub and her crystal wine glass with a bit of Chateau Margaux still left in it balanced on the edge of the tub, Allison found this sudden intrusion by armed men dressed in black rather surprising and inexplicable and unnerving, not to say, unhinging. Particularly of her jaws and vocal chords.

16

A TRULY SEMEN-ALL IDEA

✟ ✟ ✟

Peter Panzer was unavailable, but he would sure 'nuf get back to you, honey, soon as he could. He was very busy man. Oh, Lord, so busy, I don't know from day to day, he's at this ranch, that ranch doin this or that, runnin off to conventions, all such stuff, flying off all the time to hither, thither and yon. Comin and goin. Could she say what this was about?

Honey, if you're a Gator he'll be on you like smoke! You were? *A Delta Helta Delta?* Good heavens. You must be purty. What year was that? *Homecoming Queen? Citrus Queen?* You were a real queen bee, wasn't you? Good God, *Chester Dare?* Yes. Everybody knows Chester Dare. No reason in the world he ain't our senator in Washington. That election was bought. Thet air was a dirty rotten shame, we all's still sick about it. We all know it was money, everybody does. Is he thinkin a runnin agin? Oh. Oh. I see. Oh, is that the honest truth? Mr. Dare is doin that kinda work? You don't say! That good man has a heart of gold. He's gotta jeweled crown in heaven waitin for him. Oh my. Yes'm, isn't that so very fine of him. And him being who he is and all, Lordy, he could be about anything in this state and him doin that kinda work. I must say I'm surprised, but more power to him. The good Lord knows the world needs more people like that. You tell him he's got Marianne

Tallywocky's vote if he does. You tell him that now? Don't forget. Okay, I do mean it; I'll get my Bible study group fired up about it too. We'll get us a lil ole PAC goin fer him.

Oh! Ha! You tickle me. You're sweet. Lordy, you is a smart girl too. Reporter? A real reporter for a real newspaper? Oh, my goodness. Tank will eat up all this news. Thank you so much, honey, fer callin. You're a delight. You are a darlin, yes you are. Thank you, a sweet pleasure talkin to you, too. Please give our regards to Mr. Dare, heah? He has friends in cow country, you be sure and tell him that? All right now, you be good, take care. Go to church on Sunday? Good girl, that's so important. It's clear as day you been raised up right, come from good people. Tank'll catch up with you real soon. Yes, ma'am. Look for a call from him real soon. Okay, now, thank you too, honey. Bye now, God bless.

Shit. She'd probably have to wait, what? Fifteen minutes for that mindless horn toad to call back? No, five.

"Hey, Tank! Tank? Is that you? Oh, can't believe it! Oh, my God, it's been sooo long."

"Do you ever do anything but take bubble baths?"

"Garnet, look, I forgive you, okay? I'm over it. That's not why I'm here. I wanted to ask you about . . ."

"Have you heard from or seen your Uncle Smeddy since we were there that night?"

"No, darnit. I don't know how to reach him and I was going to ask you if . . ."

"No. Absolutely not. He is very busy in Klaziriwhackakakistan . . . ."

"Where?"

"A small third world country off the coast of Maine. A lot of sex problems there, the propinquity to Maine, you know? Mainers?"

"Oh yeah. Well, that's up in the North Pole, right? And then all the lobsters they eat up there? All that pink in them? It gets in their organs, so no wonder they have problems."

"Don't you know anything, Allison? For Godsake I know you went to FSU, but they teach *geography* there don't they?"

"It's wasn't required."

"And all you took were 'required' courses? Just the bare minimum to get by? Allison, how do you expect to survive in this complicated world today with all this cyborg shit that's going on, the Face Book uploads of your brain cells, not to mention the way drones, invisible drone cameras, can get through the keys of your computer keyboard and flow through your fingers into your organs and navigate down through your intestines, blast through the uterus lining and from there surreptitiously photograph your private parts and, whammo, Allison Highsmith's genitalia wind up on Twitter. There are apps for smart phones for torturing, raping and killing women, they can get into your lingerie drawer by remote control, and in a blink all your matching bra and panty sets are reduced to byte sized bits, digitized and transferred in a time warp and *10,000 miles away* downloaded to a sex fiend's laptop, and before you know it, they're on eBay with your picture, in full color, all you have to do is hit a button . . . it's all touch screen, and flush, down the drain, you're screwed, knocked up and thirty seconds later you have *a monstrous infant alien* bursting out of your abdomen that will take over the planet, spelling the doom of mankind and bubble baths too. You really *worry* me, Allison . . ."

"I don't do Wi-Fi at Starbucks or . . . ."

"That's not enough."

"I'm trying to build up my *vocabulary* . . ."

"That's *not* enough. A big vocabulary will not protect you from hackers who . . . anyway . . . . Listen to me . . . you have to understand what the words *mean* to use them. It's not just spelling or saying them right."

"I'm doing definitions too!"

"Wait. *Why* do you want to build your *vocabulary*? This isn't like you. Has Uncle Smeddy been messing with you? Has he been diddling you on his knee again? Tell me the truth."

"I'm all mixed up now. Stop it. Wait a minute. Okay, I bought this book . . ."

"You? *You bought a book?* You expect me to believe that? Why? Why would *you* buy a book? Tell me the truth."

"To improve my vocabulary."

"Something's going on here. You're changed. Something has happened to you, Allison. What are you hiding?"

"I'm trying to learn new words."

"Why?"

"To sound *smart*, I guess. There may be other uses for big words, but I'm starting with the most obvious, you know? To sound cool, be cool, be *mysterious*. People who use long words nobody understands, well, they sound hot and important, like *you*, Garnet, really unreal, way out there, and way cool, like they're communing with a higher power or maybe *distant galaxies!* And they have a lot of confidence, you know, an attitude. I dig it. I want some of that."

Distant galaxies? She'd have to think about that one when she'd had the time.

This was a serious new development signaling something. Portentous, ominous. When pigs fly, when hell freezes over, when the sun cools, when East meets West. Signs of Armageddon. Allison Highsmith wants to build up her vocabulary! Run for the hills, to the rooftops, don't look back. The Day of Judgment is upon us.

"Have you been taking drugs, bath salts, drinking hand sanitizer? Your eyes look funny."

"So do yours."

And Garnet's upper lip was twitching. She tried to stop it. Unresponsive to the urgent mental instructions she sent it, she at last slapped her hand over it. It continued to wiggle and jump like a grasshopper.

"Why is your lip jumping up and down like that?"

Through her lip-staunching parted fingers Garnet said, "Don't screw with me, Allison! How are your *pipes* doing, by the way? Have you been giving them a rest? You should, you know. It may be quite some time before Your Uncle Smeddy returns from his travels."

"Oh. I just thought of something."

"You shouldn't do that, you know. You'll get headaches, bad ones. Migraines, oh sistah, they are awful. You'll be in bed for three days, light will be a torture, you'll throw up, think you're going to die and . . . ."

"From what?"

"*Thinking*, Allison, for Godsake. You're not used to it. You believe that your *pipes* hurt, made you uncomfortable? Hahaha. Oh, go AHEAD. Fuck on. Fuck away. Fuck a friggin' duck. Fuck your pathetic brains out 24 HOURS OF THE DAY 7 DAYS A WEEK! That's nothing. Screwing is much, much safer than cogitating, ruminating, reflecting, analyzing, synthesizing, super-sizing, down-sizing, speculating, to wit, *thinking*. Your pipes are much stronger, more resilient and able to rebound and recover from extended strenuous exercise than your prefrontal cortex. Just you wait! You've never had pain like the pain you will get from thinking too much too fast. You have to work up to it, train for it, practice, eat right, sleep right, you must start with baby steps, small thoughts, a few at a time, then rest, relax, get a facial, go shopping, take a bubble bath, easy does it. It's an incremental, gradual thing.

"Think—NO. Stop. *Don't think, imagine* a flower, a tiny tightly wound bud opening ever so slowly and unfurling its tender translucent pastel petals in the warm bright welcoming morning sunshine, the dewy safe nourishing morning of its tragically short but beautiful life. Or, imagine this, a perky little bean calyx, a tiny cute little guy, pushing and pushing slowly through a seed pod until, Bingo! At long last:

Hello, world! Imma lil bean sprout. Oh, look, now Imma teenage pole bean plant, a happy little ole baby teenage pole bean plant, all green and happy, burstin beans out everywhere, waving my sweet greeny open hands in the warm soft breeze that fans my little innocent life, I'm fulla beans, dancin in the sunshine, and singing 'Imma lil bean sprout short and stout. Look me over. See me sprout . . . .

Garnet stopped suddenly. Wait. Wasn't that a *teapot?* Never mind. Never revise a moral lesson; you only confound people with metaphor swap-outs, stylistic emendations. They miss the point, forget the maxim. A crude, swift two-by-four between the eyes is preferable to textual tweaking. It was the human equivalent of housebreaking a puppy. Thwap, whap. Timely, forceful, memorable. "Allison? Are you with me? A happy little green plant?"

Allison's eyes grew distant and she smiled. "Yeah, okay, I'm a little bean sprout."

"Yes. And remember Jesus loves you. The *bibliography* tells you . . . I mean, the *Bible* tells you so, and that means everything is always going to turn out fine. You don't have to be afraid of anything."

"I'm not."

"Good. But in case anything scary should pop up unexpectedly, it's good to know that. I mean, why worry? No point in it. Follow me?"

The black cloud of Fritz darkened her thoughts, and she saw him fly out of it, swooping in wide but narrowing circles, like a deadly vortex, the nihilistic, obscurantist folds of his horrid onyx cape flaring out from around him over Allison's tiny point of light at the topmost floor in the best penthouse in Ocean One, the darkness that was Fritz sweeping, swooping down, down in ever smaller circles, like a funnel of doom, down, down, down soon to engulf and destroy Allison.

Garnet snapped her fingers in front of Allison's dilating pupils. "Hey. And say the Guardian Angel Prayer every night! Know that one?"

"No. Catholics have more prayers than Episcopalians. You've got one for everything."

"They come in handy, even if you don't use them all the time. Which I don't, as you probably know. Or know only too well. But I'll write the Guardian Angel Prayer down for you. Don't worry, it's short. Say it every single night? Promise me?"

"Whatever."

"Just do it or I'll kill you and we won't be BFFs anymore."

Allison had a hard time parsing through these instructions, the heated delivery of which left her a little open mouthed and vacant of facial expression.

"Think of that, Allison. Happy thoughts. NO. I mean *pictures*, images. *Imagine.* Don't try to figure things out by thinking. It's a dead end and the most self-destructive activity a person can engage in, suicidal ideation is the inevitable result and, I don't have to tell you, do I? *That's not healthy.* I don't care how much salmon, broccoli, alfalfa sprouts and fresh squeezed grapefruit juice you swallow, they're no protection from habitual cogitation. I don't want to be an alarmist, but you don't know what you are doing. You're playing with fire with these crazy ideas of yours. The road ahead is littered

with the wrecked lives and minds. . . of people like . . . Spinoza, Nietzsche .
. . oh, and *poor Wittgenstein*. And for Godsakes, *Woody Allen!*"

She flopped down on the floor and pulled Allison down by her hand with
her.

She took both of her hands into her own and squeezed. "Now you've
really REALLY got me worried. Context is everything. There is no meaning
without context, Allison."

"Well, I wasn't going to do it too much and I sure wasn't going to enter a
contest. And I already belong to too many clubs. All I do is get my hair and
nails done and go to meetings. I've got Junior League, the Heart Ball, the
Save the Manatee Foundation, oh you know, I can't remember it all, but a
lot of other stuff and . . ."

"I advise you, and you know how much I love you, we've been BFFs since
we were eight years old. I . . . Oh, God. I just don't want anything bad to
happen to you."

"Like what?"

"Promise me one thing so I can sleep at night and start eating again?"

"You're not eating?"

"Haven't been able to swallow anything in three days, promise me that
IF Dr. Schrump contacts you, you will call me immediately. And do NOT
under any circumstances let him in your condo."

Allison pulled out three foil-wrapped Chocolate Kisses from her pocket
and handed them to her. "Here. You gotta eat somethin, Garnet."

Garnet took the kisses and stared into and through Allison's beautiful
brown eyes into the enormity of the challenges before her. The kisses melted
in her warm, warmed to the occasion hands.

Allison's blurt broke the grim silence of her chilling visualization of the
inescapable maw of the gaping Black Hole calling her, the pit sucking her
inexorably to its event horizon.

"*Okay,* if I've found my phone by then. I ordered a new one, but it's a
custom kinda thing and I can't figure out those cheapo little pre-paid crappy
things. I bought two of them, but I couldn't get either one to work right, the
instructions are so confusing . . ."

"Bring them over here. We'll figure them out. Chester's a whiz at that tekky twaddle."

"Okay," the little albatross said. She got up and smiled the visceral autonomic smile of an infant passing gas wholly undiluted of rational thought. Pure bliss. For Garnet it was a terrifying vision of the vulnerability of innocence, the three seconds it enjoyed before it was crushed underfoot or eaten alive. "Be right back. TTFN!"

"Yeah, Ta! And hurry!" Garnet didn't have the time, patience or aptitude for tekky, oh no. That was way too useful for her to bother with, way too productive, too practical. All she was good at, good *for*, she felt, she knew now, it was perfectly clear with this latest most recent epiphany, was running her mouth off, making scenes and making and getting into trouble.

17

BOOKED

✦ ✦ ✦

Man, was she booked, was her desk ever crowded. She needed to make another list. All this whirling quickly morphing unrelated stuff demanding her immediate undivided attention, all marked urgent, number one.

As Chester was fond of saying, "Everything can't be #1 and marked extremely urgent."

"Why not?"

"Because you can't get anything *done* that way. Jesus. How'd you get this far?"

"I take exception to that remark."

"You would. You are in the truest sense of the word 'exceptional.'"

"I have my own way of doing thing things, you Pecksniff barrister."

"Few people today know that's the name of a character from Dickens. Do not, I repeat, do not use 'Pecksniff' on anyone in a drinking establishment or at a football game. Understand?"

She laughed herself silly.

Chester left the room.

Soooo, numero uno?

Wait. What was going on with *Clovis Reddick?* She had almost forgotten about him with this latest threat to Allison. Was he closing in on the tiger? Was someone else? So many balls in the air. Again.

And, *Lance*, that lazy sex-crazed quarterback of county law enforcement? Had he suffered from the jilt-jolt Allison had delivered when he got boring (boring is boring, let's face it) Was he back on the job? Paying attention?

Two people had been *murdered* in this little podunk palm frond-graced, usually safe and smiling-faced Punta Bella. And nobody was doing a damn thing about it.

There was something else, or elses, too, but these three items shrieked *now* in her brain, and now was the time for action. Where was her phone?

A squeak, squish, a spray of moisture. She looked up, her own phone in one hand and Allison's burning like a hot coal in her other hand. Chester, looking like the drowned man on a Tarot card, hung his head, stood next to her and shook his umbrella. His trench coat was soaked straight through and clinging to him like a second skin. "Looks like we might have to evacuate. Adjust your plans accordingly, kid."

She looked. She thought. Ringo jumped on Chester's wet leg, *The beach, the beach, let's hit the beach, man, let's rock.* Diesel whined and rolled over on his back in front of him. *Rub my tummy, she hasn't rubbed my tummy in an hour.*

"I'm not going."

"Yes, you are, Garnet."

"No I am not."

"Why?"

"I'm too busy."

Chester stormed out. She tensed, knowing Act II by heart. He came back, blew himself up like Frankenstein and filled the doorway. "Get your shit together just in case. It's not mandatory yet. But we need to get ready if they make it mandatory, if they say everybody has to get off the island."

"I have a higher mandate." She smiled.

He almost smiled. "What? A story?" He wandered off shaking his head.

Sensing from the soft amusement in his eyes that the time was opportune to spring her Panzer scheme on him, she launched out of her chair and trailed behind him down the hallway.

"Forget it, Garnet, I'm not going to Hendry County for anything. Particularly for a hog roast barbeque at the Panzer place."

"Why?"

"I don't want to, that's why."

"I do a lot of things for you that I don't want to do."

"Like what?"

"I do the dishes almost every day. Okay, at least three or four days a week. And sometimes I fold your *sox* and *boxers*. Sometimes I even put them *away* for you." She rested her case.

No reaction.

"You'll see lots of old friends and admirers."

"Precisely why I'm not going."

She'd been afraid of this. "You are still so screwed up and reclusive, Chester! You've got to work through it and re-join the human race, stop this penance thing, and stop hiding, beating yourself up over losing a stupid election! You fought a good fight and you lost. What's the shame in that? How can you possibly believe it's your fault?"

He left the room. She followed him down the hall. "And you can run again any time you want! For anything! You could be the damn governor of Florida if you wanted to! Everybody'd vote for you! Marianne Tallywocky's already started a PAC for you with her bible study group in Immokalee!"

He stopped and she slammed into his chest. Looking down and pulling her nose, he said, "Marianne Tallywocky? In Immokalee! Now that could prove decisive, Garnet. What a boost that would be."

"Chester, I *have* to go. And if I go by myself, he'll rape me."

"He will not."

"He'll want to."

"But he won't."

"You're coming and that's it. I have spoken."

"A hurricane is coming, Tinker Bell. And the only place you and I are going, with these canine flea bags, is inland and to the north."

"It's not even close yet." She dashed to her laptop to make sure. No sweat. Still iffy. Dilly-dallying 200 miles to the east.

Chester was in the kitchen, standing next to the counter, head bent over the sports page and eating potato chips. "I MAKE YOU POT ROAST AND MEATLOAF, YOU THANKLESS BASTARD," she screeched into his ear. "THAT, FOR GODSAKES, OUGHT TO COUNT FOR SOMETHING!"

He looked up.

"Chester, I do and you know it."

"Not in a long time."

"I'M ON A DIET! YOU SAID I WAS *FAT!*" she wailed.

He stared.

"THIS IS SO UNFAIR! I'M TRYING TO *PLEASE* YOU, MAKE YOU HAPPY. AND YOU TREAT ME LIKE *THIS*. A PIECE OF *DIRT*." She gagged out a rattling, dryish sob. She wished she could squirt out a few tears along with the rhetoric and histrionics. She'd be far more convincing. He always cratered when she did.

"And I, I, I . . . *I*, Garnet, am *not* on a diet and yet am in danger of starving to death." He pinned her with that one. "As I'm sure you have not noticed."

Maybe they could work out a deal. "Are you hungry?"

"Garnet, you have gone beyond slim, svelte and gorgeous to famished-looking. Time to put the brakes on this asceticism, this fasting of yours."

"I still have some cellulite, a little bit, here," she pointed to her hips.

"Do you still have some *brain* cells left, or have you shed those too?"

"Do *you?*" She exhaled, rolled her eyes, put her hand over her heart, generously giving ground, making a stunning concession. "OKAY. Here's my offer. Here's the deal: I quit my diet, you go with me to Hendry County to Tank's party. Take it or leave it. You have 30 seconds or I'll go bulimic on you too. My life hangs in the balance." She smiled. "As does yours."

Chester popped another potato chip into his mouth and chewed, thoughtfully. He eyed her with a baleful, gimlet eye.

"Say something, Chester."

"Okay. But *cook* something, alright? *Now? Tonight?* Can we start having dinner together again? Will you please start buying—oh, what the hell do they call it? *'Food?'*"

+ + +

Story story story. She had to work fast; her nose was to the ground. They were heading out for the Godforsaken wilderness, Tank country, the day after tomorrow, and she had *stuff to do*. Fred couldn't get enough of her tips and deliberate titillations of his numb nutz news instincts. They were not quite dead yet, but on the life support of the constant daily infusions of Garnet's blaring, swearing, impetuous updates, most carefully devised and phrased to create a maximum dose spurt, a 1000 volt charge, an electrical neurological impulse equal to the Big Bang, in Fred's head and imagination. It was similar to a hand-operated morphine pump surgery patients are given to moderate the pain of recovery in a hospital and, like an addict, Fred pumped Garnet. And pumped and pumped.

So what was the story? It was all about bastards, kicking their butts, loving well the people you loved and being *nice* to everyone else, everything else. Dogs, elephants, frogs, horses, birds, even snakes and spiders. And amoebas, protozoa, red worms, ad valorum ad infinitum infinitesimally eternally, protons, neutrons, morons effluxes cruxes. It was real darn simple. That was the truth according to Garnet. There were many varied, highly chromatic, refractory, splendiferous ways to deliver *this simple dud of a truth* and she grooved on that, often got lost in it and woke some mornings asking herself, "What have I *done?*" Which was understandable. She always had done something. She'd always put a new spin on the ball.

So what spin would she put on this simple truth today? Who struck John? What heinous excuse for a human being could she send to hell this week to protect and preserve the Good and the True and the Innocent? What nasty piece of twisted guile and malevolence was next? Priorities. Please.

Speak of the Devil. The sulfurous voicemail blew her last fuse.

"Miss ya, cupcake. Got somethin' for ya. I'll be seeing you soon, sugar baby. Gotta visit my darlin' *niece* first!"

Garnet swallowed half of her tongue. Without that, she was typically SOL. She jumped in the bug anyway and shot down A1A, on mute perhaps, but not without purpose or possible effect. *Faster.*

THE DEVIL, THE DIVA & THE DEEP BLUE SEA

In an unaccustomed act of prudence, en route she called Lance. Maybe he had silver bullets. Didn't it take silver bullets and crucifixes to repel The Big Black Booger Himself? Lance, however, perhaps still stung and smarting from Allison's rejection, balked at calling in the swat team and asking for reinforcements and technical help from the ATF, FBI, DEA, EPA, CIA, INS, NATO, the UN and other similar big guns. For some reason he had a hard time buying into the idea, nay, the *reality*, of an imminent assault on Allison by the Devil.

"You skunked me big time, Garnet, sweetheart, with that last 911 of yours. Sorry. We had to pay out of general funds to replace that $38,000 hand-carved old door from Italy."

"Is that all? I'm surprised it was that little. I thought it might have cost ten times that."

"And my guys had to clean up all that bubble bath slop and now she's tryin to nail us for the ambulance fee, medical bills, ER expenses and the shrink charges for getting her head de-bugged from the goldern 'incident.' Sorry. No way, Jose'."

"I hope you don't regret this, Lance. How could you live with yourself if something awful happened to Allison as a result of your *callous indifference?*"

"My what? Who's callin' a spade a spade here? That hussy . . ."

"You *loved* her once, did you not?"

"I'll have to get back to you on that one, darlin'.'"

"I'm surprised at you, Lance."

"Yeah, well, you let me know what happens, all righty? And give my regards to the Devil. He has met his match, I'm tellin' you. He don't have no clue to what he's in for if he has a go at 'Honey Cakes.'"

"Who?"

Click.

Pfhssst. No, not now. *Pfhissst.* The bug listed and veered to the right. Whop, whop. WHOP, WHOP. No, no, no. She was driving 90 mph, the bug's top speed, on a rim, her car leaning and swerving and slowing . . . When it stopped and she opened her eyes she was in a clutch of palmettos higher than its raggedy rag-top about ten feet from the dunes. The ocean was roaring nearby and rain was once again coming down in sheets. A seagull sat on her hood looking at her skeptically as a poor chance, an unlikely softie for a hand-out. If she died there, though, it knew, a whole new world of gourmet delicacies opened up to it. That was why it was hanging around. These suckers died sometimes. It was worth its while to stick around and see what happened. The ocean was too rough for minnows and bait fish. What did it have to lose?

What have I done, where am I? This was getting old.

Her phone was ringing somewhere. Somehow she found it.

"Where the hell are you?"

"Chester, you won't believe this . . ."

"A totally unnecessary prelude, Garnet, these days to anything you are about to tell me. Of course I won't. But where are you? Why aren't you here doing what you need to be doing? We have a lot of bases to cover, the weather is still totally unpredictable, you insist on going 200 miles down to Tank's in less than 48 hours, we might have to evacuate. We're going to have to take the damn dogs everywhere, wherever we go. What the hell are you thinking?"

"Don't be mad. Please."

"You're nuts."

"No argument, okay? The devil made me do it this time, though."

"Clovis Reddick, the guy from Peaceable Kingdom? He called the house phone looking for you."

"What?"

"He said it was urgent. But, listen, just blow him off. You do not have time for one more thing on your to-do list today, right now, do you hear me?"

"Chester?"

"Hear me?"

"Was it about the tiger?"

"What tiger? *Tiger!* Shit, Garnet."

Had she neglected to mention the tiger to Chester? Which subterfuge was that part of? She couldn't remember. Her head hurt.

"I'll explain."

"Don't bother."

"I made you fudge. It's in the fridge."

He didn't say a peep.

"Fudge, Chester?"

It was some kind of record, two different men hanging up on her in less than five minutes, but not one she was proud of.

18

THAT SINKING FEELING

✢ ✢ ✢

She deserved an Oscar for the performance she gave to persuade Chester to proceed on to Allison's place. He rolled up, madder than a hornet, seriously mad for Chester. It scared her. She'd only seen him this mad once or twice and never at her.

In silence they sped down A1A in the twilight and drenching rain. A vein, that particular portent, the uniquely Chester symptom of an impending nuclear verbal blast coincident with his trademark scorched earth advance on what had pissed him off, yes, that vein on his forehead was sticking out and throbbing as if it were going to explode.

"I wish you wouldn't be like this, Chester. It's not worth stressing out over."

"You can't keep this up. I can't live like this."

"Like what?"

"This is getting tiresome, Garnet."

The doorman, ever gracious and down-home friendly, brightened when he saw them come into to the lobby. "Hello, Miss Garnet. Mr. Dare, how are you tonight? It's been a long time! You're looking good!"

Chester forced a smile. "Hi, Brownie."

"Too bad, though. I guess you came to visit Miss Highsmith?"

"Yes?" A cold gob of something lodged in Garnet's throat.

"Just missed her. She left not five minutes ago with her uncle Dr. Schrump."

"Oh." Garnet turned to Chester, speechless.

"Did she say, Brownie, where she was going?" Chester, pleasant, casual, ever even-voiced, reserved, composed, especially so when about to detonate, about to reduce everything within a 100 mile radius to smoldering cinders and dust.

"I believe, if I remember correctly, they were going to supper." He winked. "I'm not sure, mind ya, but I thought I heard them talking about the Chart House. Down the road a piece, you know? On the ocean."

"Thanks, Brownie."

"Nice to see you again, Brownie. Take care."

"How 'bout this weather? A mess, ain't it?"

"Awful," Chester said. "Awful."

She followed him out the door like a suppliant, a penitent, the sinner that she was, the hopeless frivolous pointless useless ingrate, the piece of guano that she was, swamped with remorse and uncertainty.

"I hope nothing happens to Allison," she said.

Wordlessly they headed back north and Chester swung into the Chart House parking lot. It was deserted. The restaurant was closed because of the hurricane warning. The Chart House was only about 30 feet from the now raging 12-foot breakers. The building had been erected before the setback laws. Reeking with charm and the shabby yet dignified character of weathered cypress, people loved the place for its Old Florida ambience and the thrill of drinking and eating whilst teetering on swaying, rotting pilings that thrust 15 feet out over the Atlantic Ocean. The ocean here on this stretch of Florida coast that was subject to dazzling dolphin-hued color changes and dramatic thundering mood swings, ranging from euphoria to silent bliss to madness. The old rotter pirate hole of a place would be swept out to sea if a hurricane came through. Time was short for this old man of the ocean, the remaining number of dinners it would serve, numbered.

They paused to look at the tormented waves shrouded in the thick salt spray, the lashed palm trees and sea oats, and a nostalgic swarm of warm happy memories of times spent together there engulfed them. The tenderness and the tenuousness of their lives and all life was apparent in the view and the setting. The reality of the hurricane, its awesome destructive power and the danger they were in was manifest right before their eyes and it silenced them and dwarfed all other concerns.

"Now do you get it, Garnet?"

"Bad storm. Yep. Scary."

"Just an idea, but maybe you should take a break from trying to save Allison and the whole damn universe, for that matter, for a while. Maybe you should think about saving your own sweet ass instead."

"I said I got it, honey, okay?"

"I'm not just talking about the hurricane, kid. Maybe instead of racing all over the place muckraking the whole damn county for your stories, you should concentrate for a while on your own story, the real story of Garnet Sullivan."

The comment blind-sided and stung her. "Maybe one day I will, Chester."

They watched as a giant wave slammed into the ancient pilings under-girding the restaurant. In one crushing motion it washed away a jumble of loose timber as if it were a handful of toothpicks. In seconds the tumbling mass disappeared into the roaring angry water, gone forever.

Chester cleared his throat and coughed. Then he turned to her and looked her in the eye. She froze. Here it comes. The Point. Nowhere to run, nowhere to hide. "I would suggest to you, darling, that you hop on that story ASAP and the sooner the better. It's bigger and more important than you know."

She tried to laugh. "It would be unprintable and not at all profitable, Chester."

"You're missing the point." He stared at the ocean. His face was sad.

"Oh, no." She took his hand. "You made your point quite well, Chester. I just don't like it."

"Didn't think you would. Do it anyway, okay? For me?"

She'd do anything for him if it were in her power. But this? What was he asking her to do? "I wouldn't know where to start. It would be boring. Embarrassing. No one would be interested in it but me maybe. And, pardon the pun, but I don't see the point. Seems kinda pointless and a waste of time."

But certainly more worthy than penning snide spoofs to Fred? Yeah, it was. She should cut back some on that stuff. Really.

"I would be very much interested, but most importantly I'd be interested in the result, not the text. I would be interested in what it would do for you."

"Ha! You mean my 'plot?' How it would play out in my life? The rest of it? The rest of my story?"

"Could be a game changer, ya never know. Think of it as character development."

"That's a technique for fiction, Chester, not autobiography or psychology or spiritual formation or philosophy. And hey, I've got plenty of character, buster, and you know it. You're trying to get at that 'know thyself' maxim through the back door, using it as a pretext to punish me with it, you're insinuating there is something deficient or wrong with me of which I am not aware. Okay, ow, that hurts. Happy now? Trust me, I know my faults just as well as you do. Come off it."

"Don't spar with me and try to be cute. You know where I'm going with this."

"Not really. But if you mean take a good hard look at myself, well, introspection is over-rated, I think. Yuk, all that self-referential stuff. That 'finding oneself' crap. Tiresome. Tedious. Self-indulgent when carried to an extreme."

"How would you know?"

"Very funny. Get your head outta your butt, buddy. You know it's not about me, I mean, I'm not about me. It's all about getting rid of the bastards. My idea of heaven is to become invisible to myself, forget I have a self."

"That's crazy. Like or not, you got one. Ignoring it is bad, I'm telling you."

"I prefer to think it's selfless."

"Garnet, do you really have any idea how all your manic Joan of Arc crusading comes across? Your compulsive speeding, rushing to the rescue of every stray mot in the atmosphere or infinitesimal gnat that passes by? Your smart ass moralizing, venting, your righteous denunciations of every fleck of dust in the universe that gets in anyone's eye? For chrissake, just look at what you've done to Allison trying to help her."

"Never occurred to me. And as for Allison, my intentions were pure even though my perceptions, shall we say, may have been somewhat disordered.

But here's the thing, okay? I want my epitaph to say 'I died trying,' not 'Oh, well, I gave it a shot' or 'I made a stab at it for a while,' or 'I did what was reasonable and required.'"

"No one would ever accuse you of being reasonable, Garnet. But I'm glad you told me that. At the rate you're going, I may soon have to pass that on to some anonymous stone-cutter who could care less."

The windshield was smeared with salt spray and the ragged detritus from blown to bits foliage and seaweed. Their breath had fogged the windows. The intimacy and the rawness of the confrontation was claustrophobic under the circumstances and their angry words seemed to refuse to dissipate, to hang in the air around them, poisoning the conversation even further, making everything only worse.

"Let's not belabor this, all right? We've flogged the metaphor to death. Point made, point taken. You're mad at me, that's all. This is your way of smacking me upside the head again. Just a new phraseology and approach. A different spin to the same old same old. You ain't so perfect yourself."

"Never said I was. Whatever. Just that it's your life, your story. I'm only along for the ride. I don't think you know what moves you, that's all. And, frankly, I goddam don't think you know what you're doing half the time."

"Well, screw you too. We are made of the same stuff, Chester and you know it. We just have different methods and styles. And you're pissing away your time and talents in your job just as much as I am in mine, casting your pearls before swine, or more so, what with your morose smarting over a silly election loss, punishing yourself and me for it and other imagined sins by dedicating your life to losers. Give me a break. Who do you think you're talking to? Some moron? Now step on it! Faster! I've got work to do and a world to save. And some hell to raise and fun to have while I'm at it too."

"Shut the hell up, honey."

"Okay. And same to ya." And they did.

✝ ✝ ✝

Breaking News--

AP Newswire. Yesterday at 4:00 p.m. the geological monitors at the south Florida nuclear power plant at Turkey Point detected a shift and drop in the landmass directly below its nuclear reactor. Workers had reported a sense of movement in the floors at the plant several days before, and only hours before the monitor alarms went off, two workers in the lead lined nuclear reactor maintenance room reported hearing thunder underground and "thuds" accompanied by a shaking in the floors and walls. Washington, DC-based experts from the Nuclear Power and Energy Commission, the EPA and FEMA were called in immediately but have yet to issue a report or analysis regarding the significance of these subterranean developments.

The Florida Dept. of Energy and Natural Resources observers on the scene unofficially and off the record discounted any potential danger to residents or the environment. "Sinkholes is [sic] all it is," one said on the condition of anonymity. "Can't do a dern [sic] thing about them. Been [sic] a bad drought, going to be a bit of shuffling and shifting in old Mother Nature's big old bottom getting herself comfortable again. Floridians are used to staying light on their feet. They know how to duck and run as necessary. May have a chance to do some of that in the next few months."

Harriet Norton-Asbury-Norton, a tenured geology professor and researcher at the University of Florida in Gainesville disagreed with the evaluation of the state agent, saying, "The bottom is about to fall out of the state of Florida and deservedly so. The state has failed to regulate aquifer pumping and the Water Management Districts' commission members are on the take, crooked as h--- and brain dead to boot."

The Indian River Times, October 24, 2013
"Hold On, Gators. Things Are Getting a Little Iffy Underfoot"
By Garnet Sullivan, Columnist & Staff Reporter

"Residents of Newberry, FL on their way to work this morning were shocked to find that an 80 foot stretch of State Road 26, the main artery ('cow path' would be a perhaps more apropos word choice, but nevertheless . . .) leading from Newberry to Gainesville, FL, where most are employed, was missing. That's right. Gone. Vanished. Say what? Overnight the roadway had buckled and broken away from the underlying topsoil, and had fallen 50 feet below the rest of the road. Traffic was detoured 30 miles distant, and many workers were late for work, having stopped, en route to their workplaces, at the Waffle House in nearby Chiefland to rub their eyes, say "Duh, whut?" And swap lies and theories over a stack of pancakes about what may have "swallered" [sic] the road.

"Sinkhole activity, resulting from the recent severe Florida drought is the suspected culprit, the most likely geological cause (mostly a rock and dirt phenom), an activity exacerbated by unmanaged and mismanaged drilling and the over-pumping of water out of the FL aquifer by farmers and ranchers, golf courses and other selfish insatiably thirsty bastards.

"Specialists have gone on record as saying the aquifer water table has dropped more than 20 feet in the last nine months of dry weather, causing a very uncertain, unpredictable situation by leaving the topsoil with no supporting substrate and under which empty chasms and caverns have opened. Heavy rainfall weighs down the unsupported topsoil, and *gravity*, (Latin, *gravitas*; e.g., 'grab your ass'), a theory postulated by the Englishman Sir Isaac Newton (1643-1727), and which he demonstrated and proved conclusively as an Immutable Natural Law with the aid of an apple, his head and an over-hanging tree branch, inevitably caused the *whop ka-pow thud* incident characteristic of the formation of sinkholes.

"Unregulated, high speed, out of control heavy *gravity* is considered to be a very grave situation, according to the Academy of American Scientists and the national Atlanta-based Center for Disease Control, often with contingent adverse sequelae and having a poor proboscis prognosis. The word *grave* and the word *gravity* share the same Latin etymology, and are derived from the same root word. Over the centuries the words have acquired the implicit, explicit connotations, import, innuendos, resonance and plangent allusive nuances relative to *death, dying* and *dead,* or about to be, as in having 'one foot on a banana peel and the other foot in the *grave*.' (*Oxford English Dictionary*, vol.32, 84th edition, Oxford University Press, London [England] 2008).

"Ergo, watch where you step, guys. Although the highest sinkhole activity typically occurs in north and north central Florida, the recent drought was the worst on record and statewide. So hang on. It could happen here. Look out. Yadda yadda, the more things change, the more they remain the same. Or not. Dig it?—G.S."

Garnet stared at the newsprint spread out before her in disbelief. Fred hadn't edited out any of her customary teases and nose-pulling, the little stink bombs she stuck in her articles and pieces just so he would have *something* to edit, something to do. He always scotched *bastard*, and the pedantic stem-winder with the OED citation got not one mark or a single challenge. Had Fred even *glanced* at this drivel before he ran with it? Was he sick? Something was going on here. *But what?*

As she was considering this awful possibility, as well as some dubious hidden motive that may lurk behind his "hands off" approach to a "story" that she'd only intended as a *gag*, Allison blew through her front door without bothering to knock, breathless, exhilarated, and squealing with glee. The dogs jumped on her, her legs bowed, she staggered, hugged them, but she still staggering made it over to her desk fueled with news and high spirits.

"Garnet! You won't believe it!"

"Oh. So you're still alive? Have you been violated?"

"What's that? Made into a flower?"

"Look it up, you darling little vocabularian. Begins with a V. More like de-flowered, sweet pea."

"Okay, maybe later, but listen . . . this is so cool, such a gas . . ."

"Hold it. Where did you go last night with your Uncle Smeddy? What happened? The truth."

"We had the best good time! I'm tryin to tell you! Garnet, he is such an adorable, caring man! I'm sooooo happy to have him back in my life!"

"Are you saying the Guardian Angel Prayer I wrote down for you per my directions?"

"I lost it. But don't worry, everything is great."

"Worry? About *you*, bean sprout? Never."

"We went to Naples for dinner!"

"No way."

"Okay, sure, it was a long drive, yeah, for sure, but we got back by ten this morning. And the calamari was out of this world."

"I thought you hated calamari."

"Not anymore! And afterwards we went for a walk on the beach over there, under the stars, Garnet! He held my hand, it was so sweet!"

"What else did he hold, Bo Peep?"

"He hugged me!"

"He hugged you!"

"Yes. Real close! And the beach is different over there, doesn't have big waves like the beach here and it has soft powdery sand . . ."

"A different ocean over there may account for that."

"You mean there's more than one?"

"You should have taken that geography course, Allison. It's a big bad world out there. Many oceans. Gulfs. Swamps. Mires."

"No kidding?"

"Tell me exactly what happened. Try to stay on point."

"Oh, wow, okay. We went in his *limo!* His man Chutney drove soooo fast! He's from India, wears that thing on his head. We got there in no time."

Garnet smacked her head. "Where's this paragon of avuncular solicitude now?" She glared at the petite albatross with a strand of pearls around her neck who had become a blight and choker around her own. The guilt was leaden, the responsibility like a tomb. "Where is he? Tell me now."

"Who? What?"

"Your damn uncle, you little albatr . . . er . . . you little bean sprout."

Allison giggled. "Yeah, Imma lil bean sprout, for sure. Uncle Smeddy suddenly had to go to Salamis for a few days. But he'll be back soon."

Garnet's sense of humor had shriveled overnight. "There's a hurricane coming," she said flatly.

All her gears and wheels had become fully engaged and were whirring at top speed. She could barely keep up with the explosion of new developments, plots hatching, balls in the air, personal, professional, ethereal, temporal. She was momentarily needled by the effort of working up a plausible excuse for

Tank to have at the ready should the need abruptly arise for blowing off his "cookout," a development wholly contingent on Chester's inscrutable hurricane avoidance instincts. It may be she would have to suddenly duck out on his hog roast-skeet shooting-turkey holler whatever. Once Chester made a Decision with a capital D (as in doom), a decision meticulously reasoned, massively buttressed with flawless airtight syllogisms, precedents and case law, he trod forward like a Cyclops, and dragged her relentlessly behind him. Despite his agreement of the day before to squire her to Tank's spread for her reconnoitering on the aquifer-plundering hunch Fred had, she knew it was not a done deal.

And Fred! Fred was getting really annoying lately. Murders, aquifers, tigers, all the flotsam and jetsam of an idle mind. She was not a news staff. She was one person, for heaven sake, albeit talented, intuitive, committed etcetera blah blah, but still one over-burdened "reporter," flailing in the high winds of her own enthusiasms and the crosswinds of all her significant others' hot air and whims, buffeted, blown, hither thither and yon, dithering on and on.

Yes. Something was up with Chester, she was sure of it, she had that telltale queasy feeling that going to Tank's was not a happening thing, particularly given the weather. And that old boar hog Tank was so looking forward to showing her his new space age sperm collection equipment he'd bought for his prize bulls.

"There is?" Allison said.

Garnet jumped. "There is what?" She had almost convinced herself, day dreaming, as Allison blathered away, that a mandatory hurricane evacuation order would fill the bill with Tank excuse-wise, provided he didn't insist they scoot down to the bowels of Immokalee and hole up for the duration on his huge estate. It would depend on her impassioned delivery, and maybe other sperm bank related factors of which she was woefully unaware.

"Garnet! A *real* hurricane is comin *here?*" Allison was positively goosed by this notion.

"Look out the window, Pipes."

"Oh, yikes."

"I don't know how you could have missed it. You did drive here, did you not?"

Allison nodded gravely. "I was listening to a vocab CD, though. Ever hear of 'fungible?' It doesn't mean you got a fungus, you know."

"Yeah, so pay attention. Pack a bag. If Chester makes us leave the island, you're comin with us."

"Where?"

"I don't know, somewhere away from the ocean."

"Which one?"

"Less than two minutes ago, Allison, you thought there was only one ocean. You have gotten awfully inquisitive lately. Why?"

"Oh, you know, trying to improve my mind, I guess that's what you call it. Nothing better to do. I mean, why not? All the new words, I learn a new one every day, and they get me thinking, sort of."

"I told you not to do that. It's dangerous."

"I don't do it very much."

But Garnet, a compulsive and frequent email and text checker, was jolted and distracted by a sudden email salvo from Fred. "Get the goods on those murders and the aquifer-draining cattle bonehead or I run with your epic poem on the tiger, Ruby Begonia. The unexpurgated sinkhole piece was a warning. Think that was embarrassing? I'm losing patience. Hump it."

She was already humping it as fast as she could. Her wheels were about to fall off, she was almost out of gas. Stifling a scream, she drew a beam on the matter at hand, her BFF, and her eyes narrowed.

"Just don't make a habit of it, Allison."

"Of what?"

"Thinking! Go pack. Hurry."

"Then what?"

"Come right back here. Immediately. Understand?"

"Why?"

"There you go again. Stop it. Move your butt, now."

Things were getting a little complicated here. She needed to make a list.

19

FUSSY FISTICUFFS

✦ ✦ ✦

Allison was sound asleep in the guest bedroom. She'd stopped thinking, got her words for the day down, tried them out on Chester to no effect (he looked up for a sec, appeared puzzled as if a familiar bird had curiously chirped off key, and went right back to his newspapers and briefs). Garnet had felt a chill as the verbally disfigured words passed through Allison's pouty glossy lips and hastily corrected her pronunciation of "Aphrodite" and "aphrodisiac," then quickly followed up her elocution lesson with a severe grilling worthy of the Spanish Inquisition. Where had she gotten the words? Where?

"Uncle Smeddy, myths and stuff! He knows everything."

"He does, does he?"

"Yeah! There's, you know, a goddess? Like one day she popped out of the sea? Kind of like a human Oysters Rockefeller? On a shell? And she was very beautiful and all . . . it's about love or something." Her eyes grew dreamy and soft, distant and lamb-like.

Too many fronts. She had over-engaged the enemy. The battles were raging everywhere. At least Bean Sprout was safe within these doors. Just to make sure, Garnet checked the locks four times before turning out the lights.

Rain beat against the windows and clumps of branches and airborne junk crashed through the atmosphere and smashed against the walls outside, creating a noisy percussive presence in the bedroom. Oblivious, Chester had his nose stuck in a big fat green hardcover Westlaw edition of the Florida statutes. Leaning in toward the lamp on the bedside table, he exuded that deep ponderous absorption of a wholly engrossed Supreme Court justice. It was eleven-thirty, way past The Great One's bedtime.

"So what moronic piece of obtuse legalese are you getting off on now, honey?"

He didn't look up.

"We have to get up *early*, Chester, to make it to Tank's place in Immokalee in time for the hog waller cookout or whatever they're doing down there. And, FYI, Allison's going with us."

He rolled in closer to the light and turned a page.

She got in bed next to him and smacked her pillow. "Are you going to read *all night*, Chester? Some of us," she glanced at the comatose Ringo and Diesel on the floor next to the bed, "*Some* of us are trying to get some sleep here!" She may as well have been talking to a pile of rocks.

Then a flash of blinding red light passed before her eyes. She clenched her fist and without another word, wound up, drew back a big wallop and plowed her balled up knuckles into the hefty book in front of his judicious face, thus giving Chester a prizefighter's bloody nose, vis-à-vis the Florida Statutes. Chester was not amused.

"Chester! Look at your poor nose! You're *bleeding!* You might bleed to death!" She lurched toward the edge of the bed and rolled onto the floor. "Ice! You've got to get ice on it!"

He grabbed her arm and hauled her back into bed. "We're not going."

"*What?* You said yesterday you would go with me to Tank's after all! You promised me! We made a deal! I stopped dieting! I bought food! I made you a sandwich!"

"Old Tank's got his butt in a big wad of trouble." He let the weighty, deadly, boring (no plot, poor characterization, totally absent of wit) tome slide to the floor.

"Huh? *Trouble?* That old slug?" The dim light and the stars twinkling before Chester's swimming eyes were to her advantage. Aha. Water. His big pompous endowment of the Panzer Water Institute at UF, oh yeah. His cover for his sucking the aquifer dry. Maybe. Bad news for Chester's future campaign funds, perhaps, but it was what it was. But what, exactly, was it? She hoped Chester couldn't see the sparks flying out of her ears as her pistons roared into overdrive.

"No details. Go to sleep." He wiped the blood off his face with the back of his hand and switched off the light.

"Not funny, Chester. How could you? I swear I won't write any story, not even an eensy weensy miniscule tiny little bit about it. I promise."

Silence.

"Chester."

"If you hit me again I'm calling the cops."

"Yes, yes, as you *should.* I'm so sorry. I don't know what came over me. I love you."

"Me too you."

"Why won't you tell me then, Chester? Don't you *trust* me?"

"That question does not merit a reply."

"My hand hurts."

"Good."

✛ ✛ ✛

The following morning Allison sat in the living room on the couch with Ringo and Diesel banking her close on either side, as she studied her vocabulary book. She was a conscientious if not apt student. Ringo and Diesel were neither conscientious nor apt. They were, in fact, barely conscious. But they loved Allison and the monotonous drone of her murmuring memorization had lulled them into a state of bliss somewhere between a stuffed full stomach and an hours' long romp on the beach.

With one bloodshot eye frozen on the Weather Channel, and the other closed in exasperation, Garnet drummed her nails on the desk in sync with the rain. The hurricane was stalled 170 miles due east but had picked up strength overnight. Cat 4. Impossible. Hasn't happened in this bailiwick of Florida in over thirty years. Highly improbable. Still, the suspense was a huge pain.

Now what?

Like a laser beam fired from the outer reaches of outer space, a long forgotten quote pierced her skull. She sat up straight.

The lion will lie down with the lamb, but the lamb won't get much sleep.

–WOODY ALLEN

The phone rang and rang and she sighed and sighed. At last, a meek voice said, "Good day. It's a good day at the Peaceable Kingdom every day. How may I help you?"

"This is Garnet Sullivan returning Mr. Reddick's call."

Urgent whispers, fumbled phone. A click and she's disconnected. She sighed dramatically and voluminously. It helped sometimes. He's called about his precious tiger. Must be that. What a bother. She's not about to tell that twit where Kalimba is as long as Mr. Johnson is haunting Tommy's old place and feeding her steaks, thank you very much, every night. Calling her "kitty" and cooing, "Here, lil pussy-cat." Anything is better than a cage.

Cage. The thought was like death to Garnet. She called back. If he was up to something, she'd better sniff it out before it up and bit her. Clovis may spring a leak, let something drop. If he didn't? Looked like Chester's penniless client was going to grow old in the county jail. No bondsman would return his call.

"Yes, Miss Sullivan, thank you ever so much for ringing me back."

"You're welcome. What can I do for you, Mr. Reddick?"

"Oh, my, Lord knows I've just about despaired of ever finding my beloved Kalimba again. I do want to thank you for the concern you've expressed and your very kind help, uh (cough-cough) previously, that is, uh (cough-cough) though."

"You're more than welcome."

"I'm not bothering you today about poor Kalimba, though it certainly is a mystery to me how a Bengal tiger could so easily disappear in a fairly well developed area of Florida, particularly with a $10,000 reward offered for information leading to her recovery."

"Yes, rather odd, I'd have to agree."

"Soooo, any whoooo….actually the matter uppermost in my addled head at the present time … My word, the headaches it's given me. I can barely sleep a wink at night, even with medication."

"I am very sorry, but I don't have much time, Mr. Reddick."

"Oh my, all of which is to say, it's too horrible to contemplate, my every fiber rebels against what my senses tell me, but …"

"Yes?"

"I fear, it's too awful to say, but, my word, I do very much fear that there is a plot afoot."

"A plot *afoot*?"

"Perhaps you are aware of the unfortunate incident that led to the untimely demise of one of my former employees, God rest his soul?"

"Vaguely."

"I can't tell you the torment I'm in over this. Good God."

"What, please, are you talking about?"

"I am terribly alarmed, no, I'm in the most extreme physical and spiritual agony over the fact that the wrong man has been charged with murdering my poor employee."

"No kidding."

"Yes. And a *diabolical* twist on all of this …"

"You don't say!" Damn that Fritz. He was everywhere!

"Very convoluted, demented."

That was a positive I.D. if she'd ever heard one. "Yes?"

"Water! It's all about water. And now the precious earth is sinking beneath our very feet! These rapacious cowboys from South Florida are after me, hounding me, to drill and pump water on my land. They want to lay pipe from here all the way down to Hendry County! And, Oh! My land, I cannot for the life of me understand the connection, but a very strange coincidence having to do with this new veterinarian I've retained for the big cats."

"What's he look like, this new vet of yours?"

"The most unusual attire, long black cloak, red beret, black eye patch, my heavens. Not at all well groomed, I must say. Very seedy. And every time he shows up to treat one of my kitties something terrible happens. My 1925

Bentley fell through the earth yesterday! Yes! It did! That precious collector quality personal transportation vehicle fell over one hundred feet down toward *Hades*! It was worth, don't you know, oh my, well over one million dollars!"

"Hades! What?"

"The damnable veterinarian is in league with the cattle barons who are raping the land! And now I've lost my Bentley and God knows what's next!"

"So you got a whopper sinkhole, huh? I still don't see how this is all *related*, how it makes any sense or proves anything. You need to take a powder, Mr. Reddick. And I suggest you change veterinarians."

"The reprehensible beast purloined my keys—I'd left them in the car, don't you know? I was so distracted at the time by all the rough men in cowboy boots storming and stomping around surveilling my property and asking me impertinent questions. Then this most eccentric veterinarian showed up to give my cats some inoculations and I lost track of where he was and what he was doing. Before I knew it, I looked up and saw him, in the most reckless fashion imaginable, drive my Bentley away to a spot on the grounds at which the earth immediately collapsed! I saw this with my own eyes! Infernal is what it was! The crude cowboys thought this quite amusing! It was as if they had conspired with him, as if it were planned! As if it were a cruel practical joke!"

"Did the earth swallow the veterinarian too?" She certainly hoped so.

"No, actually, he climbed out of the nasty chasm and survived in good order. He perversely thought the entire incident was highly entertaining. The damned devil then collapsed on the ground right next to the pit and rolled around holding his sides, howling in laughter. Most offensive, most insulting. My beloved Bentley was a family heirloom!"

"My goodness." She didn't know what, but she had to give Fritz credit for something.

"And, then, oh!" Reddick's voice fell to a horrified whisper, "He made the most improper inquiries about the poor man who was murdered here. Brusquely inquisitive, absolutely rude! He imputed all sorts of nefarious behavior to me and my loyal employees. He had the fiendish nerve to ask if my Mother, my own dear *Mother,* was 'part *buffalo!* This man got right before my face and asked me if she had 'buffaloed' me all my life! Imagine that!"

"*Is* she? Has she?" Garnet had never given that particular hypothesis any consideration. That Fritz, she had to hand it to him. Out of the box, always pushing the envelope. She grinned in appreciation. Where had he gotten that idea? Where was he going with all of this? There was always a method to his madness; his dramatics were not idle entertainment, she sensed, but purposeful and effectuating toward some cause or goal. He was up to something because he was onto something. But what and why?

"Well, granted, Mother was, I mean *is*, a rather large, imposing presence. A very strong personality. Her will, that is to say, her forceful personality, will not be brooked." He sighed like her tire did before finally deflating under unbearable stress. *Pfsst*. "But recent times and poor health have, oh I don't know, sad to say . . ."

"Say it anyway, you poor, *poor* man. It'll make you feel better. Get it off your chest, Mr. Reddick."

"Mother has experienced, shall we say, an unfortunate decline. It pains me beyond measure to speak of it, but she isn't the woman she used to be. She is very diminished."

"Take heart, dear man. She may yet recover. Miracles do happen." She considered recommending the Guardian Angel Prayer to him for solace; it covered a lot of bases, but doubted she could pull it off without hooting like Fritz herself.

"I don't think so, my dear. I believe she's reached the point of no return." He sobbed softly and then honked his nose.

"There, there. Time heals all wounds."

"Thank you so much, Miss Sullivan, for the kind condolences . . ." His feeble quavering voice was riddled with stammering doubt.

"So, jumping from pillar to post here, if you'll forgive me, and pardon this abrupt transition-less query, but who do you *think* killed your employee? And how?"

She was fast losing interest, and her thoughts, true to form, were beginning to swarm unmanageably and shoot off in other directions. She gazed out the plate glass window to her side. A wind-propelled garbage can rolled by at high velocity followed by an assortment of palm fronds, and a trio of wild-eyed, sodden sea gulls whose own aerodynamic engines were no match for the wind beating the landscape.

"I absolutely have no earthly idea who murdered that innocent man."

"But why do suppose Alfredo is innocent, then?"

"Oh, my, well, I received a notice from his lawyer yesterday that Alfredo could not have possibly slain his co-worker because he was off on the day the heinous act occurred. He was not on the Peaceable Kingdom premises at the time."

"His lawyer?"

"A Mr. *Dare*? This man, this quite common and ordinary court-appointed factotum, no doubt a second-rate legal mind, you know how *those* things go, the good lawyers don't stoop to that kind of riff-raff work, but this man *Dare* actually had documentation, affidavits, the whole kaboodle, if you will, proving Alfredo was working at his part-time dish-washer job at the Tamale Emporium all day long."

After a few minutes of calm quiet reflection, Garnet stood up from her desk, picked her cell out of the trash basket and dragged her mind out of the gutter. Chester was striding back and forth through the townhouse, upstairs, downstairs, with the determined tromp of having made a Serious Decision. He had dragged out his beat up Hartman carry-on bag and stuffed some of his starched shirts into it all a-kilter, rammed in a gob of socks and boxers, and packed his briefcase so full that he couldn't get it closed. She was about out of smirks, sneers and wrenching facial contortions of heartbreak and disappointment to use on him. Like a telemarketer on auto-dial, he was calling every motel and hotel inland to find them a hideout from the hurricane.

O woe. She punched in the numbers.

"The Ruth" answered on the first ring. "State your business."

This was a difficult question under the circumstances. "Oh, I'm sorry, I just wanted . . ."

"You again. The Sorry One. You think you're sorry now? Just wait. Hey! Fritz! You evil jackass! Put your lousy drink down and come to the damn phone."

"Ruth, you crazy worthless piece of humanity! I'm gonna send you back to the state hospital if you don't shape up!"

Was that perhaps where the happy couple first met? Adjoining cork-lined rooms? Did they have, maybe, a honeymoon suite at "State?" Seemed likely. Doors slammed, furniture crashed and Ruth wailed a loony glossolalia that even Garnet could not understand. Out of nowhere the previously safely napping Allison materialized in front of her. She held up a little hand-scribbled note:

Do you have any strawbry [sic] bubal [sic] bath?

Garnet nodded furiously and pointed upstairs.

"You *do,* Garnet?"

"Is that my lil darlin'?" the fiend breathed sniggering.

Garnet faked a smile and quickly motioned her off.

"Cool beans!" Allison chirped and skipped to the stairs.

Ringo and Diesel trotted merrily after her, but shot back down the stairs, as if fired out of a cannon, the minute she turned on the bath water. They tried to make themselves invisible, certainly not in need of bathing, and slunk under the dining room table.

"I got some goodies for you, hot tits."

She gagged.

"Oh, I know you're there, sugar pants. Poopy Pipes has run off to her bubbles. It's just you and me now." He inhaled and hawed like a donkey.

"You are a lewd, lascivious lizard, Fritz."

"I ain't talking about my own junk n' goodies."

"How refreshing."

"Now pay real close attention to The Fritz. Things are heatin up. We got a *serial killer* in the neighborhood."

"Sure we do, old forky tongue."

"Don't tell anybody yet."

"My lips are sealed."

"I got all it takes to buy him a ticket to Old Sparky."

"You betcha."

"We have a very interesting situation on our hands here, one worthy of my respectful attention."

"Speak."

20

DARK ANGEL

✦ ✦ ✦

Garnet stood in the dark hallway just outside the bathroom door behind which Allison, fully "strawbry" foamed and frothed, was humming the old "Oscar Meyer Weiner" theme song. This choice of tunes by Allison would be odd under normal circumstances, but in Garnet's late stage paranoia she found it one more manifestation of the Fritzian perversities perpetrated on her BFF.

The originator and mastermind of the plot, The Fritz *(Homo Ecce!)* himself whispered urgently into her ear through her Droid.

"No one could dream this up but a dark, *dark* angel. This one will have his own bronze plaque in hell's rogue's gallery."

"You are dangerously delusional."

"You're gonna have to be nice to old Fritzie, hot stuff, if you want my help."

"What a mess of help you given me already."

"This is a *story*, baby, that will change your life! It's big."

"I'll do civil. I won't go so far as 'nice.'"

"*Deal.* I'll take it."

"Anything else?"

"Remember this, little tiger: a tiger can't change its stripes."

"More specifics, you hopeless old goat."

"We goats been around a long, long time. I'm a natural. I got the moves. The right instincts. I know where to look for dirt. I'm an expert. You ain't. Too bad. But watch out. Don't be a goat for anyone, honey. Don't let anyone get your goat."

"You are nothing but a pedantic old windbag."

"Close, but no cigar. So, anyway, duty calls, gotta run, sayonara, sweet cream, adios. Manana, mama. Don't fret. I'll be in touch."

"Wait."

"It's in the bag, honey."

"Tell me, Fritz, who are you? Are you for real? Or just another sociopath megalomaniac?"

"Who? Me? *Me*"?

I'm a movie, I'm a dream,

I'm a seeming, not a thing.

"Who said that?"

"Why, *I* did. Just now."

She threw the phone onto the floor and kicked it.

"Who was that?" First words Chester had said to her in hours.

"I have *no* idea!"

✛ ✛ ✛

She sat on the edge of the bed. Think happy thoughts. The still small point. "Teach us to care and not to care. Teach us to sit still."

A tap on the door, and Allison peeked in. She was wrapped in towels and rosy cheeked. Blandly unconcerned about hurricanes and the whole lot of challenging road bumps in the average life. The dogs stood behind her, in rapt attention, slowly wagging their tails.

"Sorry? But would tell me how to say this word?" She held out a bubble bath moistened book, heavily highlighted in bright yellow, beaming so

154

sunshiny bright from each page that everything was of equal importance and thus equally unimportant.

Garnet bent over the page. "Which one?"

"Oh, I guess, any of them."

"Okay, top to bottom, 'castigate.' Go ahead, say it."

Allison rolled her eyes. "I don't get what it means. I read the definition. It's full of other words I don't understand, like this one." She pointed to "censure" and "recrimination" followed "censure" and then there was "culpability" and many other spirit-dimming thunkers, mud clods and heaps of derision, marching across the page in grim phalanxes of doom and for pages and pages thereafter—endlessly.

"Are you really enjoying this, Allison?"

"Why?"

"Words, you know, they're just *words*. Not people, animals. Not hearts. You can't hug and kiss a word. They slip away and lose meaning or change meaning over time."

"I'm already on the C's. Done A and B so far. Tomorrow I might get to D."

"That's great." She stared at Allison. The dogs trailed around behind her totally in her thrall.

What had happened to Garnet the Good? She hadn't referred to herself with that proto-saintly moniker in weeks.

"Oh, I found the angel prayer."

"You did?"

"It was in my make-up bag. I'd blotted my lipstick on it. I started saying it again. When I found it, I thought, '*Aw*, look at that!' I had *kissed* it!"

Maybe you can hug words after all.

Allison's dark eyes wandered over the ceiling. "I wonder what happened to Uncle Smeddy. He'll be surprised when I use 'castigate' and 'censure' in a sentence."

"You should have ample opportunity to work those into casual conversation with him."

"I'll see him again, Garnet, I'm sure of that. I *miss* him."

Fonder? Or yonder? Allison was a *yonder* kind of chick when it came to absence. If she could somehow insulate her from Fritz long enough this would blow over. But how? The bastard was everywhere all the damn time! Allison lingered by the bed in a swaying trance, her head in her book. Her lips were moving soundlessly. Diesel and Ringo lay at her feet and looked up at her reverently, hanging on her every whispered, butchered phoneme, closing their eyes in rapture with every soft sigh or shift and shuffle of her feet.

"'Hope is the thing with feathers,' you know."

Allison looked up, surprised. "Hope? It's a *bird?*"

"Oh, yeah. And it's a plane. It's Superman."

"Shoot, I didn't know that. So it's a real thing?" Ringo licked her calf. Diesel leaned against her side and closed his eyes.

"Yeah, and ya gotta have hope, right?"

"Maybe I ought to get a parakeet or cockatiel then. I hear parrots are dirty. You know, I haven't seen a *canary* in a long time. Why is that, do you think? Have they gone extinct?"

"C'mon. Let's go stir up Chester. See if we can tick him off or something."

"It's still raining hard."

"We might have to book outta here tonight."

The scene in the living room stopped them in their tracks. They hung back in the dark hallway.

"Oh, no!"

"Don't worry, Allison. It's cool."

"I can't go in there! He'll be mean to me!"

"He wouldn't dare."

Chester and Sheriff Lance were sitting across from each other silently and intently leaning over a small transistor radio on the coffee table between them. The radio was blaring Gator football sports. They were hunched over in serious concentration listening to the latest skinny on injuries, starters, stats, and mumbling between themselves, nodding, smacking their knees, looking at each other, uttering short bursts of cusses or praise and agreement or disagreement with the chatter and fan folderol.

Lance was encased head to toe in something resembling a very large zip lock bag. It was a standard issue, ill-fitting, one-size-fits-all Sheriff Department rain suit, complete with what looked like a gigantic plastic shower cap covering his normally manly, proud hat. His rain gear and thick black galoshes had erased his official imposing authority and made him just an average Joe. He might have been mistaken for a wet, irritable bus driver or a mall security guard who'd been caught in a fire hydrant accident and thrown himself as a human plug at the gusher to stem the flow.

"Oh, you know what? It's *homecoming* this weekend, Allison. I totally forgot. I haven't thought about football in weeks."

They craned their necks and cocked their heads to get a read on the mood of these Gators. You had to keep an eye on guys during football season, exercise caution, and try to anticipate their reactions to gridiron events. Scores. The situation was combustible, chancy; circumstances were always uncertain and tension-filled. Gators were seasonally subject to sudden violent swings of mood, explosive shouting, fulminating. Spontaneous alcohol-fueled primitive celebrations. Feelings ran high, tempers were short. Anything might happen.

They were grumbling over something they'd just heard now, shaking their heads in disgust, making eye contact, exchanging knowing glances, sharing the swelling moment of displeasure, as only manly men can do, as a sign of camaraderie and mutual support.

Garnet and Allison looked at each other in the hallway twilight and softly giggled, hands over their mouths.

Then Chester slapped the coffee table, knocked the radio over and declaimed in his resounding courtroom voice, "And not a damn hotel or motel room to be had in the whole damned state!"

Lance hung his head and looked at his squishy wet shoes and limp rain-soaked trouser cuffs. "Shit, that's tough, man. Tough. I can't leave, but you folks should clear out tonight. Ain't there no place at all inland you could bunk with some buds for a few days?"

"Nah. And everybody's about left, looks like, dammit." But Chester soon regained his sense of priorities, life vs. football, and pumped the volume back up on the game chatter.

Both of them leaned in closer over the radio on the coffee table between them, trying to catch every subtlety, suggestion, ramification, competing forecast of the coming game.

"I got an idea, Allison. Go throw some clothes on, get your things together quick."

Garnet then blasted into the room. "Lance! Hey, man! Where ya been? Have you become a hermit or something? Great to see you, old bud! Neat! Wow! Cool beans! When'd you roll in? How long have you been here?"

The guys looked up, startled and blinking, in a genuine deer in the headlights reaction.

21

IT WAS A DARK & STORMY NIGHT

✝ ✝ ✝

Two hours later, all four of them, along with Ringo and Diesel, were barreling up I-75 through the driving rain towards Gainesville. The men sat silent in the front seat looking straight ahead, making a virile display of being in charge and control, though it would have been obvious to blind person they could see only five feet ahead into the windy foul weather. Garnet and Allison shared tight quarters with the pooches in the back, giggling, making wisecracks and firing small missiles and any wad or bit of junk they could find on the floor or in the seat pockets at the back of the stalwart, unresponsive heads in front of them.

Lance's sudden availability for the journey remained mysterious. He and Chester had huddled after hearing Garnet's convincing proposition, her brilliant airtight solution to the dearth of hotel rooms, her perfect answer to their urgent need to flee the hurricane by going north and inland.

Chester's instant objection that there would be no hotel rooms in Gainesville, either, on homecoming weekend, "What are you crazy?" was countered and rendered an immaterial fact with practiced finesse.

"There will be over a hundred empty beds at the house, trust me guys. And it hasn't rained a drop in Gainesville." They considered this additional factor without comment.

"And the rooms will be free." The men looked at each other.

Then they broke away from the ladies and retired to a dark corner of the living room where Chester pulled out his briefcase, rifled through it, and handed Lance some papers. Lance whispered earnestly in Chester's ear for several minutes. Chester nodded somberly throughout.

"Okay, ladies. Change a plans. It's official business. I'm a goin with ya'll." Lance was serious, brusque, tersely to the point as befits a County Sheriff. The ladies rolled their eyes. "That's all I can say now and all I will say. Period."

It was a humdinger that provoked peals of feminine laughter. As in a chance to go to UF homecoming, the homecoming parade, Gator Growl, the Big Game? And for free? Yadda yadda. Party, party. Road trip. You didn't need an excuse; the reasons were self-evident.

"Turn up the radio, Chester. We can't hear it back here." Garnet kicked the back of his seat. He ignored her the first few times. Then he turned around and swiftly smacked her on top of the head. "Cool it. You better be right about this."

She smiled in the dark. "Oh, I am. Positive. Can't you go any faster? Why won't you let me drive?"

Both men looked at each other and shook their heads at the same time. Negatory. Never.

There were enough plots, schemes, conspiracies, cross purposes, secrets, subterfuges and hidden agendas swirling around inside Chester's old red BMW coupe that dark and stormy night as it rattled like a bat out of hell toward the game in The Swamp to fill the Library of Congress. Most of them were cloaked under the inarguable dire need to seek safety from the hurricane. Yet if the game had been held in Punta Bella when the hurricane made landfall there, Garnet felt sure Chester would have attempted to make a persuasive case for staying put there, and riding out the hurricane in the open raging weather to watch it. Priorities were priorities. First things first. This was serious. Time to party.

The thrill of her plan and the spontaneity of this dubious but fun enterprise had sandblasted away Garnet's sticky wicket issues with Fred, blanked out her worry over Kalimba the tigress, occluded her distaste for the sappy soufflé personality of Reddick, beaned and boinked the question of Mr. Thompson's real reason for scouring Tommy Covington's old home place. The two murders, and maybe more homicides, if The Fritz wasn't lying through his teeth or completely delusional, were out of her mind so thoroughly at that moment it was as if someone had hit a delete key and erased her recent memory. All the weight of her current responsibilities had been lifted and had flown away at the tingle of a serendipitous, fortuitous adventure. Fritz had been relegated to a cypher and an uninteresting cypher at that.

That is, until an hour out of town, when Chester suddenly tossed her cell phone back to her. "Here, party girl, you forgot this." It landed in her lap like a live snake.

"I think you got a call coming in, kid." Yes, it was vibrating. She had messages, lots of them, and texts too, lots of them, from Fred.

"Did you ever call Tank, Garnet?" Chester hollered from the front seat.

Uh, no. Forgot. Ergo they would be skipping his cookout without explanation. What a bother. Put another faux pas on her losing scoreboard.

"Did you?"

"Did I *what*, Chester?" she snapped.

It was if she'd ordered a margarita but took a sip and found it was vinegar instead.

"You may have a chance to apologize to him in person."

"Why?" She glanced over at Allison's smooth, smiling untroubled face. She was quietly watching the road, her mind full of the good times that lay ahead. Ringo's snoring head was in her lap and Diesel was stretched out next to her on his back like a dead bug with his feet in the air.

"They're giving him some kind of award of appreciation at half-time during the game."

"No kidding."

"Something about that Water Institute he funded at UF."

"Oh." He must not be in that big of a "wad of trouble" then, O Great One.

Chester shouted over the noisy flaps of the windshield wipers, the rush of driving rain and the hiss of water beneath their speeding tires. "They're breaking ground for the building Sunday in Gainesville, there's a ribbon cutting ceremony, photo ops . . . Dignitaries, all that stuff . . . ."

His voice trailed off and faded to black. Chester and Lance then leaned together in the front seat and exchanged whispers punctuated with a lot of emphatic head nodding and furious head shaking. At last, having settled some serious matter, both nodded in firm agreement and drew apart. There was, she was certain, to use Clovis Reddick's term, a *"plot afoot"* in the front seat.

Garnet's sensitive snoop antennae had received a stimulus that could not be ignored. They lengthened and stretched out and up and wiggled around in the dark probing. Her ears perked and her eyes narrowed and locked on the back of their heads.

"How do you *know* all this, honey?" she asked in saccharine voice.

The silence of the grave. The Great One perhaps did not hear her?

"Huh? Chester?" He sat up there like a big block of wood, barely visibly breathing and as speechless and silent as corpse. She bopped the back of his seat with her foot. Too hard, as it happened, to suit her sandaled foot.

"Ow, dammit."

She leaned forward in the dark, hands on the back of the driver's seat, pulled herself up, and positioned her mouth two inches away from his ear. Then she scooted in closer to his implacable stolid head, full granite truths, timeless truths and the truths of righteousness and blind justice.

She bent his outer ear into her cupped hand for a megaphone effect. He didn't move. She cleared her throat. She took a breath.

And in a studied flat monotone in perfect diction and with the dull precision and persistence of piano metronome, she said, restraining her roiling, curdling nerves, *"Chester! Tell! Me! Where! You! Found! That! Out!"*

He coughed and lolled his head around on his neck. "Well, now, let's see here. *Where* did I see that, anyway? Let me think now. Oh, yes. I recollect now. It was in a state newswire squib in your *own* paper. Right next to *your epic poem about a tiger.* On the *front* page. Hey, you got top billing. You had half a page. Your picture was next to it in full color. You were the *lead* story, honey. Congrats. I'm proud of you. I always believed you would distinguish yourself in print, that your writing would receive acclaim and endure.

"Truly amazing! One-inch boldface type headlines. Breaking news. An exclusive to the *Indian River Bird Cage Liner & Mullet Wrapper*, the daily paper that is renowned for printing an itsy bitsy bit of the news that's fit to print and a whole lot of trivial stuff that isn't. There it was 'Tiger, Tiger, Burnin Bright by Thet Air Sinkhole in the Night' by 'Acclaimed Poetess Garnet Sullivan.'"

She flinched. "No it wasn't."

He tossed the rolled up paper into the back seat. "See for yourself. Proud a ya, honey. What a linguistic virtuoso, what talent. Always knew you'd make your mark."

"He did not actually put *poetess* after my name, did he?"

"Did."

"No."

"Yep."

"Oh my God."

"Blake, you know, is going to get you for pissing on his tiger poem like that."

22

ADELANTE

✛ ✛ ✛

No one in the car said a word for a long time. They were on a stretch of the interstate where radio station reception was poor. Nothing broke the steady thrum and vibration of the tires on the roadway or the white noise of the wind and rain. They'd become road stoned and dull-witted, joints frozen stiff from sitting in close quarters. The sudden swerve onto the off ramp at the Okahumpka service plaza to gas up finally broke the monotony. Everyone stretched, yawned and tried to remember where they were, what they were doing and where they were going.

"Are we there?" Garnet said through a long yawn and full body stretch. "How much farther? If you'd let me drive, Chester, we'd already be there by now."

"Fat chance, Tinker Bell."

"I'm a better driver than you are," she poked her forefinger into Lance's thick neck in the front seat, "Right, Lance?"

"I have no earthly idea, Garnet, what would make you think that I would approve of your driving."

"Oh, forget it. You know I am."

"You just ain't been caught yet. Your day will come. My guys are laying for you. They'll catch your sweet ass one day."

The giggles erupted like a geyser, piping out of Pipes in the backseat. "Lance! Hey! *Lance!*" Allison laughed, "Lance, honey? You will never, ever, *ever* catcher! Garnet is *fast,* man! *Way* too fast for you! Deal with it! Hahaahahaha . . . ." Terminal, pants-wetting mirth followed. Garnet and Allison joined hands and knocked heads. Ringo and Diesel licked the tears off their faces.

Lance had not said so much as "hello" to Allison or made eye contact with her since seeing her in the living room back at the townhouse. Garnet and Chester knew what was going on. Something was gonna blow sooner or later.

As they tumbled out of the car, Allison's vocabulary builder fell out onto the pavement at her feet. She stooped to pick it up and received a sudden galvanizing inspiration. She straightened, blinked in the blinding light of her big idea and tottered stiff-legged over to Lance. He looked down on her as if she might bite him. Chester made his escape with the dogs. Garnet watched and waited. *Nobody* could stay mad at Allison for long. It was just a matter of time.

"Lance!" Allison cried, smiling and throwing her arms up in the air, waving her book over her head. "Lance, honey! I *castigate* you!" Lance fell back. He shook his head, spread his feet and planted his hands on hips. Allison batted her eyelashes and took another step. Her smile widened, she raised her voice and looked up. "Lance, honey," she winked, "I *censure* you!"

He backed away a few more steps, a new frost springing out on his frozen features. She followed him and moved in closer, smiling and winking with her arms open wide, waving her vocabulary book around in the air wildly over her head and giggling, perhaps hoping for a great big forgiving bear hug. With an enchanting, beatific smile, she then threw her hands and arms up higher in the air, squealed, and lunged for him, laughing and giggling, and sang out in a loud soprano voice, "*Lance! I excoriate you!*"

Allison apparently had made it to the E's in her big book of new words, but she hadn't asked Garnet yet about pronunciation in that dark thicket of the alphabet, and clearly never mastered meaning and connotation of these newbies. "Excoriate" came out of her mouth something like *expectorate* or *execrate* (although *excoriate* was certainly insulting enough, plenty insulting, in fact, to knock the wind out of anyone).

Before Garnet could intervene, try to explain and make peace, Lance bellowed, "What the *hell* is the *matter* with you, woman? Get away from me! Get back! Didn't the shrink get the bats outta your belfry? We paid that dang snake oil doc ten grand already for your lil bubble bath mishap!"

Allison's smile took flight like a startled little bird. The color drained from her face. Her lips parted as if she'd seen someone turn into a pig or a toad.

"Now you listen *here,* and you listen *good,* woman!" Lance roared. "I know who you been hangin with, don't you think that I don't!" He looked at Garnet knowingly. "It's some serious bad company you been keepin. So don't you go casting no *devil* spells on me! I'm damn well over your nonsense, Honey Cakes!"

Then Lance felt for his side arm, a fully loaded Glock. Muttering something about "that damn devil woman and her evil book of spells and curses," he backed away jerkily from her, not taking his eyes off of her. Allison stood still, open-mouthed and gaping. Taking advantage of her stunned state, with his hand still on his weapon, Lance pivoted in a whirr, and took off at a trot after Chester, looking back over his shoulder several times to make sure she wasn't chasing him with any of her "dadgum satanic voo-doo."

"Poor Lance," Allison said softly, shaking her head and watching him flee. "I don't think he *knows* what those words *mean.* How sad! Isn't that just too sad, Garnet?"

Having an out of the body experience, and approaching a full blown fugue-like state, Garnet said, "Oh oh oh—you—you, you know, these things happen but . . . but . . . maybe you two could pump up your vocabularies together. . . Help each other. Anyway, don't worry, Bean Sprout. This too shall pass."

She slumped inwardly. She had hoped those verbal spit-wads would be shot at The Fritz. She might have thought about such a possibility, friendly fire accidents, an accidental launch of these fusillades in the wrong direction on innocent parties, collateral damage. Words can wound, words can kill, words can start a war—or stop one. She might as well have given Allison a loaded gun to play with. Add fifty pounds to her burden of guilt.

✝ ✝ ✝

As Chester walked the doggies on the well-trod, sparse grass around the parking lot, Lance stayed close by his side for protection from incantations and evil spirits, keeping what he hoped was a safe distance and counting on Chester to block and tackle for him if the devil's lapdog made another spiritual assault.

Meanwhile, Garnet and Allison freshened up in the restroom and tried to regain some of the larky levity they'd had when they left Punta Bella. Allison busied herself with her make-up and Garnet, with a chill in her heart, sidled off to a quiet corner and checked her messages in private. She knew they'd be full of complaints, gripes and grousing for all of the unfinished business she'd left behind.

Fred had left her several whining questions about stories she was supposed to have filed but had *failed* to deliver on, (he loved to use word on her, *failed*) and she marveled at his total indifference to any ire he may have aroused in her for running her silly poem. Forgeddabout hurting her feelings. He never mentioned or alluded to it once in the eight nit-picking texts he'd sent that day, nor in the five pissy voicemails he'd left her.

Galling was what it was. Her embarrassment over what others might think of her with the publication of the tripe was nothing compared to her annoyance and disappointment in old Fred. But then Freddie boy was an editor, not a writer himself, and lacked certain sensitivities and sensibilities that writers have. He could draft a plodding journalism school news story, yes, he had the old pyramid structure etched in his brain, but that was old school and he had never advanced any further, he hadn't kept up with reader participatory wool-gathering and today's market. He could write a decent lead, but so could a chimpanzee.

When Garnet sent Fred a reply to his most recent nagging and ragging, it was a single thought, a straight to the point reply. She knew it would surprise Fred, but not half as much as her own writing of it and sending it off to him surprised her. She'd crossed the Rubicon. There was no turning back.

This is my two weeks' notice. I'm moving on, Fred.

Had she sent that? She checked. Yes, she had. She'd finally quit. She felt like dancing a jig. Shouting for joy.

She wandered out into the hallway as Allison applied her third coat of blue mascara then wandered back as Allison had segued into scouring and evaluating the cleanliness of the interstices of her perfect teeth.

"I hate to grin and bare it you know?" She looked at Garnet who was reflected in the in the mirror to the left of her upper incisors. "Spinach, yuk! It can make you look like a Martian."

"Like Martian? Do they have green teeth?"

"Oh, yeah. They're made of spinach, ya know. Yessir, every single part a their bodies, even their fingernails."

"I had no idea."

"For real."

"Put up or shut up, Allison. Hurry up, floss those suckers. Anyway, there are bares and bears. Let it go."

"Did you know there's big ole black bears up around Ocala in the woods?"

"Yeah. There are good bears and bad bears. Those are friendly, I think."

"Let's go there sometime, okay? I heard they have something in their wieners that's like a real bone. Ever heard that?"

If this was symptomatic of a relapse in Allison, she didn't want to hear any more. She fled the oral hygiene demonstration and went outside and leaned against a wall. She expected incoming fire any minute, a return volley from Fred, at the very least a snide hand grenade along the lines, "Great, I was about to fire you anyway. This way my unemployment insurance won't be affected." A few more messages had come in on voicemail. None from Fred. But all were spine-tingling and characteristic of her other tormenter, the only one who was a bigger pisser than Fred.

"I got your back, hot stuff. Don't worry. I've gotcha covered." He cackled madly. "See ya soon."

"Big surprise comin your way, sistah. Fasten your seat-belt."

"I am with you at all times, even unto the end of the world." Was that blasphemy or literary license? That old devil.

"Have I got a story for you, pussy pie! This is your scoop of a lifetime."

She moaned. Her eyes wandered around the jammed food courts, full of tired wet evacuees from south Florida, headed north like lemmings with no definite place to go, no guarantee of lodgings. They'd have to drive to Chicago to find a decent place to hang out until the hurricane passed. Weren't they lucky, though? How had she come up with the stroke of genius, the ace in the hole, the bolt from the blue, that would get them a great place to stay and for free? Truly inspired. She gave herself an unaccustomed pat on the back.

She walked back to the ladies room to cut short Allison's obsessional grooming and cosmetology. Out of the corner of her eye she could have sworn she saw a giant crow or turkey buzzard fly into the men's room. It was a huge black fast-moving flutter and swirl. She tip-toed up to the entrance of the men's room. She glanced down. She froze. No way. A nasty raggedy red wool beret lay on the white tile.

"Allison! Get a move on! We gotta hustle. Hurry." She grabbed her by the shoulder, pushed her out of the restroom and held her hand all the way back to the car.

"Wait! You messed up my eyeliner, Garnet! Now I have to start all over again!"

"The hell you will! Move it! C'mon!"

Driving out of the parking lot, they passed a long black limo double-parked outside the food court. "Faster, Chester, dammit! We'll never get there at this rate!" As Chester pulled back onto the interstate, Allison screeched as if she'd been run through by a spear, "Wait! Stop!"

Chester hit the brakes, and everyone fell forward, then backward, like crash dummies. He pulled over and wrenched around from the front seat.

"What?" he said.

"What?" Allison said.

"Yes, *what* is the matter, Allison, dear? Pray tell, *why* did you yell stop?"

"*Why*, Allison?" Garnet said.

"Oh, no, it's just that . . ."

"Allison! Spit it out! We almost had our necks broken from whiplash!"

"I'm sorrreee. I left my vocabulary book in the ladies' room."

Chester's head snapped back around to the front.

"Can we go get it, please? I was on the F words already. I'd highlighted the important parts. I love that book."

"Allison." Garnet expelled a sigh big enough to fill a blimp.

"I made, you know, kinda notes in it? Study notes? I had turned down corners to the pages of my favorite words?"

Chester hit the gas and took off like a rocket, whipped the car around, and at Mach 5 speed, screeched to a halt in front of the ladies' room."

"Curbside service, princess."

"I'll just be a sec," Allison said.

Garnet slammed her back into the seat. "No. Sit. You stay right here and don't move."

She jumped out of the car and shouted through Chester's open window, "DO NOT LET THIS WOMAN OUT OF THIS CAR, DO YOU HEAR ME?"

Chester and Lance looked at her. Then they looked at each other. Then they looked away.

"I mean it, guys. Do not let her out of this car."

Staring straight ahead, Chester said out of the side of his mouth, "Step on it. Three minutes tops."

Garnet took off in a sprint, ran around in a circle on the grass out front and raced back to the car. She stuck her face in front of Allison's closed window.

"The angel prayer! Read it over and over again till I'm back!"

Allison tried to roll the window down, but that particular window on that particular superannuated rattle and snap BMW had not rolled up, down or budged an inch in five years.

"What?"

"The Guardian Angel Prayer," she shrieked with the ardor of a martyr engulfed by flames at an Auto da Fe.

"What?"

Garnet ripped to the other side of the car, blood roaring in her ears, and arrived just as both Chester and Lance were rolling up their windows and locking their doors. She pounded on Chester's window. He wouldn't look at her, only pointed to the building where Allison's sacred text containing the powerful words lay next to a sloppy sink in a crowded public restroom.

Lance had drawn his own conclusions. Based on the circumstantial evidence, Garnet was trying to perform an emergency exorcism on Allison. He wanted no part of that. He sank down in his seat, put his shower cap-rain gear hat over his face and pretended to be taking a nap. His hand, however, was curiously placed on the butt of his firearm.

Garnet raced off for the building hoping against the odds to beat it there and back to the car with the precious vocab builder-upper before Allison got herself Fritzed.

Meanwhile, within self-same edifice, Mrs. Maria Ortega-Emanuel, with three pint sized versions of herself hanging onto her skirts, was flipping through Allison's Vocabularium. She had dried her hands at the stinking sink, wiped her kids' noses, and almost flopped a dirty diaper on top of Allison's treasure.

Que' pasa? El libro.

Mrs. Ortega-Manuel turned it over and over in her still damp hands. She couldn't make heads or tails of it, but thought she might be able to flip it at a garage sale for 10 cents. If nothing else, she could use the pages to light her kerosene stove or for TP. So she tossed it into her diaper bag, swiped at the kids' noses one last time and sauntered out of the restroom, kids in tow dangling from her ample skirts.

Garnet bumped into her she waddled out the door. "Sorry! Excuse me."

Santos! Quel Diablo! American women need to slow down. They try to do too much. Always rushing, hurry, hurry. *Adelante!* She crossed herself, *Madre Dios!* Poor things.

"De nada," she said, rolling by Garnet and shoving her to the side with the bulk of her fulsome diaper bag.

The limo was idling behind their car when she returned empty-handed. She jumped inside. "Floor it, Chester! Let's get the hell out of here!"

"Where's my book, Garnet?"

"Faster, Chester!" The limo was following them to the on-ramp. Sick of the tension and tone of conversation in the car, Chester wanted to beat it to Gainesville just as fast as she did. He revved the engine to 3000 RPMs, gunned it and left rubber pulling into the heavy traffic headed north. The limo disappeared into the dark behind them.

"Where's my vocab book, Garnet, huh?" She'd poked her hard in the ribs. She was pulling on her arm now. She was whining now.

Garnet ground her teeth. "I don't know, Allison. Wasn't there."

"You didn't look hard enough!"

Garnet turned around in the seat and looked out the back window. Bumper to bumper headlights racing north through the wind and rain. One pair belonged to a real devil that wouldn't get off her tail whatever she did, wherever she went.

23

HOMECOMING

✣ ✣ ✣

The weary travelers in the battered old red BMW rolled onto the deserted, silent streets of Gainesville at 4:00 a.m. No one within the car had spoken to or made eye contact with their fellow pilgrims for three wind-and-rain-lashed hours. The streets were barren of all signs of life save the gutter debris of the nightlife before, tides of cast-off plastic beer tumblers, long neck beer bottles and vigorously hand-mashed beer cans. The car toodled up to an imposing white columned mansion on sorority row on the UF campus, coughed and cut its engine. This was the rabbit she had pulled out of the hat. Her brilliant idea. Garnet's old digs when she was at UF. They planned to bunk at the Delta Helta Delta House on campus for the weekend.

She'd overcome Chester's objections and Lance's reservations with inspired rhetoric and intuitive insight into the male psyche. "Man, are you kidding? There will be *plenty* of beds. All the sisters will be staying out overnight with their boyfriends. And remember, it won't cost us one red cent! We can stay there for free!"

When Chester pointed to the snoring canine heaps on the couch and asked, "What about them?" she was ready for it and sealed the deal in no time flat. "What? Are you nuts? *Dogs?* No problem. When I was a freshman before we met, Chester? Honey? Hey, listen to me. Look at me. I had a dog in my *own room* for a while." She omitted an important detail: it was a pocket-sized Jack Russell Terrier puppy, and "Puck" was only able to avoid detection and expulsion for two weeks, after which he was unceremoniously dumped off at her parents' home and quickly became her Father's constant companion. Her conscience had been at peace on "Puck's" fate for many years. But using him this way now added some sand back into it, maybe a sandspur or two.

Yet when the rumpled grumpy Gator alums stumbled up the steps to the legendary Delta Helta Delta house, hoping to flop instantly into decent beds with clean sheets, they received the crowning disappointment of a disappointing day. All of the doors were locked up tight. No one could be roused and not a light was burning within.

For the only soul inside this vast, august, swarming hive of female pulchritude and sass on the eve of Gator Homecoming was old Mother Weatherby, the House Mother for 46 years. And for 46 years, and counting, she had slept with a thick black blindfold on, heavy-duty factory-strength earplugs crammed into her ears and a loud fan droning next to her. Yes, it was lights off at 10 pm for old Mother Weatherby on sorority row, taps, shortly after tossing back her 1500 mg. Halcyon capsule, a dose that would have whacked a Clydesdale, and chasing it down with a bottle of 90 proof sherry "cordial."

"At least it isn't raining, Chester." Garnet took his hand.

"I hadn't noticed."

They shuffled back to the car in the dark, Lance in the lead with his hand on the butt of his pistol, Allison, red-eyed and in silent mourning for the loss of her vocab builder, bringing up the rear.

Midway, overcome with a strange nostalgia heightened by exhaustion, Garnet stopped, turned around and looked back at the sorority house that had been home to her for four "formative" years. "So many memories here! Unbelievable."

Chester got it and felt it too. He squeezed her hand and pulled her close. "So many yet to make, sweetheart."

In their pause in the parking lot Allison experienced a sudden burst of energy and inspiration and snapped out of her funk. She skipped ahead of them and caught up with Lance. *"Lance!"* she squealed up at him sweetly, "Lance! You are so *crepuscular* to me! Lance! I *crescendo* you!"

"Call her off, Garnet! I'm a tellin you, call her off! Do somethin or I'm a gonna." He shot off to the car like a bullet, one hand gripping the butt of his gun, the other out front as if blocking all comers. He banged into the side of the car, flung the door open, hopped inside, slammed the door and locked it.

The following morning the looming lumbering hulk of old Mother Weatherby greeted her unexpected guests with her customary cordiality and warmth. Always a lady and always gracious, she would have greeted a toad or telephone lineman or bumblebee the same way. This consistency in her comportment simplified things, kept everything orderly and got her through the day and night without undue mental exertion, something she'd always been adverse to because that sort of thing never contributed much to anything as far as she could see, therefore was most often a waste of time and could lead to other unhealthy practices and distractions which taxed the nerves. The nerves were the principle thing and hers were her principle concern. They had risen to that level of prominence and in need of careful monitoring on the first night she slept at the sorority house over 46 years ago and had remained there ever since.

Mother Weatherby's nerves had a bit of a bobble-wobble when, on her way to fetch the newspaper from the front steps this morning, she had encountered this mob of ruffians gathered at the door looking aggrieved, hungry and restless, demanding to be let in. Courtesy and good manners never failed her and were particularly disarming and effective with the sort that had never mastered those skills (or lost them, i.e., drunken fraternity boys). Confusion to the enemy, as it were.

The nerves had another bit of a wiggle-jiggle when the two large dogs jumped against her dress, tore a run in her support stockings and, and on sighting Mortie, her old cat, took off after him in a wild noisy chase through every room in the house. When they returned, panting and slobbering, the big hairy red one immediately took the liberty of raising its leg, quite defiantly, and in plain view of five adult human beings, released a three minute stream of banana yellow urine, with a surprising degree of accuracy and apparent delight, on the front of the fine moiré' wingback chair at the foot of the stairs. His fellow traveler, the other smaller ratty rapscallion, meanwhile defecated in the middle of the nice Oriental rug in the foyer, then sat next to his deposit and furiously scratched himself all over for several minutes as if infested with and tormented by millions of fleas. That finished, he fell to licking his privates with a degree of relish, thoroughness and persistence that made her distinctly uncomfortable.

Miss Garnet ineffectually scolded both mongrels and, offering no apologies for their behavior, ran to the kitchen for paper towels. Which she claimed she could not find when she returned less than 60 seconds later, thus proving she had not improved in the least since leaving these hallowed walls and the beneficent influence, benign care and nurturing solicitations of Mother Weatherby.

When the two rather rough-looking unshaven gentlemen, after only curt acknowledgement of her role as custodian and the presiding *in loco parentis*, ascended the winding staircase with suitcases to the inner sanctum sanctorum of this, *theoretically* at least, perhaps only *putatively*, or *ironically* denominated, "sanctuary" for virginal high-minded young women, Mother Weatherby finally excused herself. With a loving, kindly smile and a passable rendition of *noblesse oblige* and pleasant word bouquets and best wishes for a "happy safe stay with us," she gracefully took her leave and beat a strategic retreat.

She had found that she was getting slightly nervous, the prelude to becoming very nervous, the sure sign of impending tremulousness and trembling-palsied musculature, symptomatic of the first stage of a "total nervous breakdown." She knew the drill. She wanted to avoid another one at all costs.

Murmuring something about clean towels and sheets in the linen closets to Garnet Sullivan (Oh, you *bet* she remembered her. The minx.), and pointedly omitting the customary "make yourselves at home," she clop-clopped her size 11 scuffed, but presentable, black patent leather pumps down the gleaming old hardwood hallway back to her quaint immaculate quarters, closed the door, locked and bolted it and filled an ice tea glass to the brim with her high octane sherry. Then she downed her "tonic" in a lady-like jiffy with two hefty Xanax boosters, dabbed her lips with a linen napkin, stuffed two pairs of new earplugs deep into her ears, turned her largest fan on high, closed her window shades, put her black velvet blindfold over her eyes and keeled backward onto the bed like a large felled tree, fully clothed and shod.

As an elderly sleeping beauty, safe at this stage from a fresh kiss from a rash, passing prince, she could remain entirely unaware of the tipsy debaucheries, vainglorious and highly improper dramas, carnal excesses, pranks, practical jokes, subterfuges, hijinks and hilarity and social travesties raging around her in the parallel universe outside her pristine private quarters, a parallel universe of high spirits with similar and frequent recourse to anodynes as regards their nervier nerves.

It was prudent, calming, and good for the nerves and the only *lady-like* thing to do.

24

I LOVE A PARADE

They were late, no surprise, for the parade, because Allison had lost her make-up kit and curling iron and only finally found them after everyone tore apart the car and their messy encampment in the sleeping dorm, and then discovered them under the bed she'd claimed. Subsequently, once in the car on the way to the Homecoming Parade and in heavy traffic (since 50,000+ other Gator fans, students, and alums, pick pockets, shop-lifters, and shift-less shifty-eyed types drawn to large crowds opportunistically, were also hell bent on converging on University Avenue and Main St. in the little *ville* of Gainesville at the same time) Allison suddenly insisted, through copious tears, on stopping at Barnes & Noble to get a new vocabulary builder—first.

Allison's plaintive voice was so annoying and unappeasable due to the emotional tatters she was in and traumas she'd experienced as the result of the tragic loss of her original vocab pumper-upper, that everyone agreed: a trip to the moon and back would be worth it to stop this torrent of strident, grating nonsensical mourning and breast-beating. They got there in record time, given the incentive, even though it was on the other side of town eighteen miles away.

Once there among the stacks and the boggling selection of thousands of books, Allison became confused, disoriented, couldn't make up her mind, and so she eventually bought fifteen of them, but only after Garnet's lengthy patient assistance, through which Garnet ground her teeth and weathered Chester's withering glares and shows of disgust and all the while trying to keep an eye on Lance's increasingly weird behavior.

Lance himself skulked and sulked in a dark corner of B & N, his hand on his gun and his eyes locked on the risible proceedings among the vocab books in the suspiciously denominated "Language and Reference" section of the store. Unnerved by Allison's recent interest and utterance of strange words, imprecations and expostulations, to his ears delivered with undue volume, and with unusual force/emphasis and with a lot of weird gesticulations and arm waving, and always, it seemed to him, eerily *preceded* by directly addressing himself, as *Lance!* Lance refused to be comforted or reassured that this activity was not malign nor supernatural nor "of the Devil," but only a result of Allison's pure and harmless effort to "pump up her vocabulary."

No. Oh, no, no, he knew lil' ole "Honey Cakes," and purty dern well, as matter a fact. This was no way "self-improvement" in his view, oh, HO, noooo. No sirree, good buddy. It fit the pattern he'd discerned in her behavior over time and from which he now recoiled. Having been dumped, reviling and demonizing this little witchy woman was an acceptable and preferable alternative to dragging his painfully disgraced butt all over town about it, weeping in public over losing her, and standing under her window in the rain all night begging her to take him back, it seemed to him. Heck! No brainer, man, hooo-eeee.

Taking this tack for his rebound and recovery, he'd immediately latched onto Garnet's desperate appeal for help the night she called outta her wits, screamin the *"Devil was after Allison!"* as a critical most useful clue, an essential piece of the puzzle, most helpful in shoring up his position and advancing his recovery.

Thank you, ma'am, Garnet, honey. He caught that there clue in mid-air, as it flew right outta her screamin mouth, and—bang—slapped it into his own growing dossier on "Honey Cakes," particularly his up close recent personal highly intimate experiences with this hussy, and his growing suspicions about her downright evil behavior and treatment of himself, not to mention her previous lusty amazingly powerful "powers" over him, somethin which he still thought about a lot and still found quite diabolically "powerful" and magnetic, making him continue to think stuff he shouldn't be thinkin normally, and her own formerly wild unbridled insatiable appetites and unstinting interest and curiosity in certain parts of his "anatomy" at certain times and occasions. Made his head swim, it did.

If he couldn't have her, he dang well might as well *hate* her, *revile* her, he reasoned, though maybe "reasoned" would be a gussied up word for the vague subterranean mental processes by which he arrived at this conclusion. Yet, prima facie, it seemed to him an easier way to live than loving her unrequitedly forevermore, disconsolately, hopelessly and in an interminable jolted state of angry jiltedness.

This stratagem was, for Lance, an approach fraught with perils for which he lacked the faculties to perceive, let alone the resources with which to repel, the emotional blowback that this inevitably entails and the self-injurious boomerang effects of his mis-applied efforts. Simply put: this was only an instance of the male version of "the lady doth protest too much." That is, "the gentleman doth *detest* too much." Lance was about to kick himself in the balls and didn't know it, and stab himself in the heart, rather than heal its brokenness.

At this point in time, in view of the mounting evidence and the clear as day unnaturalness of this voo-doo woman, he was *aghast* that he could not see it all before. It dadgummed showed you he was under a spell and a curse at the time, bewitched, rendered helpless, and it only made him more alert and watchful of what she might have up her sleeve (or in her under garments) or ready to launch from her mouth to lasso him in once more.

It all added up to a perfectly hellish combo in Lance's view. She might be a suck-up or suck-up-a-guss, whichever, or something like that, or something even worse he hadn't heard of yet. At any rate, she was hurling these nasty sounding, hair curling, nail biter words at him every chance she got, and he dang well knew if he wasn't careful, one of em was gonna stick, maybe get under his skin and turn him into something, he didn't know what, but somethin nasty and quite unlike the well-scrubbed, honorable, law abiding, decent person he was. Maybe it would take possession of his body, maybe his soul if she could find it, and make him do all kinds of hideous indecent things that'd he'd be ashamed of and would never be able to live down.

If one of those longer word goblin suckers hit him between the eyes, or in the heart? It might instantly turn him into a little devil himself that she could put a collar and leash on and then she'd be able to walk him around town like a little pet dog, put him in her purse, kiss him all over the head whenever she wanted, and make him wear little suits and sweaters, and pork pie hats, Good Lord, and nobody'd ever know it was him because, some a those little dogs are so blame ugly and weird looking, for all he knew, maybe they was little devils too, formerly fine folks who'd gone missing one day and was turned into one of those ornery little things with eyes that bugged outta their heads, a god-awful under bite, bad crooked teeth, their faces so screwed up they could hardly close their mouths, chew their kibbles and bits, or breathe right through those nasty twisted-around, flattened-up and pushed-back noses. Damn little things wheezed all the time, pore little noses never stopped runin, their legs was short and puny, even if they tried to get away, run as hard as they could, they couldn't get far fore they was scooped back up and stuffed back down into a *purse!*

Good gosh. Just think: *Him* winding up a little Pug dog with a bashed in face, stumpy little body and a tail like a pig, stuffed in Allison's big fancy purse, carried around like a toy, fooled with and tickled and teased in every nasty way, and nobody'd ever *know*, or dream of what had happened to him. He'd have to go right straight to hell with her and back, no doubt she made regular trips, visiting her friends, relatives, and other satanic evil creatures that smelled bad, were horrible ugly, did unspeakable things, and danced by the light of the full moon nekked on graves, and basically scared the livin crap outta anybody they wanted to any dang time they felt like it.

Standing there, loitering at the far end of the "Language and Reference" section in Barnes & Noble, Lance considered all of this and what he might do to avoid a similar metamorphosis and fate. He twitched and tensed at Allison's every sputtering pronunciation as she "tried out" new words and considered possible books to purchase, and her habitual arm and hand gestures, flinging and flailing the air over her head and around her (a result of the huge effort all of this required for her to "say it right") did not do a thing to calm the Sheriff. The tipping point came when she happened to look at Lance just as she attempted, flinging her arm up into the air, "MY-ZO-RHN-CHUS!"

Their eyes met for a fleeting moment and locked for a fateful few seconds during which she *penetrated* him—that was the only word he could think of that fit what she'd done. She'd penetrated him. During that time, the penetration, Lance was sensible of a galvanic electrical transmission out of Allison's eyes into his own, compounding exponentially the crippling effect of the curse she fired at him out of her mouth. When she finally dropped her glance back to the book in her hands, Lance was released from the evil energy she'd injected him with, and like a suddenly unplugged lamp, his lights went out, everything went black and he swooned and fell to his knees. Recovering some, he rose to a ducked and crouched position, and started taking evasive action from residual fallout from what he was sure was a High Velocity High Impact verbal gob of hellish crap, a curse or spell with an infernal lot of torque and traction. Crouching low and keeping his head down, he scrambled through the narrow alleys between the bookshelves closest to him to a safe distance.

Then he stood up like a jack-in-the-box and sped in a green blur from the back of the store, head down, hand on his gun, in a flat out run for daylight, heading for the glass entrance doors. In his flight, he respected no obstacle, did not swerve from his singular goal, took hurdles such as boxes of books, like an Olympic sprinter, knocked over floor displays as if they did not exist, throwing carefully merchandised piles of bestsellers helter-skelter, scattering annoyed customers, and during the last 15 yards or so of his breakneck streak through the store, was shouted at and chased by two observant young clerks who were sure he'd shoplifted something—or worse—never mind that he was wearing a sheriff's uniform, had a big gold star of a badge on his chest and a side arm with his hand on its butt—this was The UF Swamp—he was a con artist. He was impersonating a law officer. That's nothing around here—besides, it's Homecoming weekend. Holy Shit. He may be in some asinine costume.

The part-time student clerks' interest in catching him was more than casual or passing for there was a cash bounty on book thieves' heads paid for by B & N, and employees were regularly exhorted to take all possible measures to apprehend them for prosecution for shoplifting. As the cash-strapped, cash-inspired student clerks were furiously competing for the reward for this particular book ripper (himself in flight from the Devil's own harlot and personal lap dancer), the race between them in pursuit of the suspect and the subsequent conversations and mutual interrogatories in the parking lot outside among all three parties became quite heated and contentious and of the tenor/tone and level of comprehension worthy of the top floor of the Tower of Babel.

25

A TANTRIC TANTRUM

✛ ✛ ✛

So, yes, they were late for the parade. No big deal. They made it finally and the conversation in the BMW on the last leg to the parade, that is, post-curse and cussing, was nil. The only noise in the BMW came from the Gator Football news network radio station, so everyone could relax for a while and safely pretend to be listening to that and not plotting and scheming the best way to get even with or punish everyone else in the car for multiple recent affronts and insults.

Chester and Lance had pushed and shoved, serving as blockers and shields for Garnet and Allison, through the rowdy, roaring, raucous inebriated mass of sweaty bodies swarming, surging, swirling along the parade route. They'd made it to a vantage point of about three feet from the curb at the intersection of University and 13th Street. Not bad considering, though not ideal for Garnet and Allison who often had to hop up and down to get a peek or a glimpse of what was going on, depending on the restiveness and tidal surges of the unruly crowd as it responded to the passing pageantry.

The Mardi Gras Parade and the Gay Pride and Puerto Rican Pride Parades in New York are standouts for levels of outrageousness, energy, raucous enthusiasm, wild celebration, shock value, color and conniption fits. They

THE DEVIL, THE DIVA & THE DEEP BLUE SEA

have well deserved reputations for blowing the minds and offending the sensibilities and eardrums of onlookers. The Gator Homecoming Parade is a junior version of these unspeakably loud, surprising, imaginative, sometimes offensive, frequently hilarious public pageants and spectacles. Sure, the UF codes, official rules and regs try to put a lid on things, and the blasts and bursts of the offensive and original stuff are intermittent because of the presence in the long caravan of cornball ordinary uninspired plodding duds and plugs, such as high school bands, starched stiff ROTC dudes in uniforms, Future Farmers of America chapters from high schools, VFW and Rotary geezers, grim-faced and seriously in step or buzzing around on their tiny motorcycles in tiny safe obsessive circles.

But the lid of the rules and regs and the presence of the conventional types only increases the steam pressure under the lid, the urgency and impatience, and serves to inflame the mad desire of the kids who have the urge to make a public statement as performance art or to pull off an amazing stunt (or to maybe moon everyone that stands for order and convention all the way from the board of regents up to and including the Pope). So the tension and expectation, the eager anticipation and restless watchfulness of the spectators builds and builds until it's almost unbearable and seems about to explode. Everyone knows something's gonna blow, it's gonna be big, and, man, they don't want to miss it.

Garnet and Allison were in a funk because they were sure they were going to miss it. It was clear they were doomed to miss everything about the parade that made going to it worthwhile. And it was horribly hot and humid, no wind, the blank white death ray of the noon sun was roasting the tops of their heads and the stinky nasty wet bodies next to them were totally grossing them out. People were getting sloppy drunk, rude, stepping on their toes, elbowing them, shoving them from behind, and bumping them. They'd had enough, were getting angry and were about to puke, faint or sock the next sucker in the face that rubbed them the wrong way or looked at them funny.

"I wanna go."

"They aren't gonna leave."

Chester and Lance were engrossed, rubber necking it, laughing, shouting, clapping. The newly rehabilitated, but just as wildly talented as ever, Florida

A & M Band was going by, the coolest of the cool, and the crowd was roaring with appreciation; the band was getting down, doing the boogie and dance routines that made them famous and fun and everyone's Homecoming Parade favorite.

But the ladies couldn't see any of it. For they were trapped in a mass of thick, towering, disgusting-sweaty bodies and plain stuck—SOL. Garnet ground her teeth and seethed and perspired then seethed-sweated all the more a-seething most a-sweatingly sweating as she was. But Mademoiselle Allison, with increasing ire, irritation and noise, groused, grumbled, fussed, made nasty faces, and shot her angry-getting-angrier by the second eyes right and left under a dark and furious frown.

"I don't care, let's me and you go. I wanna go *now.*"

"Don't be a cry baby. Grow up. We're stuck.'"

"No! *C'mon. I'm hot. We can't even see.*"

"Stop it, Allison, you brat. Chill. We can't leave. Tough rocks."

"I'm getting really pissed off, Garnet."

"So? I *am* pissed off. That's two of us. Suck it up. We'll live—I hope." She was going to slap her silly, maybe break her jaw, if she didn't stop this.

"I mean it. I'm super mad *now*, Garnet!" she then shouted. Garnet whipped her head around to Allison nearly snapping her neck in half at her childish hissy fit. But Allison only glowered, grimaced, stomped her foot, folded her arms—and sneered at her.

A few people were looking at them, elbowing one another. Allison's voice was fraught with emotional pain and anxiety and loud. She was adept at soap opera histrionics. Yeah, there was little drama going on here, a few folks thought, and they'd become curious about what was going to happen next.

She was a ringer for every three or four year-old brat about to stage a massive noisy temper tantrum in a crowded grocery store. You wanted to knock the crap out of the kid, it had earned it, and the viable convincing threat and freedom to do so in private would have prevented this disgusting and humiliating melodrama. But here? Here hundreds of eyes belonging to total strangers were glued on you, all of them belonging to self-styled parenting experts, each of which was a spy for the department of child welfare and protection. The kid knew this. The leverage was inspiring to the brat, hamstrung the parent, and—BAM—everything blows up on the spot, gets way outta control.

There ensues a terrible scene, the kid cries and wails and performs a truly inspired act convincing all of the horrified morally incensed onlookers that it is a victim of ongoing extremely savage child abuse. The kid cringes, rolls on the floors in the aisles, flees your approach wailing at the top of its lungs down the aisles, pushes empty grocery carts at you to protect itself, its lamb-like terrified innocent little self, that knows only too well the horrors and pain you will inflict because of the relentless inhuman brutalization it has suffered for oh-so long.

The desperate child then flies away shrieking in fear, waving its panicky hands wildly into the air over its poor little noggin, and dashes off to the meat department where it scrambles up into a refrigerated display and fran-tically tries to cover itself with the hamburger packages to protect itself from the agonizing blows sure to follow. Then it tumbles pathetically out onto the floor in cold terror as you approach and pleads on its little knees, tears bathing its sweet lying demonic face, a face which by this point is beet red, hot as a coal, and seems suspiciously *swollen* to the gaping, aghast, now very much emotionally involved witnesses, some of whom are fumbling for their cell phones but never taking their eyes for a second off of *you*. The kid drags its butt across the floor as you patiently and gently take its hand, trying to help it up and comfort and console it, yelling at the top of its lungs of hair-raising horrors.

Nice things like, "*Noooo!* Mommy! Noooo. . .!!!! I don't wanna go outside, noooo.... YOU'LL BEAT ME WITH A TWO-BY-FOUR UNTIL I BLEED AND PASS OUT, JUST LIKE YOU *ALWAYS* DO EVERY NIGHT... Please! *Noooo!* Whaaaaaa! Sob sob sob . . . . *Help!*"

Garnet resented her BFF intensely at that moment and considered demoting her from that status. She almost hated her.

26

AN OLD PIRATE

✛ ✛ ✛

The sun was a white hot, blinding furnace overhead. She could not stand the presence of the whining tearful brat Allison for one more second. In the humid, unrelenting early afternoon heat, Garnet's clothes were soaked in "Essence of Garnet" and clung to her moist, nubile, nimble-witted, motor-mouthed self like a thousand damp hands. She felt woozy and swoony with nausea from the claustrophobic presence of what surely were millions (to her near-hysterical-hypersensitive close to hyper-ventilating nerves) of rowdy, shouting, sweating, drunken parade watchers—endless waves and mobs of them—bumping, groping, grabbing her and slamming into her and jostling her from all sides. Under these insufferable equatorial conditions, Allison's keening, glowering, tear-streaked face was no longer supportable—it was as simple as that. Garnet put one foot in front of the other, then another, and like a sleepwalker, pushed her way through the dense jungle of reeking human flesh, aimlessly, with no direction whatsoever in mind, her only goal being escape, her only desire to save herself by ridding her senses of any awareness of this possessed little witch.

But alas. Allison pursued her like a harridan, wailing, *"Garnet! Garnet! Take me home! I wanna go home! I'm so HOT, I'm gonna DIE!"* Finally she caught up with her in the sweaty mass of swirling humanity, grabbed her by the arm and spun her around. Garnet stared at this infantile, spoiled little monster in silent disbelief. Her face was crushed and crumpled up in anger almost beyond recognition and bathed in hot furious tears. The urge to strangle her was almost overwhelming, and so powerful under the circumstances, she felt as if she would flat out fall down in a dead sweat-soaked faint trying to resist it.

Then, marvelous to behold, the clouds parted, as did the crowd, and Allison's eyes suddenly lifted and softened and the anger melted from her face. *"Chutney!"* she squealed in delight. She clapped her hands with glee. "Hey! Chutneeeeey!" She launched like a rocket, whizzed past Garnet and the very backdraft of her urgent forward propulsion whirled Garnet around after her.

Yes, it was indeed the tall turbaned Speedy Go-For, and as per the usual, impeccably dressed and pressed. He put his hands together, bowed from the waist once, twice. This was an evil portent, baby. And in an evil hour.

Chutney Patel, New Delhi native, Gator Fanatic, Man Friday and Speedy Go-For, Diabolically Dangerous Driver and Chauffeur for perhaps the Devil Himself, turned theatrically to Garnet, nodded, smiled and took a step forward. He bowed deeply. She saw he had something under his arm that he held close.

"Most esteemed and very fine and most beautiful lady," he said, with a bow that was so profoundly admiring and respectful and deep that it practically put his forehead in contact with pavement. He rose and with a flourish graciously extended his hand to her. His smooth, long, tapering, almond-hued fingers held a beautiful large white vellum envelope.

"Please, missy?" he said, "The Story!"

Those very words had been lettered exquisitely by an expert calligrapher in black ink on the face of the envelope. She turned it over. The envelope had been closed by large black wax seal that had been embossed by a signet ring with a huge trident.

Proteus. Proteus' sign, symbol. The wave rider, spirit of the ocean. Commander of the Waves, changeable, ever-changing, ebbing, flowing, whispering, roaring. Forever shifting form and shape and mood. Never the same. Capable of infinite variety, surprising, creative, powerful.

That old goat. He'd studied up for this latest stunt of his. How very clever to further confuse her with an ostentatious display of erudition camouflaged as apparent clarification.

Pure B.S.

Maybe.

Proteus wielded a *trident*. The dirty old Devil tossed his shit with an ordinary *pitchfork*. There was a difference, a big difference.

Oh she'd rather hang with Proteus, surfin and riding the waves any day than roast with the Father of Lies in the fires of Hell for all eternity. Wouldn't anyone?

Clues mount, fructify, entice, and tease. Mystify. Ensnare and fire the imagination. Her wheels, gears and pistons were spinning, pumping and whirling in overdrive. She was accelerating. The chase was on.

She looked up. Chutney was gone. And Allison/Poopy Pipes/Bean Sprout had a very dangerous expression on her face.

"It's *him*!" she suddenly shrieked, piercing the air with a voice that could have shattered crystal and did shatter nerves and ears. The crowd swirled and faced her.

"Garnet!" Allison launched herself straight up into the air in a spring from the ground worthy of a grasshopper or a leprechaun.

"Look!" She cried and up she went again into the air with rocket booster's payload effect, a bounce of such intense excitement, *boing*, she went up at least three feet off the sidewalk. Was she on a pogo stick? *"It's Uncle Smeddy!"*

The crowd swayed and whirled around to face the road again and the parade. An oceanic roar of laughter erupted from the spectators closest to the curb, hoots, hollers, guffaws, *Oh my God! Oh that's awful!* women said, laughing loudly, helplessly.

The mass of howling hooting sweating human flesh developed a seam, then a narrow alley in the middle of it, and convulsions of hilarity and conniptions, and cackles increasingly troubled and roiled it. Waves of incapacitated rolling, knee-walking, knee-slapping, belly-holding, hyena laughing lunatics parted in a widening swath through which strode a swaggering piratical skinny old man wearing a large fake bushy black beard with a cocky over-sized pirate's hat on his head, a black eye-patch and wielding a fake sword high in the air. He wore a smart, snappy pirate's jacket with epaulets and brass buttons and he walked atop long scaly white legs he'd maybe borrowed from or stolen off or killed a stork for.

Argh! Argh! He growled, slicing the air with his preposterous fakey sword, leering and lunging at women, grabbing boobs and butts with impunity, whacking and smacking heads and shoulders with his sword, and threatening in the most breathtakingly obscene, lewd, offensive unrestrained manner anything female with thrusts of his pelvis in a richly revolting repertoire of lusty bumps and grinds. The visual point of interest, the area the eye was ines-capably drawn to and to which it stuck paralyzed in shock and disbelief, lay south of the pirate's equator and immediately above the fork in the stork legs.

Garnet, girl, what is this? She laughed out loud and too loud. *Oh no get outta town Oh God Fritz you are so disgusting jeese what on earth are you doing Don't you dare come over you old sleaze bag don't you old nasty bastard don't come here I'm getting outta here now this is Soooo oh now God bless America why am I laughing He's probably dangerously over-ginned his gin I am going freakin faint The cops! Call the cops! Someone is going to oh my god that is the most disgusting I'm gonna throw up what the hell is that what is he doing What the eye saw or thought it saw and then questioned the veracity of the conclusion it drew was C'mon on Garnet move your freaking feet, he's aimed, he's locked in on Oh God he's launched like torpedo at me and Allison Haul ass A pair of grape fruit sized something or other Awful to imagine Everybody is clapping and dancing egging him on Don't encourage him someone doing this Fritz! Oh my God get away from me Going to these lengths so to speak and then going out in public Too many shocks, questions, alarms bells going off at once, grape fruits, Eeeek Eeeew Get away don't you dare come near me Act like you don't know him maybe what all is in there anyway what's he doing? Where is he going with this a kind of bulging fruit assortment protuberance seemed to be the effect but question remained my God what else does he have in there and THIS IS HYSTERICALLY FUNNY WHY AM I LAUGHING SO HARD IT ONLY ENCOURAGES HIM STOP LAUGHING what are his intentions don't make eye contact don't tick him off staring is going to IT LOOKS LIKE going to explode is he a suicide you have be truly insane to do this bomber rapist sexual deviant what kind of mind cooked this whole deal up it was suggestive of an maybe arrangement derangement of fruits and vegetables he must be joking but maybe do not don't look at him run run and very briefly and tightly covered by a pretend you don't see him run run run. Chester. Oh my God—a purple speedo bathing suit.*

The purple speedo bulged unnaturally with, apparently, and in addition to and on top of, his own personal apparatus, two maybe tennis balls? Or perhaps oranges? Or other round things? And the largest cucumber or jumbo zucchini or who knows *what* that Publix had in its produce section the day he'd plundered and pillaged it for this horrid gross-out get up.

He was advancing on them quickly. At all of this swagger and braggadocio, Allison uttered a tiny squeak and then opened her arms and flew toward him like a little dove. He caught her in mid-flight and threw her over his shoulder like one of the Sabine women of rapine yore, her butt in the air, head facing backward and hanging down behind him. She squealed with thrills and chills and joy, kicked her feet excitedly and the pirate threw back his head and roared, *Arrrgh!*

And the crowd that had been clapping, dancing, hooting and chanting *go man go get down do the dirty* answered him in a deafening appreciative roar, *ARRRGH!*

It was the grossest, most obnoxious gross-out involving so many people Garnet had ever seen in her life, wholly unbecoming and inappropriate for a man of his age to be inciting and performing, and the impact, the ambush, the surprise of it, knocked the wind right out of Garnet Sullivan and blew her every synapse, shooting her into a state of fade to black shock. As the Pirate swept through the crowd with abducted Poopy Pipes hoisted over his shoulder, Garnet held her hands up toward the receding Allison and fell backward onto the sidewalk, a wild irregular melody winding out of her mouth. She looked up at the blue indifferent sky overhead and whispered, *Fritz, you BASTARD, you got me!*

"Chester! Help!" A few of those bleats and yelps and Chester and Lance, who'd been separated from Allison and Garnet, were on the scene. Gravely they listened to the preposterous unbelievable synopsis of the recent incidents and no, they didn't believe a word of it, but Allison was gone, and Garnet said they went that-a-way and that some man had carried her off screaming and kicking, and part of it might be true, and better safe than sorry, so off they went, Garnet holding on to the back of Chester's belt and following as he and Lance pushed and shouldered their way through what was now a mob of drunken rioters clapping and dancing around and enthusing to, grooving on, the blatant derelict decadence of the homecoming float of—

Garnet stopped in her tracks and sighed. Oh of course, she should have known, Chester had been a member, she'd gone with him to several of their parties until they together decided one bleary morning after just such a party, and in the throes of terrible hangovers, that maybe such quantities of grain alcohol might not help their GPAs or IQs all that much—Yes, it was none other than the typical disgusting float of the doughty haughty Pirate Crew, an elite and notoriously bad boy drinking club at UF, which was anchored there.

Nothing new to the Pirate Crew float as far as she could see. Her eyes swept over it and saw only the same old privileged drunken horn toads of a certain age in their traditional garb, acting out adolescent gross outs before they passed out, just the same old rot, the same old garbage. Nothing new, no, but with one big exception: an unusual tableau had been created in the center of this year's float featuring Allison crowned as queen of these puling little league pirates with Fritz standing next to her thrusting his purple speedo vegetable-fruit basket back and forth and looming over a wild animal cage in which a frightened little man in a tiger costume sat morosely, his eyes sticking out on terrified stalks, wringing his hands and watching the rioting crowd. As she stared struggling with Fritzian exegesis it became clear that it was none other than Clovis Reddick in a cheap tiger costume, ludicrous ears and whiskers, long tail, the works, who quivered and trembled inside the cage.

Tyger! Tyger! Burning bright
In the forests of the night

Now Fritz, the genius and impresario of this immorality play, was on the curb standing in front of them like the master of ceremonies. He shoved a big file and fat envelope at open-mouthed speechless Lance who took them from Fritz with staring unblinking eyes. This wasn't Lance's jurisdiction, but had it been, Fritz would have been tasered unconscious on the spot for the high voltage shock he'd given Lance in that get up, pants stuffed like that, shaking his booty, dancing around yelling like the devil himself.

This sucker was a ghastly leak from the nether regions, an escapee from somewheres Lance didn't want to know about, hideous, hair-raising, and there was Allison sitting up there with him just as proud and happy as punch about it. Why, sakes alive, she was his goldern crowned queen! And this same woman, why she had freakin penetrated Lance this mornin right through the eyes; she'd laid a nuclear powered word curse on him. He knew it was bad but had no idea.

The blood left Lance's face. He doubted bullets would work on fiends like this, that the ordnance, whatever it took to take out whatever this dangerous shit was, existed anywhere, was anywhere to be found. Any second the curse she put on him could start takin effect. What would he be turned into? What god-awful things would she make him do? A Pug dog didn't seem all that bad compared to somethin like this putrid, hellish, old thing on long water bird legs, with scary stuff bustin out of his underwear, Satan sized equipment, and urges so dark and disgustin they made his head spin. Would she make him wear a purple speedo? Good Lord, he did *not* want to have put on a speedo and go around like that in front of everybody. 'Course if he was a monkey wearin it, nobody'd guess it was him. He sure hoped not to become somethin so smelly he'd have to always be lookin to be upwind of hisself and have to go round holding his nose all the time at the stink comin off hisself. Goldern— he looked at his hands—they'd started getting hairer on the tops. Could be a werewolf he was growing into or, aw, he sure hoped not a monkey. He felt behind him—No tails yet that he could tell. Look. More hair was growing on the tops of his hands. All that time, he glanced up at Allison, Lord, all that time he'd been rolling around in the hay with the Devil's Queen herself, his queen, not just an old girlfriend or former sweetheart! HIS DADGUM QUEEN, THE QUEEN OF HELL! He prayed it'd just be a Pug dog in her pocket book with pork pie hats and all--

Fritz threw his head back, punched the air in front of him with his purple pelvic vegetable basket and growled, "ARRGH!"

What the *hell* do you suppose he meant by *that?* Lance wondered. He'd never laid his dadgum eyes on anything like this. Never imagined it even existed. Tryin to be friendly—looked like he was gonna have to get along, maybe, with this scary shit from hell for a little while at least, least till he'd planned his escape out good—"Ahem, *Grrrrr*, yessir," Lance said as nice and polite as he could.

From behind his squirrel's nest of a black beard and slicing the air with his silly plastic sword, Fritz roared, "Sheriff, arrest this man! He is a serial killer!"

"Yessir," Lance said respectfully. "Anything else, sir?" Why on earth had he said that last part? Oh, what a mess of horror he'd opened up now. Lance cringed. Good golly. He's gonna tell me to do something so awful I can't stand it. Why did I ever, ever say that? His face squinched up, his nose wrinkled, dadgum say it, just say it, the sound of it may kill me, then it'd be over and I could leave this life with a clean record and without a tail--

"Everything you need to send that fiend from hell back to hell is in your hands, Sheriff."

Lance swayed, his wide dilated glassy eyes fell to the hefty file and thick envelope in his hands, and swam and blurred at the septic toxic enormity of the horrors, the unspeakable perversities—sins so vile a fiend from hell with a record this long and this fat must a done. Reckon nobody knows better'n his boss there, the Top Dog Devil hisself, oh my word, this was awful bad, an absolute stinkin mess. What, oh, his knees buckled, if any of it leaked out and got on his hands or clothes? He'd triple bag it, wrap it in a hazmat suit for sure, cover it good with several bags of toxic waste-blocking charcoal, thow some shovels of sand on it--

"All the Lab reports, dates, affidavits, meticulously detailed descriptions of the hideous pervert's savage brutality and bestiality are there in your hands, Sheriff."

Ho, buddy, then sure 'nuff, he'd thow some gravel on it too, put some cinder blocks on top of the whole mess in case the heat got to it, swole it all up it, got it all blown up and gaseous. Lordy. If it got to that, it'd pop the trunk wide open whilst he was drivin and turn into an—oh my oh my Lordy Lord—an environmental hazard. No. A blame catastrophe—it'd spread quick--

"This is unspeakably horrifying material, Sherriff, and damning in every way. You've got an air tight case right there, everything you need."

This was super-hot, like radioactive unholy shit, oh Lord, the wages of sin, it's an environmental catastrophe waitin to happen. Don't drop it, whatever you do, don't drop this shit—It's all over if you do. Maybe he'd call the EPA, have them run the whole nasty mess. Dadgummit, just give his cruiser to them, let them park it at state's office, let them take complete charge of this evil Devil bidness. He didn't have the trainin to take custody of hellish shit like this—Never took those courses. Precautions, hazards he wouldn't know about. Couldn't think a anybody he could call on the QT, unofficial, get some tips, this is god-awful worse than that fiendish bacteria from Lee County, never could get the full story on that hissin squirmin zombie tar baby crap—Disappeared was the official line, no paper trail, officer quit was the expert on it--

"*Fritz!*" Garnet's voice was a shot fired into the air. The hysteria and mob behavior had to be stopped.

A little man in a tiger costume sat in a wild animal cage at the center of this mob riot, this primitive harvest festival, an alcohol-inflamed bump and grind drama-ritual thing. He had been publicly accused of being a serial killer by a retired Florida dermatologist in a pirate costume. This oddest of oddballs, through truly original inspired theatrical means, had persuaded a Florida county sheriff in uniform to arrest him and, handing him few packets with brief instructions, convinced the Sheriff that everything he needed to convict him was contained therein. The Sheriff accepted all of this demented phantasmagoria without question.

"Chester?"

The Great One was disgusted, though not surprised. "Don't look at me, kid. You started this. You convinced all of us to come up here to get away from the storm. I want no part of this. It's your show. These are your friends and associates. I'm here for the game."

Lance walked up to the cage, in a trance it seemed, and read the Miranda rights to the caged man in a tiger suit. "You're under arrest, you have the right to remain silent, you have the right to . . . ."

Chester put on his courtroom face, folded his arms, watched and listened closely.

"Chester, help me with this, will you? I guess we'll take him back to the sorority house, stash him there for the duration and book him in Punta Bella."

"Sounds reasonable to me."

"Allison, come on."

"I want to stay."

"We're leaving." She took her arm, yanked her up, and pulled her along. She'd punch her out if she had to and drag her along by her hair.

"Owch!"

"Owch yourself. Move it."

"You owe me, cupcake!" Fritz hollered from somewhere overhead and out of sight.

She didn't stop walking. "Phone home, Fritz! The Huns have invaded Cleveland and Ruth is out of celery!"

"You'll thank me one day!" A fake sword fell out of an over-hanging tree as she and Allison passed by and hit her on the head.

Through a narrow slit in her front window drapes, old Mother Weatherby watched as a car with a caged man in a tiger suit strapped to its top pulled into the parking lot. Garnet got out first and marched up the steps, followed by the other one. Behind her, the men carried on their shoulders the caged tiger man down the walk and up the steps. The late afternoon sun caught Garnet's hair and seemed to set it on fire for an instant as she opened the front door.

"That one," Mother Weatherby said. She closed the drapes and reached for her cordial glass and refilled it. She had always been wary of redheads. And that one, that one, she had a russet mane that lit up in the light as if from an inner flame, an unquenchable fire within. A deeper more suffused hue. She sipped her sherry. And then Mother Weatherby sat up suddenly very straight, held the glass away at arm's length, reached for her bifocals and got up and held the glass under the lamp. In the glass, under the lamp's golden glow, Mother Weatherby, inspired by a long cordial quiet afternoon, thought she saw Garnet's smiling face glimmer and sway in the amber liquid. It gave her quite a start. A bit of a fright. That poor man, the tiger man. What do you suppose she intends to do with him? She shivered. It would be an early night for old Mother Weatherby. My oh my. Land sakes, she was plain tuckered out. Lights out soon, good and gentle woman. Sleep will knit up your furrowed brow, and yes, there will be joy in the morning. But that one, oh my.

27

MY BLOOD RIOTS

✝ ✝ ✝

En route to take care of some serious prisoner bidness, Lance sped past The Reigning Queen of Hell HRH Allison seated on a big couch on the sun porch. She had a book open on her lap, scads of books around her and on the floor and was engaged in her dark arts and practices, the manufacture of curses and spells. He saw her out of the corner of his eye and increased his speed, nearly became airborne, with new urgency and his application to the task at hand.

"Lance!" she cried, with a sniper's accuracy, "You cute old pookie-pook SWAIN you!"

Lance stopped dead in his tracks and fell to his knees. That *swain* was a knee-capper, a cussed hot ball of birdshot, and hurt like hell--

"Yes, ma'am?"

"You are, oh . . . *Lance!"*

She was revving up, loadin up for something big, knee capped as he was his chances were---

"Lift THINE VISAGE UNTO ME, sirrah!"

He was gonna have to at least learn a few words, enough to get by, of this Devil talk. No way he could high tail it in this crippled state, goldern look at him he couldn't even stand up--

"Lance!"

Here it comes, he fell forward, bowed his head, he'd be wagging a tail any second now, pork pie hats plopped on his head, doing embarrassin tricks to maker laugh and do that giggle dance she does--

"Lance?"

"Ma'am?"

"My blood riots."

Good *golly.* Hell has really changed this woman. "You pore thing."

His tailbone itched; he prayed it was just bubbles and nothing more serious--

"Lance?"

Get it over with, oh my, I never dreamed a woman could be that kind a shot, look at me, I am freakin turnin into somethin, a—No! A wild animal noise is going to come out of my mouth! Maybe it's just all them bubbles rushin around inside—a terrible rush a bubbles in my head--

"My loyal vassal, *Lance!"*

I knew it was in the vessels, see there--

"*Lance!* A queen demands her rightful OBEISANCE."

Good God. Maybe I could tell I don't have none on me right now, but when I get some I'll sure enough pay her? But what *is* it? Where do you get it? *No* idea what that means, and I'm not gonna ask, the shameful things that woman comes up with playing around—maybe, maybe she'll forget, and I'll get off, but the bubbles—God what's she gonna hit next? He put his hand over his heart, covered the space twixt his eyes. But his vitals, Lord, he couldn't cover everything with two hands--

He was cookin now within, the heat, oh my Lord, the pizzin her penetration was puttin his eyes. She had shot in a tank, a full tank already, and was toppin it off. Oh, secret bubbles that did things you even don't want to repeat. He didn't. And he wouldn't, sure 'nuff. She'd knee-capped him. What next now? He's got all kinds of ticklish itchy bubbles in his pore ole blood—*Would she please, please just turn him into a monkey and be done with it?* Bubbles, bubbles are going everywhere, flying around—God God God, his hair, oh my word, look at that, the little hairs standing up on his arms—she

she done done made the hairs into tiny little devils, they're standin up and wavin at her—Good Lord Good Lord, knee-capped bad--

"Lance?"

Here it comes, he looked up, and, Lord, she penetrated him—zing!—just like that *again!*

"Ma'am?"

She had him in a lock-up penetration now, pumpin the pizzin in again, oh Lord, this ain't no church picnic, I can tell you, it hurts--

"Lance, honey? Wanna work on vocab? Pump it up?"

If that devil woman pumps any more a them bubbles in me she'll be takin her clothes off and takin a bath in em, she's dang near waltzing around inside me now, teasin and ticklin and gigglin—Lord, they can shrink down, and get right *inside* a man—the things women can do! She's a devil *hussy* about bubbles--

"Just tell me what you want me to do, ma'am." He was of the devil now, one a their own--

"Lance? C'mere! Look!"

Lord, I am a goner, it may be a donkey I'll be, I'll be carrying her around on my back, pork pie hat between my jackass ears—she, she done took out a real big nasty book now a curses, oh no—keep your head down, man, protect what you can—

Don't know why, honest to God, but this brings to mind that news story—A man in Tennessee woke up one morning with a *rhinoceros horn* where his nose used to be oncet, it was in the paper with a pitcher, gawdawfullest horn where his nose was. Turned out, his nose took fright or didn't like bein a close neighbor of what'd moved in and went and stuck itself on his pore behind—Didn't find out till he was havin breathin problems each time set down—

Went to the Doc, and he said, 'Well, hellacious goldern! Ain't that the just cussedest thang! I'll be! Never did see anything like that, son.' Ast him what he'd been eatin, was he doin anything unnatural—'Nossir, Doc,' man said, '*I* aint but my little *gal* is, she's a devil, she is.' Doc snapped his fingers, 'Hot damn! That done it, son! Always does! Careful there, that gal is playful, watcher, she needs it.' His nose had to be froze off in Siberia—Had to go there in a dog sled in the middle of winter. Worst long trip—Dang near froze to death, then, goldern, they welded it, had to, near burned his face clean off, *back* where it was in the first place. Never did work proper, all that freezing and welding—Part of it totally useless, even after they worked a two-man auger on it. Nearly killed the man, that auger work—

All *that* and it *still* looked off center next to the rhino horn. Man suffered pain rest a his natural his life—Then dang, wouldn't you know it? If *another* dern nose didn't sprout on his backside come spring in the *same place?* Must be fertile for noses, that part a his hide or the first nose that homesteaded that area—guess you could call it his bottomland—or lower forty—seeded it before it got froze off in Siberia—wonder why—But a man can only take much, truthfully, and I doubt I'd go that far—'Let it be,' he told the Doc—'A man gets weary messin, nitpickin, always strivin fer perfection—Good enough is good enough fer me. When I need to breathe I'll stand up'—

The pore man didn't ever have the horn took off, has it to this day—Got used to it, he said, and found it useful in some ways—He's still with that little gal, paper did a foller up few months ago—she don't care much where a man's nose is long as the rest of him is fairly orderly, he said—

Lord, get this over with please—

"*Lance!* Come on! Sit next to me so we can pump up together, please?"

"Yes, ma'am, Allison. I'm a comin."

GitRDone Garnet was on a terrible tare and had overthrown and silenced Garnet the Good and Garnet the Great; she had effectively sent them off to their Time Out corners to contemplate their recent bad behavior. For, whoa, now, ladies! Enough of this. She was going get to the bottom of this tonight. This was crazy. Even she had to admit it. She needed a clean sweep, bare floors. What was going on here? What was the story? What did she know? Cut the crap. The Chapter Room was the perfect setting; it would be her war room. She carried her notes and laptop inside and spread out her piles and lists under the great overhead lights, refusing admittance to any and all fairy dust and costumes. This was going to be *who struck John boilerplate*. Period. What could she know with her five senses, all five senses in agreement? What were the facts? No nuance, implication, suggestion admitted for this session.

The objective was to settle accounts with Fred. She owed him these stories. She had to finish her outstanding assignments minus teases or gags. She had to go with what she knew *now,* not what she hoped for tomorrow. So then, down to business. Who murdered Tommy? Who murdered Reddick's employee? Is Peter Panzer engaged in illegal activity to obtain water from the FL aquifer?

She shuffled and sorted what she had over and over again and soon fell into a stymied stupor.

This is so freakin boring, I hope to hell I can stay awake and get it done. I hate this shit. Might as well be balancing my checkbook. And, wouldn't you know it, look. Ugh. I cannot think straight or get organized when my nails look like this. Emery Board! Bastards! Oh God. I want coffee, but I don't feel coffee. I want something else. Absinthe would be just the thing, the perfect beverage for this kind of slow-death deskwork. Too bad it's illegal now. So many fun things are now . . . Sambuca, maybe. Too sweet. Campari is too Italian, nooo oomph, hardly any sizzle. I don't know why anybody bothers with Campari.

"Garnet!"

Was that A FREAKIN *megaphone* he used on her ear?

"Dammit, Chester! I *hate* it when you do that. What do you want? Hurry. Work in progress here. Speak."

"Hi, Garnet."

"Hi, Lance. Hey? Look at me. You feel okay?"

"Listen, Faery Queen, where do you want the tiger you bagged today?"

"Oh. Best place is in the '*catacombs*,' Chester. If some of the girls wandered in and found a little man in a cage dressed up like a tiger, God, I can't even think about it."

"And what the hell and where the hell are the 'catacombs' in this bat house and home for hellion women, please?"

"Hahaha. It's where all the old stuff is stashed. Oh, uh . . . and some other stuff we kitty cats, uh, put in there, uh, oh ya know, from time to time."

"Is that right? So, okay, too much information already, Lucille on the Ball. Now where is it, that is, if you don't mind—and still have the use of your own highly questionable mind."

If he wanted to be a smart ass, she was more than ready to hand it right back to him. This was not the time to test her patience. "Not one of your better ripostes, old sport. But anyway, go all the way down. Down, down down—go *all the way down*. Take the stairs all the way down *six* flights. There's a landing there? Turn right under the big hole in the ceiling, not the little one, they're close in size, so really look hard and make sure you're under the *big* hole, then from there, walk five or six steps, and take an *immediate 70 degree* angle turn left through the small narrow space, you're gonna have to squeeze through guys, but line backers and defensive tackles have made it through so I'm sure you can, it's the narrow space where the old house was hooked onto to the new house, but then mysteriously, one night there was this *groaning noise*? No one wanted to go down there? To see what's up, you know? So we all went down together finally? And all the lights had gone out? And there's not enough oxygen to keep a candle lit down there? So it was hard to see even the nose on your own face, but we could *feel* something *rending*, you know, in the atmosphere? Where the fabric of the universe has gotten thin, you know? The rending noise it makes before it rips and whatever is behind it flies out, or *in* as the case may be, and can find comfort? It made that noise that night, and *that's* the night the two houses pulled apart. Something came out, and into the world, was oh sorta *released*? But we couldn't see it, the lights were out. Whatever. It's been a long time, I'm sure it's long gone by now. Only the narrow space where it squeezed through is left. It's a small black shaft. You can't miss it.

"So there, right *there*. Look straight ahead. You'll see a mark—it's probably faded now to pink, used to be red—it's a mark shaped like a *hand*, see? Like my hand here. See? So push it, and then the wall will move forward. Then step down three short steps, 1-2-3. And you're there. That's the 'catacombs.' You'll have to duck to get in, but you can stand up mostly straight once you're in. Light's not too good down there and it's a little damp cause it's below ground, oh maybe ten feet or so, but that won't kill him for one night."

"How many other cats are down there, Garnet?"

"Lance, Lance. Let me think a minute. Um. Oh! Mr. Reddick will be the *only* cat down there tonight. He'll have the whole place to *himself*."

"I mean to tell you, woman, I ain't never *combed* a prisoner before, I'm flat out tellin you right now, I ain't gonna start tonight with a *serial killer*."

"Calm down, relax, Lance. I don't blame you. I don't *where* they keep the cat combs now anyway. He'll have to get through the night somehow without catacombing. Get him some dinner out of the fridge in the kitchen. He's hungry by now and get some blankets outta the closet next to the bathroom. There's a chill down there, the walls drip *constantly*."

"Good God Almighty! Chester, let's get this over and done with, man, okay?"

Chester didn't move a muscle or an eyelash.

"Chester, if you have something to say, I wish you'd damn well spit it out and not stand there lookin at me like that. I've got a shitload of work to do."

"Garnet, get an ice pack for your head, okay? Stick your head in a freezer for 15 minutes? You're over-heating, too many RPMs."

"C'mon, Chester, you're rapier is getting rusty. Stick it in your ear. The sand in your brains should clean it up. OH! Wait. Wait. Forgot. Forgot guys."

"Forgot *what*?" His eyebrows had locked up in a terrible frown and he had the purse-lipped pissy face that was often his prelude to delivering a devastating quip intended to send her reeling end over end like a misbehaving puppy.

"Goodness, don't get mad, Chester! Jeese, *chill*, honey! Okay, so there have always been weird sounds and noises down there, especially late at night, but it's probably just the house settling or the earth moving a little. The earth does move, Chester. Did you know that? It turns around on itself and turns itself around the sun?"

"You know, I know that, but I still don't get why we don't fall off."

"Me neither, Lance. But hey, I'm probably spinning faster than the whole whirling deal, and may spin right off the face of the earth any minute into outer space, just ask the expert here, Chester Dare. Anyway. Back to the weird noises down there? It's no biggie if you hear anything like, oh you know, *AAAAhhhhhhhhhh*, it used to do that a lot, or *AAAArrrrrrrrggghhhhhh* or *UUUUggghhhhhhh* or, um, like *Yi yi yi yi yi yi yiiiip?* Don't worry. That's normal down there."

"Hey, Chester? Did you get all those goldern directions, good buddy?" Lance shifted from foot to foot and his eyes roamed around the room.

"Yeah, I got them all right."

"Oh! Forgot. One other noise I've heard it make?" She lowered her voice to a ghostly whisper, rolled her eyes up in their sockets until they almost disappeared, and hissed, "Sometimes down there you hear *StickItInYourEarChesterDaaaaarrrre!* In fact, it did that just tonight. Kinda weird, but probably harmless."

"No doubt. The spirits of dead cats are known to do that—and certified lunatics."

"Well, I wouldn't know, Chester, honey. You're so much smarter than I am. And it's just the kind of info you'd be up on. Maybe so. Anyway, toodle-loo, now. I've got tons of work to do tonight. Bye-bye, guys. Good luck."

28

CRIES & WHISPERS

An hour later she was still shuffling papers and piles, almost despondent at what lay ahead, the mountain of material she had to go through, sift, sort, check out, compare, put through the mental meat grinder of skepticism, then smack together what came out the other end into some kind of shape, some kind of organization, before she even wrote a single word. She hadn't yet so much as touched the stinky time bomb that Fritz had planted in this mess under the guise of evidence. He was a tempter, if not the Master of Temptation. He'd burned her so many times already with his imaginative theatrics and "gotcha pranks" she didn't think she could withstand one more. She was sure the vellum trident stamped envelope was sucker bait and refused to fall for it. If she did, she wouldn't get any work done at all.

She was swimming hard, trying, but the undertow was pulling harder, slowing down her thinking and actions, and it was wearing her out. She needed to swim harder, get her brain on the page, start sitting up straight at the desk, drilling down; she needed to be sharp, keen, shrewd, with some fire in her blood, but she was drowning in the mess and nothing but a dullard in spite of all her efforts.

Wait. She sat up with a jolt. Where were Ringo and Diesel? They were zonked out on her piles just a minute ago. "Ringo!" There will be hell to pay if they crapped up anything else here. "Diesel!" Maybe those rotten dogs are in the kitchen. "Ringo!"

Garnet went downstairs. "Diesel?" The lights were off for the night and she had to feel her way along the bannister and railing. "Whoops!" She'd collided with a man on the stairs in the dark.

"Sorry, Garnet! You okay? Didn't see you! It's dark as midnight in here," Lance whispered. "Hey, would you and Chester mind takin a look at this and tellin me what's in it?"

She pulled away from him, suspicious and alarmed. "What *is* that, Lance?" He was cradling a bundled up wad of white plastic in his arms. Her first reaction was that sinking feeling one gets when a small animal has been killed and wrapped up for burial or the chilling to the bone sensation at the sight of a dead baby. She had tightened into a knot of tension and apprehension on seeing the package in his arms. Something was in there that was seriously sad and maybe even tragic.

"What *is* it?"

"I don't know. I wrapped it all up in a hazmat suit. Didn't want it to get damaged, you know, that's against the regs for handlin evidence, or Good Lord, didn't want any of it to leak out and spread. This is toxic, man, real dangerous stuff. You gotta think of the environment, public safety. But inside is the evidence that old devil gave me today. I don't need to go through all these papers. And I don't wanna look at those blame photos of the murders and crime scenes. Not that I'm a chicken shit or nothing, but you know in my job I've seen plenty of God awful things that people done, things that'll ruin your day and sure enough inject goblins and horrors into your dreams and ruin your sleep for months and years. I don't need any more evidence of how bad, sinful bad, people can be and the terrible things they can do. Lordy, I got a whole library, a damn evil bacteria hot house, and more, in my head. And, sorry, but I don't want to stash anymore up there and have that crap stinkin and oozing in my brain at night when I'm tryin to sleep."

"I can understand." A dark stairway late at night. Speaking of unspeakable things. Perfect place for chit chat about dirt bags and demons.

208

"Listen here, Garnet, my job is to book that little man prisoner for somethin, fill in the blanks on the forms. Doesn't have to be charges. State does that. Suspicion of crimes is good enough to arrest him, let the State's people sift and sort through this pile of evil shit. That's their own bag a bones, their job."

"All righty, sure." Too good to be true. She wouldn't be surprised at anything in those packets or if nothing was in them at all but old newspapers. Too much "evidence" was floating around now, and most of it Fritzian.

"Allison wants me to do words with her. That's where I need to be. Helping her pump em up and all."

"You go help Allison, Lance. Chester and I will look at this."

Lance sighed and groaned. "You know, the prisoner is an unhappy little cat down there, Garnet. He ain't said a word, not a peep, since we took him off the old devil Fritz."

"Oh, I'm sorry. He may be scum of the earth, but it's a bad place he's put himself in. I'm sure he's hurting. Damn." She twisted inside with a bad ache, the discomfort of compassion pushing against revulsion at what the man was alleged to have done. Poor excuse for a human being maybe, but still, he wasn't a rock or a stone and neither was she. Little bastard said some stupid things about Chester, but don't we all say stupid things, diss people, commit social sins all day long? Her rage over his silly words about her hometown hero and honey were gone at this point.

"Yeah. You can't help but feel a little for him. Hard to believe such a little feller could be such a fiend, that he could do all that they say he did."

"That's sad isn't it? And all alone down there with his sins, crimes, whatever. Turning them over and over in his head, scared to death of what's coming next." God forbid she ever got thwacked for even ten percent of her own errors and mistakes. She'd disintegrate on the spot.

"They may juice the lights outta that sucker, ya know. If they can prove it all, he'll get the chair in Florida. Unless some bleedin heart judge and some good appeal lawyer are his luck of the draw, he's a goner."

"Yeah. But lots of times that's not enough."

"Guess he's got the bucks for those kinda lawyers. They can drag it out so that he dies of old age or gets killed at Raiford."

"That tiny tiger won't last long in Raiford, Lance."

"Three minutes maybe."

"Did you get him anything to eat?"

"Not much in that fridge, Garnet. I made him a little cheese sandwich and took him a glass of milk."

"That's all? That's not much, Lance."

"He's little, he'll get by. It's only one night. I'll go get him some burritos or somethin in the morning. I gave him a blanket."

"Just one?"

"That's enough. Ain't that cold down there."

"Damp, though, and just sitting in that cage all night in that clammy place? Anyway, okay, so here, give me the toxin texts. I gotta get to *work*, dammit. Have you seen Ringo and Diesel?"

"No."

"Do you know where Chester is?"

"I'm right behind you, drama queen."

"You damn sneak." She turned around. "How long have you been there?"

"Taking the fifth on that one."

"Have you seen Ringo and Diesel?"

"No. I walked them and fed them. Your part of the deal was to keep track of them. I'm hitting the sack. Big game tomorrow, unless you've lost that part of your head too, remember?"

"Help me with these evidentiary papers first."

"No."

"What?"

"No. Can't. Would be unethical, maybe a crime given my job as PD."

"Oh you bastard! At least help me find the dogs."

"No. I'm getting *Sports Illustrated* out of the car, going to read a bit, then lights out."

"Chester!"

"You started this. You finish it. Paddle your own canoe, darlin'. I sure as hell don't get much help from you paddling mine. 'Nite, Lance."

"Get some good rest, man. Gonna be a good game."

"You too, Lance, buddy."

"Chester, wait. What about Tank? Tank Panzer? How am I gonna get to see him tomorrow? When he gets that award for the water institute he's setting up, the dirty crook, at half-time, how am I going to get to him before he leaves?" That was going to be the toughest piece to do for Fred, she had nothing but a suspicion, though she knew it in her bones, that he was sucking the aquifer dry and breaking the law too.

"I don't know. How?"

"Chester, you can be a real irritating little shit sometimes, ya know honey?"

"So can you, sugar." He pinched her butt and went down the stairs.

"You can be a royal pain in the ass too!" she said in an angry sawmill whisper as he went by.

Maybe Tank's secretary Marianne could tell her where he's staying while he's here, yeah, girl, call Marianne in Immokalee. Holy freakin crap, how in the world was she gonna get all this done by Monday? Absinthe. Ah the fuel and inspiration for great artists and poets. But she may have to settle for brewing some Dunkin Donuts or plain old water. There was too much to do, she'd never get it all done, it was humanly impossible, she was insane to try, this was totally unreasonable. So she would, one way or another, hell or high water, just do it. *Some*how.

She wandered around in the dark downstairs with the hazmat-wrapped bundle of evidence whispering "Ringo! Diesel!" and feeling like an unwed mother from an 18th century novel with her newborn illegitimate baby cradled in her arms searching for a haven on a dark and stormy night. Yeah, all of this was slightly illegitimate and this was her baby. The tough situation was only her own fault. The dogs were in here somewhere. They couldn't have gotten loose. They'd show up, she'd clean up or pay for the mess they'd made. None of which would be a total surprise to Mother Weatherby. She knew her and already had too much logged in on her in her *Chronicles of Chronic Trouble Makers* within these walls from "yesteryears."

"Ringo! Dammit! Diesel! Where are you?" The words buzzed like a swarm of angry hornets out of her mouth and disappeared into the dark with no effect.

"Garnet? Is that you? Garnet?"

"Oh! Mother Weatherby! I'm sorry, I AM SO SORRREEE. Good grief. I hope I didn't wake you?"

Mother Weatherby had made the mistake of removing her blindfold and venturing forth from the safety of her private rooms before daylight. Her nerves had been thus exposed, and now they were taxed, very much so, to be perfectly frank. She stared at the small white bundle cradled in Garnet's arms and an icy chill ran through her, her heart banged against her chest once like a sledgehammer and she stiffened as if she'd been turned to stone. Every joint in her body froze solid. She was in her long white flannel nightgown and fluffy pink bedroom slippers and was holding an empty cordial glass, a glass which she'd very much hoped to refill from her emergency reserve stock of sherry in the locked cabinet in the kitchen. Her ear plugs were still in her ears, something she'd forgotten, and which Garnet did not observe, as she apologized at great groveling length for having disturbed her, giving her a highly embroidered, quite imaginative line of lying crap about what she was up to, what was going on, what the bundle was, where she was going with it. But no matter, even if Mother Weatherby had been able to hear her, nothing she could have said would have erased the conclusions Mother Weatherby had instantly drawn from this chance encounter in the dark hallway late at night with Garnet Sullivan and the small white bundle she held cradled in her arms.

"Again, Mother Weatherby, Soooo, soooooo sorry! I'll be up late working but will be quiet as a mouse, I promise!"

Then she turned on her heel, raced off to the stairs and, cradling the horrifying bundle in her arms, hopped up the stairs like a jackrabbit, taking them two at time.

When Garnet was gone, and long gone, old Mother Weatherby stood a long, long while in the dark hallway like a tall marble Roman statue from antiquity, implacable, stoic-faced, with blank staring unseeing eyes. Her large old gray cat Mortie rubbed against her numb unfeeling legs, purring and meowing. Poor little tiger man. He'd been caged, she wondered, for how long? And for this? Is that all that remained of him? That girl, that one. Oh my. A jagged spear of ice had been thrust through Mother Weatherby's already enervated entrails. That one. Ice crystals had formed on her every nerve.

It behooves me to lie down, she decided. Little feet, way down there, little feet in your little slippers, shall we? Shall we? Please little feet, come along now, be good little feet and take me back to my rooms.

29

QUEEN OF THE DAMNED

✝ ✝ ✝

The Queen of the Damned and her consort sat in the center of a plush white brocade couch in the middle of the dark living room. They were bathed in the golden glow of a floor lamp. Books were scattered across the lush crimson carpet at their feet.

In Allison's lap a book lay open, a book entitled *The Language of Shakespeare: A Lexicon & Guide to the Diction of the Elizabethan Dramatists.*

"Lance, catacombs are where the heathen devils sorted and stashed the dead Christians. If they kept any cats in em, I don't know, but it was like, you know, a wine cellar for dead Christians. After they'd killed em and all."

"Well, did they *comb* em for a reason? Maybe to clean em up before logging them in and putting them away?"

"Maybe. Why not?"

"I didn't see *any* dead Christians down there, Allison. There was a bunch of old ball gowns, shoes, hats, things like that. Although, come to think of it, I may have stashed one dead Christian in there myself. Or one soon to be dead."

"Oh, no. They're gonna kill that little tiger man?"

"Who?"

"The heathens?"

"Where?"

"Here?"

"You don't mean to tell me, Allison, that there are *heathens* in this place?"

"None that I've seen. But I don't know what they look like. Do you?"

"No. But when I hear the word, I think of an alligator or a shark."

"Look at this picture, Lance! I just love this book. She's a queen. I *love* this book, it's my favorite!"

"Oh, my Lord! She could be Garnet's granny! Lookit that hair, them eyes. Wouldn't want to mess with *that* lady. She's one bad bar fight I'd be willing to miss."

"Avaunt, Satan!"

"Oh, no! He around tonight? He don't get jealous does he? You know, me and you together like this?"

"*Lance!* Did you know that Shakespeare had a dark lady he loved a lot? He wrote lots of poems for her."

"Men just can't help but love devil women. It shouldn't even be a sin."

"The heart wants what it wants."

"You can say that again! There ain't no accountin for it, just the way it is."

"She said it, *Emily*, not me. Look in this book over here."

"You know, Allison, if I didn't know better, to look at you here tonight, I'd might a taken you for an angel."

"That's pretty, Lance. Look at this. 'O me! My heart! My rising heart!'"

She leaned into Lance and brushed his cheek with her lips.

"Aw, don't do that, you don't have to kiss me."

"Lance! You *know* I don't do anything I don't want to do unless I have to do it."

"That I know, yes, ma'am, of that I am perfectly aware."

"I want and have to kiss you."

"That's extreme duress then. You won't be breakin any law if you do."

"This is fun."

"I don't mind it myself, either, Allison, to be perfectly honest about it."

"*Lance!* Do you like *poetry?*"

"Never thought about till now, but, yes, I think I do."

When Garnet made it to the door of the Chapter Room with her hideous bundle of damning evidence that was supposedly going to get boulders of Fred-induced guilt off her back and the hooks of obligation out of her mouth and gills, *and* earn Clovis Reddick a one way ticket to hell, she hit the brakes. Beyond that door was her war room of paper piles, shreds of clues, notes, her laptop, pens, and she was about to dump this questionable shapeless mass onto the already plenty confused mess. Fritz was the source of all of the recent information and his antics had been responsible every new suspicion she had.

She was about to spend hours sorting and sifting through what? The products of a genius madman with an overheated imagination? The dramatized outlandish accusations of a bad actor? That did not strike her as a good use of her time, let alone a pleasurable one. She wasn't a pathologist, criminologist, criminal psychologist, and could not interpret lab reports, crime scene jargon, and other specialist data. She'd spend hours Googling terms to get through the mass of material and even then might not get it right. Fred would insist on verifiable sources and grill the bejesus out of her.

She couldn't just ignore what Fritz had delivered, though. It could contain hints and suggestions that could point her in the right direction and help her make better sense of the data she already had, material that was sourced and quotable. Was there an alternative, an option, to all of this? Five minutes passed as she hemmed and hawed, made excuses and ran through scenarios. Finally, disgusted with her procrastination, she put her hand on the doorknob, resigned to hours of tedious methodical research that may result in nothing she could use at all. She had to do it. There was no getting around it.

As she turned the knob, a sound like the cry of a lost soul in hell expressing its unspeakable agony filled the house. It was a spiraling geyser of inarticulate torment and it seemed to throw her up from the floor and hold her suspended in a dark funnel of fear and horror. Then it stopped just as suddenly and mysteriously as it had started. The silence that followed seemed to shudder and throb with shock. She raced downstairs to the "catacombs." She pushed the wall, and just inside a gray cat, every hair on its body standing on end, with yellow eyes so alarming and ghastly it could strip the color off the cheeks of a cupid on a Valentine's Day card, arched its back and hissed like a fiend, dancing on the tips of its toes and baring its fangs. Just behind it stood Ringo and Diesel, their chests heaving and jaws dripping stalactites of drool. She lunged for their collars and the cat shot past her with a snarl so nasty and vicious it would have made a corpse sit up and curl its toes.

"Damn your ass, Mortie!" she hissed after him. She leaned forward into the dark. "Mr. Reddick? Are you all right?"

A disembodied, high-pitched, wavering voice several yards away said, "How nice to see you again, Miss Sullivan! What a pleasant surprise! Won't you please come in?"

"Do you need anything, Mr. Reddick?" She had Ringo and Diesel by the scruff of their lousy mis-behaving necks and leaned deeper into gloom.

A thin ribbon of a voice wound out of the dark and threaded its way through her heart. "Yes, how very nice of you to ask. Thank you. I was hoping, actually, that you would ask. You see, I need to tell the truth. I'd like to tell you what happened, why I'm here, don't you know, it's all so hurly burly, dear me. What a commotion and so very odd. But, oh heavens, bless my soul, it's so damp in here and dark, but I'd like to tell you, you most particularly, I couldn't possibly trust anyone else to listen properly, and not miss anything, and you've always been so very kind and compassionate, very considerate, and Kalimba, you seemed to care and understand. I'd like to tell you a true story, not a pretty one, the story of, oh, don't you know, of what I did. Atrocious, oh my, I can't believe it. Things got out of hand, I can't believe it, but what they've got is only half-right, and not everything. And, say, do you think, I wonder, I don't want to inconvenience you, but would it be too much trouble for you to bring me another blanket?"

"Sure! I'm so sorry you're cold! I'll go get one right now! Be right back."

"Wait! Miss Sullivan! I did some terrible things. But the truth will out. Hahaha, as the saying goes, you know? So let's give it a little push shall we? What happened and how, why I did these awful things? Do you think you might put this story, a summary, perhaps, that would do, in your paper? Having this inside of me, I'm in, and if you will pardon me, but I don't think I'm exaggerating one bit, but I'm in agony."

✛ ✛ ✛

When the piercing cry rent the house and split and exited out of the top of Garnet's skull, driving her downstairs in a reckless rush to the rescue of whatever the hell was down there making this god-awful noise, Allison and Lance were under the stars looking for the Big Dipper. The vocab pump up on *Celestial,* say it, write it, use it in a sentence, had launched them and— twinkle, twinkle little star—had lured them outdoors. One twinkle leads to another and you never know where, but it doesn't matter, if wonder, wondering and wonderful are your reasons for wandering, for then it's not aimless or a waste of time or killing time, for time has been cancelled, you're never late and you're never early, for you lose track of time when you're on the right track.

"*Lance!* Look."

"Is that a star or a planet?"

"Stars twinkle."

"So do you, Allison, all over, inside and out. Sure you're not an angel?"

"*Lance!*"

She'd sure enough had made a monkey out of him, but it wasn't all bad. She may not be a devil, but she had the powers, maybe part devil, only had a little of the devil in her ever now and then, but goldern it was a hot sauce in a woman he had to have and he'd pay more for it to get it if he had to. He was getting used to acting like a monkey, it felt almost natural now, and when it come right down to it, if it'd make her happy, he'd wear a pork pie hat too and learn to speak Eye-talian and tippy toe around in a pink ballerina skirt long as she was lookin at him and he could make her smile.

The scream of screams had popped Chester's eyes open and jerked him rudely out of a deep soft dreamy sleep. His *Sports Illustrated* had slipped from his hands and into his lap when he dozed off reading it, his glasses had slid down his nose, and after a half an hour of light pleasant twilight sleep, he turned over, switched off the light, put his glasses on the bedside table, and the magazine slid onto the floor. It was nice and quiet in there. And cool. He chuckled at some of the memories he'd filed away in his mind of the parade, particularly the boogie funny sassy woogie routines and high-steppin of the Florida A & M Marching Band. Man. They had the rhythm and the attitude! He sometimes felt like that, but where in Punta Bella, Florida could an attorney, especially one who worked for the state, get down like that, wail to the music, let it all hang out, show his stuff, wag his butt, prance, do some high steppin,' wave his arms in the air, growl, sing, yell and let it all hang out in public as part of a public celebration, an annual blow-out, dedicated to high spirits, where could a sober-sides like Chester Dare drop the armor of office, and express the zest and exhilaration of being alive, the sheer joy of it? Bill Clinton, yeah, he got away with it. Chester smiled. Lucky devil. Chester wasn't comfortable taking the risk, feeling that it would somehow compromise the authority he had in the public eye, the respect for him as a professional and maybe the respect for the office itself. He was, after all, a public servant, not an entertainer. And he had to run for re-election every four years. Made him a little sad, not having the liberty and latitude to throw his hands up and shout for joy with everyone else, dance to the music outside, loud and with the strength of feeling he had deep inside his sober-sides. Oh, hell. Piss on it. No big deal. Sure was a kick, though, watching others get down, rock and roll, show their stuff, and behave like adolescents. He enjoyed it, yeah.

The last image before his eyes before his tether to the world of responsibility and duty was loosed and the undertow of deep sleep carried him away, was the trombone player in the Florida A & M Band wailing on that horn, grooving, swaying back and forth, head rising and falling emphatically in sync with the rhythm, his knees like pistons rising to his chest, feet plowing back down to the pavement in perfect time to the rhythm, he was so cool and full of life, and then Chester sailed away in a mild contentment, satisfied, at peace. And THEN the scream ripped through his parade of dreams and his eyes snapped open.

Garnet, I love you with all my heart, my life would be dullsville, dusty and gray without you; you entertain me, inspire me; you are always there for me, as I am for you; but tonight, tonight, I will not, I refuse to jump up and haul my ass out of bed to see what you've stirred up now, what crack you've got your butt stuck in, what heinous crime has filled you with stuttering stammering outrage; I won't race to the scene to discover what crisis or urgent errand is making you bounce off the walls, bang your fist on your desk, what shocking mistake you've made yourself and only now recognized, what error or over-sight of yours, has caused you to slap your forehead and sigh, slam your fist against the wall, slump, moan, fly around a room cussing yourself, and others, yelling "The bastards! The bastards!" to only, once your ravings and rants have let enough of the steam out of your disappointment with yourself and anger at others, watch you run right out, juice up once more, get another tank of gas, and petal to the medal, go out and do the same damn thing all over again.

Woman, you are more than equal to anything you meet in the road, at a bar, in an office, at a club, anywhere. You can take care of yourself when it comes bad asses. By now you've got whatever or whoever caused that scream to split my ears and my jar my sweet peace, handled, I'm sure of it, and I would venture to say if there is a malefactor or a perp you've I.D.'d who pounded or scared that scream out of a person, you are on him and his ass is grass.

He closed his eyes. Honey, tonight, I'm tired, I'm comfortable, and I don't want to get up. Tell me about it in the morning, when the bad guys are smithereens, the victim is comforted, you've cooled to room temperature and can speak in a normal voice. Till then, sugar. He smiled, and slid away from the shore of chores, conniption fits and noise, down the lazy river on a cushiony magic carpet afloat on the gentle current of sleep, and what a lovely, lovely feeling it was.

30 (A)

THE EPIC TORMENT OF OLD MOTHER WEATHERBY

✝ ✝ ✝

The Return of the Red Devil

Faint and drear, Old Mother Weatherby sat bundled, her head wrapped round and round with scarves, on the ledge of her of bundle-besieged bed. She had swathed and bandaged her damaged vision from the foul and fearsome bundle assault by the Bundling Red Devil Garnet, whose devilish evil hands held the dear bundle of the loathsome remains of her savagery, her pillaged gains, torn from the flesh and bones of The Innocent, the virtuous child-man, The Little Tiger Man, bundling it away stealthily, bundling it in a bundle away into the night.

The lady enscarved her stinging stabbing pain with banners black, banners vain, mourning bundles of bundles of woe, frantic bleak festoons of grief, emphatic of the deep she felt within her now empty cranial attic and befitting The Abhorrence, now entered her and which within now dwelt her, bundling sullen, bundling snarling, a bundling misbegotten bastard toothsome, amid the ruined dripping empty caverns, all of sense foresworn, within her upper story, the storehouse of herself, you know, the Her That Was, but is not now, and from whence her Panicked Brains had flown, the flight from the Red Devil's bundling blows, the fate, the roundly ruinous plight, of all that opposed her or stood before or aft her, or in the furious path of her, or in reach or sight of her, or the mighty might of her.

The Flight from the Red Devil

The cry of flight, the preface, prolegomenon, prelude, epithalamium, wisely, madly heralding, caroling, pressing press of pressing events, among the frank, speaking frankly, and the heart faint feeling faintly, on the news of the advance of her, whence comes striding and striding, striding, unswerving, dark-purposed, preening, the price exacted from all, the toll excised by the rampaging Red Devil, the Raging Red Hornet Garnet.

30 (B)

A TALE TOLD BY AN IDIOT

Garnet ducked into the "catacombs" with a bundle of three blankets, several sandwiches, a Dr. Pepper and another bundle of the tools of her trade, including her laptop, emery boards, a smidgeon of a bottle of absinthe she'd found (shock of shocks) in the broom closet in the kitchen where she'd hidden it as a sneaky literati hotsie-totsie poseur her freshman year (wow, she knew she was good at sequestering, but had no idea how good), pens, yellow legal pads and a long pearl cigarette holder (she couldn't find any cigarettes to go in it, but so what?), a tall sterling silver cigarette lighter (a prop to lend ambience, cache, atmospherics) a sterling silver candelabra and eight tall fluted candles. It was a tight squeeze, a big pair of bundles, but it would be a long night. She needed the necessary provisions for what lay ahead. She hated the sight of an animal in a cage, loathed it, any kind of animal.

"You came back, my dear!"

As the candlelight flickered against the dusky damp walls, with cigarette holder between her teeth, and taking ritualistic tiny sips of absinthe, not enough there for a buzz, she filed her bastard fingernails and listened—rapt.

GIRLS JUST WANNA HAVE FUN

"Oh my, let's see now. I want to be very, very careful and not leave anything out. I suppose it all began when I met Mother on the stairway rushing in absolute flat out haste, all dressed up to the very nines, she was wearing the gown she'd worn for the portrait Sargent had done of her, we gave that to the Metropolitan years ago, bee-yuu-tiful painting but a bit grandiose for our place here and not at all oh "Floridian" or tropical décor, don't you know? It's in the museum in New York now. So she was rushing down the stairs, something that stunned me in and of itself because, you know, Mother is 98 years old, for heaven sake, and most days she can't walk, perhaps doesn't want to since there are so few places of interest here to her and poor thing, almost all of her good friends, bosom buddies and fox hunting galloping gals are all dead now, and she doesn't have anyone to race around with and have high times with, no one to go to the theatre with or a Broadway show or do lunch at 21, or to fly off to go on safari, or to pop in on Amelia Earhart, you know, or toddle off to Paris for a week to hit the café scene, shop the designers, pick up a painting here and there—she got some nice Dali paintings that way, and Picassos too, you got to get them while they're available, don't you know? They're one of a kind, but anyway, and those painters were young then and not at all well known, so back then you could pick up a Picasso on the cheap, and now and then, if you were lucky, you could practically steal a Van Gogh because he hadn't become fashionable yet—It was the high life, I'm telling you. Mother and her little friends would, you know, wander off to Paris to do the Charleston at the clubs on the West Bank, or hop off to hopscotch through the museums and cathedrals in Florence on a whim, whenever the spirit moved them or a bee got in someone's bonnet. Back then it was 'Well, why not? I feel like it. Shall we then? I miss the lemon sole and the Pino Grigio at Ratroisie' on the boulevard' something or other, and off they went, zoom-zoom! On a moment's notice they'd cook up an enthusiasm or notion to go take a few days to go flirt with the gondoliers in Venice!

NOT HER FAULT SHE'S A RICH BITCH

"And Poor Mother, I do sympathize and sort of understand. I mean, oh, they did have so much fun together and, I know this sounds silly and hardly anyone could sympathize with her or feel sorry for her, but, you know? It wasn't her *fault* she was born rich, married rich, had a grand old time for many, *many* years and all the money and privileges that anyone in the world could have. She is not going to get anyone's empathy or commiseration because she mourns the loss of those times and her beautiful rich girlfriends. But, you know, with ageing, it's so sad but too true, you lose and lose and lose! It's quite painful from what I myself have observed, from what I've seen myself and not just in Mother's case, the losses just keep coming, and it's so very devastating—Oh here I go again, my apologies, Miss Sullivan! I'm running my silly mouth about nonsense maybe but—

"Forgive me for the tears, but anyway, to continue, Mother always said I was too sensitive and I talked too much, that I carried on like a *girl*. 'You're no *jeune fille*, Clovis, you little SOB! *Be a man!*' she'd say. 'Act like a man, Clovis! Shame on you! Stiff upper lip!' she always said. And 'Shut up, for Godsakes! Shut the hell up, Clovis!' she'd say. 'Men don't carry on in public about those things. You're an embarrassment to the family! Your father is profoundly disappointed in you, your girlish concern for little birds and music and writing poetry. My Lord, what next? You and your simpering around, playing with kitties and puppies all the time, reading all those books, your head in a book all the time, and picking flowers! Get out of my sight! I can't stand to look at you! Go to your room!'

"I tried, but I honestly do not believe, no matter whatever I did and how hard I tried, I could not please Mother. Actually, I don't think Mother found *anyone* entirely satisfactory or tip-top, if you follow me?

"Anyway, oh don't you know, and Lord have Mercy, but I don't want to be a bore or bore you with this, but, to tell you the truth, I believe the pain of losing in advanced age is the same the world over wherever you go, whatever your financial happenstance. Very sad, sad. Oh, I don't know, I'm rambling on here. But Mother is a fish out of water gasping for her last breaths … *nobody* dresses for dinner here, that I can tell anyway, I mean, maybe there are that sort somewhere in Florida, but even in Palm Beach, my word. Everything's gotten so casual. Anyway . . . .

"So there I am standing dumbstruck on the stairs with my mouth hanging open, sure I'm either dreaming or witnessed a real miracle in my own home, and Mother almost slammed into me—she had some of her diamonds on and the giant diamond brooch Papa gave her, and was wearing the big emerald ring she'd inherited from Grandmother—and, to tell you the absolute truth, I was perfectly astonished! This woman could not even walk on her own the day before and sad to say, but she is in the last stages of dementia. Dementia can be *terminal*, Miss Sullivan, did you know that?

WHAT? DEMENTIA CAN BE TERMINAL? AS IN KILL YOU?

"All along, during the last several months, I'd been fearing the end was near, she had only radishes and capers—at the most—left in her noggin, talk about being a vegetable! But this happened over time, her decline was gradual, but, true to say, she's always been a bit rash and 'demented,' don't you know? Imperious? Impulsive? Dramatic? Rushing hither, thither and yon? All with the greatest urgency and speed. She used to beat the poor crackers out of Jimmy-James' head, he was her long suffering chauffeur. I'm telling you, Papa must have given him some good stock options he could only exercise if he stuck it out for 30 years. She was the 'Queen of Demanding and Faster,' I mean to say. Wherever she went, 'Faster, faster, you fool!' she'd cry, 'I'm late to pick up Florimell Rockefeller and Lily Tiltwilly Vanderbilt.' And she'd smack his poor pate with whatever she had handy. I don't know how he put up with it for so many years! Maybe he'd started stuffing his uniform hat with newspapers before he came to work.

"So here I am with my poor mouth hanging open, shocked out of my wits, positively speechless over what I'm looking at on the stairway, and thinking, good heavens! Has Lady Lazarus Risen from the Dead? Did *Jesus* stop by and say, 'Betsy, take up your bed and walk? Get up quick, sweetheart! Go get ready and rush along now, hurry, *Orfeo* is being performed at the Met and Florimell and Lily Tiltwilly are waiting for you to scoop them up for the eight o'clock show?' I was absolutely positively floored. I have never been so shocked in my life about anything. I mean to tell you, this was very, very unexpected, and Mother says, standing there on the stairway in all her grandeur, bedecked head to toe like the society queen bee she was, the perfect potentate of rich-pretty and pretty-rich, as they used to say, but that was oh a century ago almost, don't you know? Practically ancient history. Incredibly, Mother then shouts quite regally in her old manner of ordering everyone around, *'GET OUT OF MY WAY! I'M LATE FOR THE OPERA!'*

"At that point I happened to notice she had a big old nasty looking *butcher knife* that she's trying to hide in the folds of her gown. Yes! Oh my dear. You have no idea. I mean to tell you, I very nearly lost every single one of my tiny little marbles. Where on earth she ever got it, I have absolutely no clue. Maybe she bribed a maid, gave her some jewelry or something to get it for her. She has no cash in her possession that I know of; I handle all the finances and shopping, you know? Maybe she found it by accident puttering around, though she has not been able to putter under her own steam for a number of years.

"Anyway, may heaven forgive me, I simply cannot believe that I did this, but I confess, I am so ashamed, embarrassed, you have no idea, it's agony, the remorse and regret and guilt I feel for what happened afterwards, but when she stood there and demanded the keys to the Bentley with that ugly knife in her hand, God forgive me, but I gave them to her! I took them right out of my pocket and handed them to her! I did not object or do anything to counter or avert the disaster that followed. It was as if I was 14 years old again and she was the monarch of New York society and my Almighty Mother, and not to be brooked. One simply did not argue with Mother. Her word was the absolute law.

"And so there she goes! She trundles right out to the Bentley, hops in and off she tears at 100 miles per hour! Over hill and dale, racing all around the grounds here, slamming into buildings, backing up at 100 miles per hour too, taking off in every direction, blasting through fences. She destroyed, just tore to pieces, the Peaceable Kingdom! Many animals got loose, some were very seriously injured, many were killed, and my loyal and valiant, yes, they were valiant, employees gave their very all to catch up with her and stop her, to protect the animals, to wrest the knife from her—but she actually went after them and some bison with the knife!

"Somehow, I don't know how, she got out our gate and onto to the road that runs by our place and took off. We chased her all over creation, lost her, then found her, and on it went, an insane and deadly chase. I was amazed the police didn't stop us, often we were driving 90 or 100 miles an hour, and yet there was not a single police car anywhere in sight! But thank the good Lord there was not very much traffic on the road that night. She never did hit a car that I know of, nor injure a pedestrian, but—oh, my living God, the damage she did, and the poor animals, all because I gave her the keys to the Bentley, just like the obedient, good little boy I was 'supposed' to be!

A TIGERESS AMISS

"Finally, after some hours of this madness, the Bentley ran out of gas. The chase ended somewhere out in the woods near the home of an older man who heard the ruckus, all our shouting back and forth, and I guess he came outside to see what was going on, what the trouble was and . . .

"Oh. Oh! Did I mention that ... this is unbelievable! I still cannot believe this part. After Mother had blown a hole with the Bentley into the big cat enclosures, don't you know? Their habitats? The kitties, my kitty-cats, got loose, you will find this as astonishing as I did and still do, I'm sure you will, my word. I mean to say. The whole thing is the biggest nightmare from hell and it's my fault. I have no one to blame but myself. Somehow Kalimba climbed into the backseat of the Bentley when a door flew open from the force of impact, and Mother raced off our grounds onto to Florida public highways at 90 to 100 miles per hour with a Bengal Tiger in the backseat of her car! Yes! A tiger sitting up like a passenger in the backseat of the Bentley and Mother in her ball gown, jewels, opera glasses dangling from her neck, flying down the road at 100 miles an hour to what she thinks is a performance of *Orfeo* at the Metropolitan Opera in New York! Talk about crackers, my dear. Yes, it was crackers. I'm still amazed Kalimba didn't kill or maul her, but she did not do anything at all improper, not even scratch her. The only thing the sweet thing did was go along for the ride, as far as I could tell.

"The older man out there in the woods was most concerned about all of this, as you can well imagine, and tried so hard to help us. He chased the tiger, he chased Mother, oh my, he tried so hard. Yet this is part is still all mixed up in my over-taxed and never too bright mind. But this much I do remember: it was dark, Mother was uncontrollable, raging and ranting and storming around out there the woods, out there in nowhere, in the dark, in her ball gown and diamonds and emerald ring, her opera glasses on a ribbon and dangling from her neck. Kalimba leapt from the car when it stopped and Mother got out and started yelling for Jimmy-James, oh don't you know, her old chauffeur so many, many years ago, good Lord, he's been dead now, bless his soul for at least 30 years! My employees were running all over the place, and trying to catch the tiger, subdue Mother, the good man tried to help. I honestly don't know, but I think the dear old man might have been injured in all of this. I was terrified, just out of my mind at what had happened. I should have stayed and checked on him, but Kalimba had run off into the woods, and Mother was raving at the top of her lungs and waving that knife, and then—

"Oh my Lord, she collapsed! The crazy old doll had a heart attack! Well, my word, who wouldn't? I cannot believe I did not have several multiple ongoing and finally fatal heart attacks myself. I wish I had. Just look at me now. Look at me here in this cage. This costume, this humiliation. We did not know what had happened to Mother, though of course it would have been a blessing if she had died on the spot. I certainly wish I had. So we raced her to the hospital. We had to leave Kalimba behind, and there was no time to inquire after the kindly older man who'd rushed out and tried to help us.

"The most tragic part of all of this is that one of my brave employees, during this fracas, died as a result of his injuries. And, as you now know, an innocent man has been charged with murdering him. I have said nothing because I'm trying to protect my 98-year-old demented mother and I, myself, gave her the keys to the Bentley.

"After all of this happened, I thought what on earth had launched Mother like that? *The Devil?* I mean, I seriously considered the possibility that the Devil was somehow involved in this. That's how bizarre and unlikely it was, and everyone around her who saw her every day agreed. We could *not* imagine what had gotten into this woman who the day before lay in her bed with her mouth open, eyes glazed over, drooling and unable to talk. She had not walked in months, and if she said anything at all, it was bursts of nonsense like 'Caviar! Faster! Tiffany's! Go to hell, Clovis!' She'd often shout between drools and snorts, 'Faster!' But Good Lord, she was always banging on Jimmy-James to 'Hurry damn up, Jimmy, faster!'

"But there I am, stunned into a stupor thinking, good Lord, it had to be something *like* the Devil, though quite honestly, I've never taken that notion literally. I think people are evil *inside* and it's up to them to manage their own devils. Quite frankly, I think the old guy with horns and a pitchfork?

It's a cop out. He's not out there; he doesn't make anybody do anything. It's something dark in everyone's heart always agitating, tempting us to be selfish, to live only for ourselves and our baser instincts, trying to stir things up all the damn time, and our responsibility is to manage it, oh don't you know, like don't sin, don't be cruel, don't hurt anyone?

Rx FOR MADNESS

"So this incident! Oh my word! It made me seriously reconsider. Was she possessed or something? It was horrifying, just demonic, her behavior! Oh, sorry, I didn't mean to alarm you! I can tell by the look on your face, Miss Sullivan, that this upsets you, it disturbs you. I, oh no, I don't want to upset you! But I promised you the truth. So I'm telling you the truth! She acted possessed, if you will forgive me, as if something, an evil thing, had got ahold of her and used her to destroy and wreak havoc.

"And then I thought, oh I just wonder, maybe it was the new medicine the doctor put her on! The medicine to mollify her symptoms, to treat the dementia? It is actually an experimental drug, don't you know, and the side effects might just be unpredictable? And so I found that infernal bottle, poured all the pills into the john and I *flushed* that nasty business. And that was the end of *that* course of treatment, I mean to tell you. Good heavens.

"And it must have been that, that horrid prescription, because she was very shortly all radishes and capers in the noggin again. Can't walk and can only barely talk again, poor thing, just as she was before.

"And that's the truth as I can recollect it, Miss Sullivan. I promise you."

Garnet had listened closely to Clovis Reddick's "confessions," as speechless as a clam, no questions, quips or smart-ass comments, lips zipped, and when he said he gave his demented hyperactive Mother the keys to the Bentley, she recalled Fritz's antics with the Bentley at Peaceable Kingdom. When Clovis at last fell silent, Garnet visualized The Fritz posing as a veterinarian and sending the Bentley to "hell" via a sinkhole, a sinkhole that opened up at the precise moment he drove it to a certain spot. With a push from Fritz, the engine of doom and death was flushed into the earth, thus ensuring that neither Clovis nor his crazy Mother could ever toddle or barrel it anywhere else again—even to go the opera. In the ensuing silence, Garnet tapped out the last gooey drop of ancient absinthe from the bottle into her glass. She tossed it back, swallowed hard and stood up, her powers of speech somewhat restored.

"Clovis, are you warm enough now? Please excuse me for a few minutes. I won't be long."

The big white vellum envelope with the wax trident seal on the back was empty and the thick packet and file were stuffed with comics from a Sunday newspaper.

The Fritz had sent *Clovis* to her. Clovis was the story. "The Story." The "big" story that would "change her life." The other things were props and teases to heighten her interest, spark her imagination, get her attention, and get her involved. What, in the in the Fritzian scenario, as things played out, did he hope or expect her to do with Clovis and his stupefying tale of woe? More to the point, maybe, what did he expect Clovis' story to do to her?

Like an aimless wandering wraith, her nightgown rumpled from hours of restless sleepless ruminating, and with exhausted staring eyes and blurry vision, Garnet stumbled down the dark staircase toward the pitch-black kitchen. There had to be some coffee in there. She fumbled around, dropped things, bumped her head on a cabinet, said oh shit, and winced. Then Mortie shot through the air, just like that, out of nowhere, a gray whiz, in the kitchen right in front of her at very high velocity and literally airborne when she dropped the coffee canister. He shot back in the opposite direction two feet off the floor right in front of her when she dropped a spoon. His hair looked all stuck out, moussed up, and "punk" Goth, she noticed, not wondering why. Cats! Cats could get away with anything. People said, "Cats! He's a cat, whatdya expect?"

231

Soooo Mortie's doing a Goth look and strut. Okay. He's into that right now. He's into Goth, spectral wild staring eyes, yellow eyes the size of the full harvest moon, and indulging in full frontal *joie de vivre*. Mortie, zestful, full of the devil, having fun just for the sheer fun of it, executing phantom torpedo passes through the kitchen at 90 MPH six inches from my face as I sit here at this tiny table stirring brownness, exhausted, his antics of choice of the moment, trying out new routines, showing off, what the hell, his aerodynamic acrobatic skills. Whoops, there he goes again. "You da man, Mortie. Dig it." That was fast, really fast.

Thank God, she'd locked up Diesel and Ringo upstairs. She could not deal with something like that right now. She could hardly stand up. Bone tired. Brain dead. God, how was she going to get through the day? The game at the stadium, all those noisy sweaty drunk obnoxious people, the sun beating down, no air, no breeze. She was dead tired. Coffee.

As she was stirring a miserable watery thin excuse for coffee, a freeze-dried pastiche of powdery brownness with no taste, and doubting it had any caffeine it at all, she heard a noise and looked up.

Now isn't that something. I didn't know cats could do that. "Mortie, what on earth are you doing, dude?" This cat would not do this during daylight in the company of a group of people. No, cats reserved this kind of weirdness for when you're all alone, exhausted, it's dark, you're uptight, worried, have a thousand urgent things on your to-do list, only no time at all to do any of them because you have to go to a damn freakin football game, jam your way into a stadium with 90,000 other people, squeeze by them, rub your butt over some leering jerk's face just to get to your freakin seat, constantly have to excuse yourself, your ears assaulted by insane yelling shouting bumping pumping deafening noise, all of it mock tragic or triumphant, and you can't see a blasted thing for all the people jumping up and down all around you—

"Mortie, old man, all your blood is going to rush to your head, man, then you're going to fall with a big thud right on top of this swill." Why am I trying to gag down this vile sickening brown stuff, telling myself, 'hey, self, it's coffee, drink it, you need to wake up?' Cuz it's Game Day—Wake up! Isn't that the best reason in the world to go back to bed?

Will you look at that? I did not know cats were like that. That's a new one to me, that a cat could stick to a ceiling like a spider, look at down at you with its head turned all the way around backwards on its neck and *smile* at you.

"Nice smile, Mortie. Yeah. I'm impressed. What do you want, Mortie? No tuna on me right now, sorry."

Did that damn cat just give me a *thumbs-up* or what? Is that what that cat is doing? Cats don't have thumbs. How many digits are on a cat's foot? "Okay, wow. You are very talented, get an agent, dude, you could get big bucks for that kinda mid-air loop de loop, Mortie. Bravo. Here, thumbs-up back atcha, bud."

What? Was that a *bird* finger he just gave me? Just ignore him.

"Now scat, cat. Leave me alone, you dark cloud of feline insanity. Get lost." That cat ate roach poison or a bug that tripped it out.

Whoa. Coffee, coffee. Hold it. That cat did not just fly through that wall. I know it didn't. This is disgusting. Only way to do this is to use a funnel, pour the swill down my throat. Wait. That cat swooped down off the ceiling and shot through that wall like a cannon ball. No, it did not. I didn't hear a noise. If it went through the wall like a cannon ball, there would have been a noise. There is no mark on the wall. No hole where the cat went in. The cat did not do that. The cat did not do that. You are all pooped out. Groggy. I've never seen a cat smile like that before, but shoot, different breeds, in-breeding, genetic screw-ups? Didn't the Siamese in a Disney animated film smile?

"Okay, Mortie, how're you *doing* that? I know you're holding onto some-thing, Mortie, that's impossible. It's okay, let me come over, yes, nice smile, little guy, I'm not going to ruin your act, but I only want to take a little closer peek, not going to touch any part of you."

Something is in this coffee. Somebody musta put hand sanitizer in it or something. Just ignore him. This is not normal— even for a cat. I still do not understand how he can hang out there suspended in mid-air and look at me that long. That *is* a smile, isn't it? I swear, that cat is *possessed!* If I didn't know better, I'd think Fritz was behind this, staging it, pulling the strings.

Yikes. Will you get a load a *this.* Holy Moley. Where did *she* come from?

"Mother *Weatherby?* Is that *you?* Hi, there. Ohhhh . . . Is your head cold? All those scarves . . . Have a bad headache, do you? Oh, gosh, I hope I didn't wake you up again!" Good Lord, why is her head all *bundled up* like that? She can't possibly *see* anything—

Whereupon the good and gentle woman declaimed sadly, sonorously and with exquisite sensitivity:

Little lamb, who made thee?
Dost thou know who made thee?

"Why Mother Weatherby! Blake, yeah, man! I didn't know you were a fan too! The partner poem of that one I like better myself, a matter of personal taste, I guess. The image, Mother Weatherby, you know, is maybe more, uh, like *me?* The one that goes:

Tyger, Tyger, Burning Bright
In the Forests of the Night?
What immortal hand or eye
Framed thy fearful symmetry?

"Yes? No? Maybe? Don't like it all, huh? Ultimately, it's a matter of personal taste, of course. *Songs of Innocence* and *Songs of Experience* just knocked my socks off first time I read them, totally blew my mind. But that's 'the story of my life' you know, I'm a little, uh, oh, I don't know, whatever. Anyway, both are certainly wonderful poems and universally admired."

From deep within the thick silken swaths of her scarves, Mother Weatherby abruptly interrupted Garnet with a deep guttural "*Lo!*" She tilted her shrouded head upward and opened her palms. Her large lantern jaw dropped open. In onerous portentous tones, tones worthy of the great epic poets, Homerian and weighty, the leaden verses rolled off her tongue like huge relentless waves crashing onto the beach.

Godspeed, Tiger Man, fare thee well.
Violated, lost Tiger Man soul.
Bundle bundling bundling,
Bundling bundle, athwart.
Fore and Aft
Bundling
Sta'bbard and Bow
Bundling
Cast off, Alack and Alas, Bundling Tillerman.

Make all bundling haste with bundled oar.
The Red Devil, maw unslaked
Commeth bundling forth.
The Red Devil Dragon
Mutilator, Torturer, Ravenously Hungry—Red Whore.

"Oh my gosh! You know, Mother Weatherby? That knocks me out. You might consider volunteering with the 'Reading for the Blind' programs! You have a *very* expressive voice. You'd be great at that.

"But I'm not at *all* familiar with *that* poem. It's certainly epic in style, yeah, man, sounds sort of Germanic to me, and maybe like it lost a little something when it was translated into modern English? To me it sounds sorta Old English, kinda 'Beowulfy;' it has that signature dread and *kick-butt* to it. Just my first impressions, course. And, shoot, what do *I* know?"

Mother Weatherby's palms remained open, her chin still thrust toward the sky, her feet rooted to the same two squares of linoleum she had chosen for her bardic bomb drop.

"Heavens! I've lost all track of time. It's getting *late*. I gotta get going here! Sorry, excuse me, hope you feel better, Mother Weatherby. Rest today, okay? Take it easy. Take care of your sweet self!"

30 (C)

ONE ENCHANTED EVENING

Once upon a midnight dreary, Garnet Sullivan pondered weak and weary, her sunken eyes cast upon a dusty plaster bust of Pallas Athena that she'd found rummaging around in the sorority house "catacombs" while searching frantically for other items. On her desk the candles in the candelabra flickered and sputtered their last. All that the sorry scene in the Chapter Room lacked was a smart-ass raven muttering *Nevermore*. A mere ten miles distant—at that very instant—an event transpired that rent the fabric of the whole blinking, winking universe and a confined spirit in need of comfort was set free.

Specifically—it was a dark and slightly stormy night. A small figure in an old-fashioned strapless tangerine evening gown appeared at an I-75 northbound on-ramp. Tottering atop high tangerine stilettos, it held onto a big floppy magnolia-flounced tangerine hat, its brim fluttering madly in the whimsical wind. In less than sixty seconds, a long sleek black limousine came to a screeching halt beside it and a dignified, turbaned chauffeur leaped out, bowed deeply and offered the delicate figure his hand. The tangerine apparition swiftly disappeared inside. The driver gunned the engine until it screamed like a wildcat and the limo vanished into the night.

"Oh don't you know—it all happened so *fast!* It was soooo confusing. But to the best of my recollection, don't you know, that's the absolute *truth*. That's what happened. Good Lord, *what will happen next?* My word. What a surprise. It was very, very unexpected, I can tell you that. And the driver, he was absolutely diabolically fast, heavens, faster, I would guess, than the speed of light itself. What a thrilling trip! It was like flying, oh my goodness, my heart was in my throat all the way. I was holding on for dear life! Mother's driver Jimmy-James, even he never drove *that* fast. Oh no. Not even when she was bappin-boppin the blessed crackers out of that poor man's head, yelling 'faster, you dirty bastard, faster!'

"Oh, my goodness, but I must say, I do have admit, it was very, very exciting and so much *fun!* Heavens. And I just *love* this dress. *Perfect* attire for the occasion! Such sartorial splendor! I mean to tell you, with all the matching accessories? I was *dressed to kill*, honey, don't you know? Oh, my! I almost exploded for *joy*! And, as the good Lord knows, *I hadn't been to the opera in years!*"

✝ ✝ ✝

There was a lot of jostling crowded around the coffee pot mid-morning. It had been an unusual night for everyone.

Garnet sat at a small table stirring a fresh cup of brown swill. Lance had been standing over her for three minutes. Ignoring him had gotten boring. She looked up. "Something on your mind, Lance?"

"What did you do with him?"

"With WHOM?" you gentle knight, pricking and ticking and starting to tick her off.

"Where is he?"

"What are you talking about?"

"Honey, did you see *this?*"

"What, my darling Chester, O Great One, my *raison d'etre?*"

He waved a newspaper under her nose. "Take a look at this. Tank got killed last night."

"No!"

"He was sucked into a sperm collection machine and drowned in a vat of bull sperm."

"You are *kidding* me! My, you're feeling perky and devilish this morning. Musta gotten a good sleep."

"No, I'm serious. Old Tank was showing off his new high-speed state of the art bull semen collection equipment at that cookout we were supposed to go to and something freaky happened. It all of a sudden went ka-flooey and sucked him right in. He drowned in a whopper vat of bull semen before they could get it open and fish the poor bastard out."

"Good grief. I'm not sorry we missed that scene. But I never *RSVP'd.* He died thinking I had bad manners. He left this earth thinking I had callously ignored his gracious invitation to a wild hog roast and a demonstration of the latest in large scale, warp speed bull semen collection equipment. I don't know if that bothers me or not. I think it actually *does* kinda bother me. I hope I didn't hurt his feelings. I don't want to be impolite to anyone. Oh, heck, he was, after all, a *bastard.* Maybe that makes it excusable? But I could not *make up* on my *best* day in La-La-Land something like that. You swear? No kidding? For real, Chester?"

"It's the honest truth. Look at this, they've a got shot of the bull semen vat. That thing's bigger than average Florida backyard swimming pool."

"Unbelievable. Wait a minute. So Tank actually got sucked in by his suck machine that he bought to suck something out of something else and instead of sucking them, he sucked up himself?"

"Apparently. Death strikes again—the schmucks, the sucked, sucks, suck-ups, suckers… like in . . . or as in . . . they were . . . a circle of sucky sucks sucking endlessly . . . end to end—man. It's a snake with its tail in its mouth."

"Try to be more *positive,* okay, honey? Don't always dwell on the downers? Try to look on the *bright* side?"

"'You are my sunshine, my only sunshine, you make me happy when skies are gray.'"

"I'm gonna overlook that, Chester. I know you didn't mean it the way it sounded. Sarcasm is the tool of clods and so unbecoming. But boy, oh, boy. I'm getting dizzy. Know what? It's a *mandala.* Eternity, it's a symbol of it.

This is too much. Nooooo, buddy. Think about it. So, like, it was a fluke accident?"

"Yeah, damn thing went haywire, I guess, just had a crazy malfunction."

"Soooo . . . the fancy machine thing kinda went on *The Fritz?*"

"That would seem to be the case, yes."

"Go figure. That is amazing." That old freelancing devil got around. Bravo. He must have picked up on Tank's tricks and antics while he was sniffing around Clovis's place. More power to him.

"Guess I won't get to serve that dang warrant on Panzer at the game then, huh, Chester, man?"

"That would be a fair surmise, I would say. Yep, Lance. You've lost two prisoners overnight, Sheriff. Tough luck, man."

Garnet's head spun around like a top scoping out the pair of earnest brown-eyed legal beagles. Were they pulling her leg?

"Say *what?* You guys. So *that's* what your sneaky whispering was all about. You had the dirt on Tank. You were going to arrest him?"

"No big deal now, honey. You might as well know. State's attorney got a tip from a retired doctor. It panned out. Then another one came in from old Johnson, Tommy's long-time bud. He found some threatening correspondence from Panzer Properties in Tom's papers at his house."

"I knew Mr. Johnson was out there looking for something serious. I just had a feeling. This is hot. I can break this, run with it. Now *this* is a story I can write. Hold on, Freddie!"

"Where is he, Garnet?"

"Wait. Show me the warrant first, Lance? That's money in the bank for me. What a story!"

"Where's the tiny tiger guy, Garnet?"

"Lance, for heaven sake. *Why* do you ask?"

"What was in them envelopes?"

And the envelope, please . . . . "I haven't read any of it. I've been busy. Honestly. That's the truth, I swear, so help me God. In plain English, Lance: I have not read it. I've been busy . . . truly, truly."

"Garnet!"

"How's the vocab pump-up, goin?" The dragon went that-a-way, Lance.

"You are *impossible,* woman. You are downright *evil* sometimes."

"Thank you." Awww, Sir Lance-Uh-Lot, pricking, ticking, trying now to tick her off, Lance the Knight Inconstant in a Constant Huff.

"Lance! O, me! I am compelled by the force of my rising heart to confess—you are the cutest little ole *knightly* thang!"

"And you, Garnet, are the most goldern difficult, dadgum confoundin witchy woman I, as sheriff of a fruitcake Florida county, have ever had to deal with."

"Why, thank you very much, Lance."

"You know what, woman? I had *nightmare* last night you were flyin around on a *broomstick* and that I was chasing your sweet ass tryin to ticket you for *breakin the sound barrier* and drivin everyone plumb crazy. Yeah, truly I did. You, little sister, you."

"That is too cool. You did?"

"What happened to the little striped cat in the basement, Garnet? Helping a prisoner escape is a felony in Florida. What sweet satisfaction it would be to slam your bouncing around little bottom behind bars."

"So answer me, Sheriff, you never did, you dodged the question. Vocab pump-up? You are showing some signs of having made surprising progress. How much are you pumpin now, and in what kinda sets? How *heavy,* Lance, is your vocabulary now? Be honest."

"Heavy enough, you devil woman. I *swear.*"

"You swear? Forward or backward? Can you foreswear and make a point? That's really hard. It's like kicking yourself in the balls, a kill shot for sure—and a very good incentive, little girls and boys, to always tell the truth to your own sweet self."

"Get outta town, Garnet. You are so full of crap."

"Lance? Don't get *mad.* It's a *word game,* silly. Vocab! Up! Up! C'mon, pump it UP. Dribble and shoot. Practice, practice!"

"Huh?"

"Forehand, backhand, foreswear, back-swear, keep swearing along, bounce-bounce-bounce, an 'I swear' is a loose ball in the air. It can land anywhere, bounce off . . . Hey, look at me! Lance? Get it?"

"Get what?"

"Keep your promises. Be true to your heart. Hoop a truth. Shoot, shoot, dunk it, do it, move it, do it, swear it, *swear it*—huh? Lance? What'dya say? Foreswear, backswear, this swear, that swear, I swear, you swear, he . . . Get in the humble honest crouch and *shoot.*"

"I *swear* I love Allison with all my heart!"

"Slam dunk! Winning point! Okay. You can do it. See? Let's play again."

"How does Chester tolerate you?"

"Simple, he loves me! Okay, now. Do you want to play? Are you in the game? Lance? If you love her, want to be her lover forever, no if and or buts—do you truly *swear* that you love her, that you love Allison Highsmith, with all your lying, out of bounds, bouncing heart, forget your lying big bounce-bounce mouth—c'mon now, keep the ball moving at all times."

"What the *hell* are you talkin about, woman? Lord. What happened to the prisoner, Garnet?"

"Bounce, bounce, Lance, watch this. Look! There's freakin fairy up there! It's waving to you! Slum dunk. Pay attention."

"I swear, you are awful. I swear I love Allison. I think I'm done with swearin for today. God, you are a fiend—what happened to that little cat? I was gonna book him. I already read him his rights."

"Okay, I'll play. What happened?"

"He's not there."

"You know, Lance, I *swear*, I noticed that myself. Point. That's the game. I won. Whoooopsss. Scoot, scoot. Wow, it's late AND I'M LATE FOR THE OPERA!"

"I swear."

"Loose ball."

"That I love Allison."

"*Awww*, that's sweet!" Allison said, appearing at the doorway. "You *do*, Lance?" Their eyes met, she locked him right up and penetrated him—*again!*

"Yes, Honey Cakes, I swear."

"Great game, Lance. Now get me that warrant, please. I've got a story to write. Freddie will wet his pants when he gets this one." She got up from her chair, stiff as a board, picked up her coffee cup and shuffled off toward the stairs, shaking her head. By what strange accidents and agencies lives are shaped and altered.

"Where are you going, Garnet?" Allison said. "Don't leave! This is a cool game! I wanna play!"

"Maybe later. I've got to get ready, Allison."

"For what?"

"More fun and games."

Garnet put her hand on the railing and looked up the dim winding staircase. She blinked and shook her head. For a second there she thought she saw Clovis at the top swishing and spinning around in a sparkling aura of tangerine taffeta and tulle, just having himself an absolute ball in the ball gown. And in that shaft of light on the dark landing, wasn't that Tommy Covington with a puppy under his arm, smiling and waving hello—or was it good-bye? Her heart turned over. It had been a long night. She was seeing things that maybe weren't there. Yet maybe they were. "Uncle Tommy?" Yes, it was. It was. She lifted her hand and whispered under her breath, "Tommy? Hey! Oh! Tommy! Oh my God! Tommy! Hey! Oh! Hi!" ❦

ACKNOWLEDGEMENTS

Special thanks to my husband Bruce R. Barbour, super-agent and publishing impresario extraordinaire, Founder & CEO of Literary Management Group LLC; and to Bob Bubnis, creative genius & principal of BookSetters.

ABOUT THE AUTHOR

Margaret Jean (Peggy) Langstaff has written more than twenty books, both under her own name and as a ghostwriter for others, and countless feature articles and book reviews for prominent national periodicals, such as the *L.A. Times*, *Publishers Weekly*, *BookPage*, and the *L.A. Times Book Review* and *Business Page*.

She is a member in good standing of the *National Book Critics Circle* (NYC), and former board member of the *Book Industry Study Group* (NYC).

In spite of her many travels and years of work in publishing and book-selling in NYC, Nashville and other places, "home" for Langstaff has always been Florida. Today she spends most of her time on a small farm in north Florida with a raucous animal menagerie and thousands of books, reading, writing, noodling and hatching plots.

Readers and other like-minded interested parties can find Langstaff on Goodreads.com, or her literary blog at www.margaretlangstaff.com, or can email her at Margaret@margaretlangstaffeditorial.com.

Margaret Langstaff is also a writing and editorial consultant of many years, and owns and operates *Margaret Langstaff Editorial*, a professional full service writing and editorial service.

www.ingramcontent.com/pod-product-compliance
Lightning Source LLC
Chambersburg PA
CBHW070050260626
47160CB00004B/1159